Plaster [illegible]

"A delightful small-town Maine sleuth . . . Solid and entertaining . . . A pull-no-punches mystery."

—*Midwest Book Review*

Spackled and Spooked

"Smooth, clever, and witty. This series is a winner!"

—*Once Upon a Romance*

"Bound to be another winner for this talented author. Home-renovation buffs will appreciate the wealth of detail."

—Examiner.com

"I hope the series continues." —*Gumshoe Review*

Fatal Fixer-Upper

"A great whodunit . . . Fans will enjoy this fine cozy."

—*Midwest Book Review*

"Smartly blends investigative drama, sexual tension, and romantic comedy elements, and marks the start of what looks like an outstanding series of Avery Baker cases."

—*The Nashville City Paper*

"Polished writing and well-paced story. I was hooked . . . from page one." —*Cozy Library*

continued . . .

"There's a new contender in the do-it-yourself home-renovation mystery field . . . An enjoyable beginning to a series." —*Bangor Daily News*

"A strong debut mystery . . . Do-it-yourselfers will find much to enjoy." —*The Mystery Reader*

"A cozy whodunit with many elements familiar to fans of Agatha Christie or *Murder, She Wrote.*" —*Nashville Scene*

"A great whodunit. Fans will enjoy this fine cozy." —*The Mystery Gazette*

"A fun and sassy journey that teaches readers about home renovation as they follow the twists and turns of a great mystery." —Examiner.com

Berkley Prime Crime titles by Jennie Bentley

FATAL FIXER-UPPER
SPACKLED AND SPOOKED
PLASTER AND POISON
MORTAR AND MURDER

MORTAR and MURDER

JENNIE BENTLEY

BERKLEY PRIME CRIME, NEW YORK

THE BERKLEY PUBLISHING GROUP
Published by the Penguin Group
Penguin Group (USA) Inc.
375 Hudson Street, New York, New York 10014, USA
Penguin Group (Canada), 90 Eglinton Avenue East, Suite 700, Toronto, Ontario M4P 2Y3, Canada
(a division of Pearson Penguin Canada Inc.)
Penguin Books Ltd., 80 Strand, London WC2R 0RL, England
Penguin Group Ireland, 25 St. Stephen's Green, Dublin 2, Ireland (a division of Penguin Books Ltd.)
Penguin Group (Australia), 250 Camberwell Road, Camberwell, Victoria 3124, Australia
(a division of Pearson Australia Group Pty. Ltd.)
Penguin Books India Pvt. Ltd., 11 Community Centre, Panchsheel Park, New Delhi—110 017, India
Penguin Group (NZ), 67 Apollo Drive, Rosedale, North Shore 0632, New Zealand
(a division of Pearson New Zealand Ltd.)
Penguin Books (South Africa) (Pty.) Ltd., 24 Sturdee Avenue, Rosebank, Johannesburg 2196,
South Africa

Penguin Books Ltd., Registered Offices: 80 Strand, London WC2R 0RL, England

MORTAR AND MURDER

A Berkley Prime Crime Book / published by arrangement with the author

PRINTING HISTORY
Berkley Prime Crime mass-market edition / January 2011

Cover design by Rita Frangie.
Cover illustration by Jennifer Taylor / Paperdog Studio.
Interior text design by Laura K. Corless.

ISBN: 978-0-425-23926-1

BERKLEY® PRIME CRIME
Berkley Prime Crime Books are published by The Berkley Publishing Group,
a division of Penguin Group (USA) Inc.,
375 Hudson Street, New York, New York 10014.
BERKLEY® PRIME CRIME and the PRIME CRIME logo are trademarks of Penguin Group (USA) Inc.

PRINTED IN THE UNITED STATES OF AMERICA

10 9 8 7 6 5 4 3 2 1

— Acknowledgments —

No writer is an island, and this book couldn't have happened without the help of a whole lot of people.

As always, thanks to my wonderful agent, Stephany Evans, and everyone at Fine Print Literary Management, and my equally wonderful editor, Jessica Wade, and everyone at Berkley Prime Crime.

Thanks to my publicists, Tom Robinson with Author and Book Media and Megan Swartz with Berkley, without whom this book would be nowhere.

Thanks to the Penguin design team for another beautiful book: Rita Frangie for art direction and cover design, Jennifer Taylor for cover art, and Laura K. Corless for interior design.

Big hugs to my critique partner, the wonderful Jamie Livingston-Dierks, who saves my posterior over and over again, and to all my other writer friends, too numerous to mention, who have loved and supported me through it all.

Thanks to Angela Burns, my favorite breed of human—a librarian!—for donating her name to a good cause and for tirelessly pushing my books on her patrons. Thanks also to all the other librarians and booksellers out there, along with all the reviewers, and most especially the readers, who have made this journey possible.

Finally, thanks, hugs, kisses, and undying love to my family, especially my husband and two boys, who know the real me and love me anyway. You guys are the best!

—1—

On April Fools' Day, Derek started work on his dream house. If I had thought about it, I would have realized that that was a bad sign, but no, I was just too excited that he finally had something to do to worry about anything else.

The house was a decrepit 1783 center-chimney Colonial on Rowanberry Island, about thirty minutes up the coast from Waterfield by boat, and he had fallen in love with it six months earlier: leaking roof, leaning walls, broken windows, and all. He'd wanted to buy it right then and there, but we were in the middle of renovating another house, a project where all our money was tied up, and with winter coming on, the timing just wasn't right. But as soon as the snow melted and the ground thawed, and we sold the house on Becklea Drive and put some cash back into the coffers, Derek was back to harping on about the Colonial on Rowanberry Island. He's nothing if not persistent.

Derek Ellis is my significant other, as well as my business partner. We'd met the previous June, when I'd inherited two cats and a house in tiny Waterfield, Maine, from my great-aunt Inga. Once I decided to spend the summer fixing it up, Derek was the handyman I hired to help me do the work. And in spite of a rocky beginning, I fell for him like a ton of bricks. When I chose to stay in Waterfield instead of going back to New York and my textile design career, going into business together seemed like a no-brainer.

At this point, Derek was owner and I was resident designer of Waterfield Renovation and Restoration. There were no other employees, so Derek was also plumber, electrician, painter, and general contractor, while I did a little of this and a little of that, including some painting, some tiling, some wall treatments, and some other stuff. I do what I can, in other words, and what I don't know how to do, Derek either does himself, or he gives me a crash course on the subject and lets me loose. It's worked for us so far.

The house on Rowanberry Island would be our fourth—and most ambitious—renovation project. After Aunt Inga's Second Empire Victorian in the historic district, we'd spent most of the autumn redoing a midcentury ranch in a suburb west of Waterfield (the aforementioned Becklea Drive place), before coming back to the Village to spend the early part of the winter turning my friend Kate's carriage house into a romantic retreat for her and her new husband. They'd gotten married on New Year's Eve and had flown to Paris for their honeymoon, and we had just managed to get everything into place for their return.

Since Waterfield was still blanketed under a foot of snow, Derek was forced to spend the first couple months of the new year doing small handyman jobs for other people, while I had agreed to teach a couple of textile design and history classes at local Barnham College. Both of us waited eagerly for enough snow to thaw to allow us to start work on the Rowanberry Island house.

The big day turned out to be April first: The weather was beautiful, most of the snow was gone, and the top couple of inches of ground had thawed. We brought all of Derek's tools down to the harbor and loaded up a little motorboat we had borrowed from Derek's friends Jill and Peter Cortino. That done, we locked Derek's black pickup truck and set out for Rowanberry Island.

The island was only accessible by boat. It was inhabited year-round, but just barely. A handful of houses clung stubbornly to the rocky ground on the northwestern—lee—side, but every year it seemed another person or two gave up the fight and moved to the mainland. Kids went away to college, never to return, and the elderly died or were moved to assisted-living facilities off island.

For those who held on, there was a little ferry that docked in the tiny harbor a few times a day. Our house was clear across the island from the village, and Derek and I didn't want to be dependent upon the whims of the ferry, so we'd arranged with Peter and Jill to use their boat. It was too early in the year for them to use it themselves; the Maine coast in April isn't conducive to pleasure-boating.

April first was a perfect example. The air was crisp, the sky was a lovely, clear blue, and the wind was strong enough to make me wish I'd put on my down-filled winter jacket instead of a padded vest and the knit sweater with reindeer and snowflakes I had spent a couple of months slaving over. The life jacket Derek had insisted I wear helped a little, but not enough. I couldn't feel my fingers or my ears, my Mello Yello–colored hair was stinging my face where it blew in the brisk wind, and my lips were turning blue under my lip gloss.

"How much farther?" I squeaked over the sound of the motor. And had to repeat it, louder, when Derek couldn't hear me. "Derek! How much farther?"

"Not far," Derek answered bracingly. He was upright, steering the boat, while I was huddled in a miserable, shivering bundle on one of the seats in the back. And, of course, he didn't look at all cold, even though he was wearing less than me. A pair of faded jeans hugged his posterior, and a cable-knit fisherman's sweater was covered by an orange life vest. The wind whipped his hair, which looked more brown than blond now, after being covered by a hat most of the winter. In the summer, the sun lightened it in streaks through the front and crown. His cheeks were flushed, and he looked happy. "See that?" He pointed to a low, green shape rising from the water in front of us. "That's it. It'll take another ten minutes, tops, to get to it."

"Great." I huddled deeper into the life vest, shivering.

"You'll be OK once we get there," Derek promised. "It'll take me a while to hook up the generator, but then we'll have heat."

"The little bit of it that won't escape through the holes in the walls."

"There are no holes in the walls," Derek said.

"Fine. The cracks, then. The cracks between the planks that are wide enough for me to put my fingers through."

He didn't answer that. Couldn't, when he knew I was right.

"A week from now we'll have it insulated and all the rotten wood replaced," he said instead. "After that, heat loss won't be a problem."

I grimaced. And then I took a breath. "I'm sorry. I'm being grumpy."

He flashed me a grin over his shoulder, which after ten months together still gave me a thrill. "You really are a city girl, aren't you, Tink? The ocean and the wind and the wide-open spaces freak you out."

I shrugged, pouting. That pout, coupled with the yellow

hair I often pile in a knot on top of my head, and the fact that I'm a measly five foot two, is what had originally earned me the nickname. Tinkerbell. Now I was stuck with it. My mother thought it was adorable, Kate thought it was hilarious, and Melissa James, Derek's ex-wife, thought it was cute. She didn't mean it as a compliment. But then Derek's nickname for Melissa had been Miss Melly, so I don't know that she had a whole lot of room to talk.

Melissa and Derek had gotten divorced almost six years ago, and Melissa had been shacked up with my distant cousin Ray Stenham ever since. Until just before Christmas, when something happened to change that, and now Melissa was back on the market and looking for someone to replace Ray. My big fear was that she had realized what she'd lost when she let Derek go, and now she wanted him back. I felt like she'd been coming around rather a lot lately, like I was stumbling over her every time I turned around, although I suppose it could have been my imagination. It's just that she's so damned *perfect*. . . .

"There it is," Derek said. I looked up.

The island was closer now: close enough that I could see the craggy coast, with its big boulders and rocky coves with grainy, grayish yellow sand. Most of the interior seemed taken up with pine trees, tall and dark, outlined against the china blue bowl of the sky.

I squinted; we were heading northeast, it was fairly early, and the sun was shining. "That's not our house, is it?"

"Can't be," Derek said, "our house is on the other side of the island. Where?"

"I can't see it anymore. But there was a building of some sort in the trees. Big and white. Look, there it is again. Are you sure that isn't our house? It looks exactly like it."

"Not exactly like it," Derek said, squinting into the sun,

the corners of his eyes crinkling. "That house looks like our house will look three months from now. When it isn't falling down anymore."

"But it is a center-chimney Colonial, isn't it? It looks like one."

"I'm sure it is," Derek said, navigating the boat around the south end of the island, away from the other house. The one that looked just like ours, no matter what he said. "There are two of them. Twins. The man who built them had two daughters, and he built them each a house."

"Those were the days."

"Apparently the girls couldn't get along, so he built one house on one side of the island, and one on the other, facing in opposite directions. That way, the girls never had to look at one another again if they didn't want to."

"How do you know all this?" I asked.

"Irina told me. The first time she showed me the house. You didn't want to come with us, remember; you and John Nickerson were busy picking out furniture to stage the house on Becklea Drive, and I went on my own."

"With Irina." I nodded. "I remember."

Irina Rozhdestvensky is our Realtor, a Russian transplant who lives just down the street from the house on Becklea Drive that we renovated in the fall.

I had met John Nickerson, the owner of an antique store on Main Street, around that same time, and he had let me pick some things out of his store to stage the house for showing. That's what we'd been doing when Irina first drew Derek's attention to the house on Rowanberry Island.

"Did Irina know anything else about them?"

"Nothing she mentioned." Derek aimed the boat toward a small cove and rocky beach and cut the engine. "There's our house. See it?"

I nodded. It was big and square, positioned with its rear

against a backdrop of dark pine trees and bare birches and oaks, getting closer every second as we drifted toward shore. The chimney had fallen in, there was a hole in the roof, more than half the windows were broken, and there wasn't a speck of paint left on the entire front of the house, the old planks faded to a silvery gray from the constant onslaught of wind, sun, and salt. I shuddered.

"Isn't she a beauty?" Derek said, and meant it. His entire attention was focused on the house, his eyes soft and dreamy, and his mouth curved in an adoring smile. Another woman might have felt a twinge of jealousy—I don't think Melissa had ever understood why he'd look at a run-down wreck of a house with more emotion than he ever showed her—but I've gotten used to it. It's no reflection of how he feels about me, it's just how he feels about old houses. It seemed a pity to disturb his no doubt beautiful dreams; however, I didn't have a choice.

"Derek? Look out. You're about to hit the dock." Literally.

"Oops." His eyes came back into focus, and he made the necessary adjustments to bring the boat up alongside the decrepit-looking dock leaning into the water at a precarious angle. "Sorry about that."

"No problem. Is the dock safe, do you suppose?"

"I'm sure it is," Derek said, looping a rope around a pylon and bringing the boat to a rocking stop. He bounced out and onto the dock, which looked to me as if it could break into pieces under his booted feet at any moment. Miraculously, it held. "C'mon."

He reached down. I grabbed his hand and used the support to get to my feet, unsteadily. Growing up on the coast of Maine, Derek had been in and out of boats his entire life. I was born and raised in Manhattan, and the closest I'd ever gotten to a boat was the occasional trip on the Circle Line ferry when friends from away came to visit.

"Upsy-daisy." He lifted me onto the dock. Sometimes it's nice to be petite. Especially when your boyfriend is a strapping six feet or so and used to hauling lumber and other heavy objects. I tottered—just slightly on purpose; the dock was slippery and about as wobbly as it looked—and he put an arm around me to steady me. I leaned in. The puffy orange life vest made cuddling less fun than usual, but his arm was nice and warm and solid through the wool sweater, and the brisk wind hadn't managed to eradicate his particular aroma: Ivory soap and shampoo mixed with paint thinner and sawdust. Mmmm!

All too soon he let me go, though, and turned to survey the house again. I sighed. "You're more comfortable in the boat than I am. Why don't you hand the stuff up to me, and then we'll carry it to the house together."

"Sure." He tore his gaze away and went back into the boat. We unloaded for a few minutes, and then we picked up what we could carry and started across the meadow toward the house.

I'm not sure what the reason was; whether it was that this was the first time I'd seen the place clearly, in bright sunshine, since early November—and the light hadn't been that good then, with the fog and the rain—or whether it was because this was the first time I'd seen the house uncovered by snow while we owned it . . . but I was aware of a horrible sinking feeling in my stomach. Had it really always looked this bad? Or had the winter months and the snow done a number on the place so that it now needed another ten or twenty thousand dollars' worth of work above and beyond what we had expected to put into it? Had the hole in the roof always been so big? Had there always been so many broken windows? And how was it possible that I hadn't noticed how the whole thing tilted to the right like something out of a Dr. Seuss book?

"What?" Derek asked when I stopped dead in the middle of the grass, my eyes round. "You OK, Tink? You look like you're gonna faint."

"I feel like I'm going to faint," I said. "Did it always look this bad?"

He stared at it. For a long time, before he turned back to me. "Pretty much, yeah."

"Oh." I bit my lip. "I didn't realize . . . I mean, I knew it would need a lot of work, but I had no idea . . . This is, like, a hundred times worse than Aunt Inga's house!"

Derek examined the house again. "Not quite," he said judiciously. "I mean, yeah—it's rough. It's gonna need a lot of work. A *lot* of work. But it isn't a hundred times worse than your aunt's house."

My voice reached an uncomfortable, hysterical pitch, even to my own ears. "The roof has a hole in it! Big enough for a helicopter to land in the attic! If there's an unbroken window in the entire house, I can't see it, and the whole thing is *leaning*! Like the freaking Tower of Pisa!"

"Maybe we can turn it into a tourist attraction?" Derek suggested, a smile tugging at the corners of his mouth.

"I can't believe you're laughing at me! It isn't funny, dammit. We're gonna sink every dime we own into this place, and it won't even make a dent, and then we'll have to rob a bank or something to keep going, and when we're finished, assuming we aren't caught and sent to jail, it'll be years from now, and we'll have spent so much money we'll have to sell the house for a couple of million to get our money back, and no one's gonna wanna pay that much for a house on an island in the middle of the ocean where it isn't even warm!"

"You'd be surprised," Derek said. He dropped a rolled-up tarp he'd been carrying across his shoulder on the grass. "C'mere, Avery." He put his arm around my shoulders and began steering me in the direction of the house again, murmuring encouragement the whole way. The medical profession lost a great doctor when Derek retired his license; his bedside manner is excellent, both in and out of the bedroom. "It'll be all right, you'll see. It won't cost as much as you think. And it won't take as long, either. And you'd be surprised how much someone might pay for a place like this, all fixed up. That other Colonial we saw? It belongs to Gert Heyerdahl."

"The author?" My feet were moving, independent of my brain.

Derek nodded, prodding me gently along. "The same. He's only there for a few months in the summer. The rest of the time he divides between his penthouse in Miami and his villa in Tuscany."

"What a life. Maybe *I* should become a thriller writer."

"Or maybe you should just stay here with me," Derek said. "There are a couple of other houses like that, too, here and on the other islands. All of them summer homes; the only people who live here full time are the ones in the villages. And I guess maybe some of the big houses have staff. Or maybe not; they may close them down for the winter and only open up again for the season."

"M-hm." We had reached the front steps now, and they appeared in no better shape than the leaning dock down by the water. "Think this'll hold our weight?"

"It's held mine every time I've been here. Along with Irina's. And she's a lot bigger than you." He dropped his arm from around my shoulders and started up the wooden stairs. They creaked under his feet but didn't break. Something that had been underneath must have shared my misgivings, though, because it streaked out from under the porch and disappeared in the brush. All I saw was a blur of fur going by at warp speed. I squealed.

"What?" Derek said, turning around.

"Animal. Furry."

"Mouse?" Derek said.

I shook my head, knees knocking together. "Bigger. And blue. What kind of animal is about this big"—I held my shaking hands a little less than a foot apart—"and blue?"

Derek thought for a moment. "Cookie Monster?"

I rolled my eyes. "Don't be ridiculous. Cookie Monster is much bigger. And it wasn't that kind of blue. No animal in nature is Cookie Monster blue."

"More of a blue gray? A squirrel, maybe? Or a rat?"

"Not a rat. We don't have rats." At least we'd better not. "I think the legs were longer. And I didn't notice much of a tail."

"Hare? They're gray. With white stubby tails."

"Maybe. Although it didn't hop."

"We'll find out," Derek said. "If it lives under there, it'll be back."

"True." And wouldn't that be lovely?

The distraction of the blue gray furry thing—and the fact that Derek had been jumping up and down on the porch—had alleviated one of my fears, anyway. If it could hold him, surely it could hold me. I crept up the steps while Derek fumbled in his pocket for the key. He turned to the heavy front door. While he wrestled with it, he gave me a crash course in architecture, most of which I knew already—from mandatory architecture classes at Parsons School of Design—but some of which was new to me.

"The center-chimney Colonial is the first distinctive housing style in New England. It started out as a very simple one-story design: two rooms around a central chimney. Then it got expanded to one-over-one: two stories, four rooms. Three bays wide."

"Bays?"

"Doors and windows." He grunted, trying to turn the key in the lock. "This house is five bays wide. Center door, two windows on each side. That style came later. After 1750, say. And we've got two stories. Plus an attic. And a tight run-around staircase. That, there."

He pushed the protesting door open and pointed. I nodded, stifling a moan.

It wasn't the staircase so much. The staircase was fine, really. Narrow and cramped, yes, sort of doubling back on itself, but compared to some of the other features, not a big deal. Quite attractive, really.

The floors were wide planks, and if they'd ever been sanded and polyurethaned, it wasn't in my lifetime. The windows were small and deep set—and dirty and broken—and the light filtering in was pale and weak. It didn't help that the ceilings were low and made the rooms seem even darker. At least in Aunt Inga's 1870s Victorian cottage, the ceilings had been ten feet tall. Here, they looked like they'd brush the top of Derek's head once he started walking around. I made a mental note: no hanging light fixtures. They'd all have to be flush-mounted or even recessed. Except maybe in the dining room: a chandelier-type light fixture is really de rigueur above a dining room table.

The temperature was freezing; it was even colder inside than outside, and although spring had officially come to down east Maine, it was really only warmer compared to the frigid dead of winter. If I couldn't quite see my breath in front of me, I felt like I ought to.

Derek rubbed his hands together. I'm not sure if it was the cold or the anticipation. Probably the latter. When he turned to me, he didn't look daunted in the least. "Guess we'd better get started."

"I guess."

"Can you help me carry the extension ladder from the boat? That way, I can get the tarp off and start patching the hole in the roof."

"Sure."

He looked at me for a second before he reached out—with both arms this time—and pulled me close. With the stupid orange life vest gone, I could snuggle in and put my cheek against the scratchy wool of the sweater. His body was comfortably warm through the layers, and his heart beat steadily against my ear.

"It'll be OK, Avery." He said it into my hair. "Come June, you won't recognize this place, I promise. And you'll feel better once we start working. You felt the same way about rebuilding Kate's carriage house, remember? You didn't think we could do it. But we did, and it was great. You did an awesome job. And you'll do an even better job this time. This house is going to be a showplace by summer. I promise."

"If you're sure."

"I'm sure." He tilted my face up and kissed me. "Now shake a leg. The sooner we get started, the sooner we'll be done."

"I'll drink to that," I said and followed him outside and down the stairs and across the meadow to the dock again. In the corner of my eye, a small blue gray shadow darted through the brush and under the porch.

—2—

Derek was right: I did feel better once I started working. Even if all I did for the first two days was hold the ladder while he climbed onto the roof, and then stand below to make encouraging remarks and watch him like a hawk so he didn't fall off and plummet to his death.

He spent the first day rebuilding and tuck-pointing the substantial chimney: making sure the mortar holding the bricks together was strong and not crumbling. Once the new mortar was set and the chimney was safe, he tied a rope around his waist and looped the other end around the chimney; that way, if he fell—through the roof or over the side of it—he wouldn't fall too far. And then he proceeded to walk around up there holding on to the rope with one hand. Just wandering back and forth, peeling off old layers of roof shingle and decking and assessing the damage, whistling as he worked. All while I stood below with my heart in my throat, stomping my feet and twitching with worry. From time to time he'd even turn to give me a cheerful wave or thumbs-up, as if to make sure that *I* was all right.

By the time he finally came down, two and a half days later, I was wrung dry emotionally. To the point where, as soon as he had put the second foot on the ground, I said, "I need a break."

Derek looked surprised. "OK. Um . . . from what, exactly?"

"The worry. I've been worrying for two days straight."

"Except when we were doing other things," Derek said, a reminiscent twinkle in his eyes.

I blushed. "All right. Yes, except when we were doing other things. But I've been standing here for the past two days, worrying that you'll fall off the roof, and I need to do something else for a while."

"You can start working on the inside," Derek suggested, since I had refused to do that while he was outside.

"Other than that."

He sighed. "Fine. What do you want to do?"

"I want to take a walk," I said firmly.

"A walk?"

"Across the island, to the other Colonial. I want to see it. Up close."

"Oh." His face cleared. "Sure. Go ahead."

"You don't want to come?"

He smiled. "I'd love to come. But the sooner I get the holes patched and the windowpanes replaced, the sooner we can hook up the generator and get some heat and power going. It's been a while since I had to work only with manual tools, and I can't wait to get my electric drill plugged in somewhere."

"Oh." I nodded. Totally understandable. I'm not good at roughing it, either. A hotel without room service is about as far as I'll go. "OK, then. I'll just take a quick walk across the island—it shouldn't take much more than ten minutes to get there, do you think?—and have a look around, and then I'll come back. Thirty minutes, tops. Just to see what they've done to the place, you know?"

"Be careful," Derek said. "Knock on the door before you start peering through the windows. Just in case someone's there. You don't want to catch Gert hanging around in his boxer shorts drinking beer and watching NASCAR."

I shuddered. "Definitely not." Derek watching TV in his boxer shorts was one thing, gorgeous specimen that he is. Gert Heyerdahl, with his beard and long hippie hair, was another, and not one I wanted to experience firsthand. "I'll be careful."

"If you're not back in an hour, I'll come looking for you." He turned and headed up the stairs to the front door. I went the opposite way, around the corner of the house and along a narrow, partially overgrown path that led away from the ocean and into the woods.

The state tree of Maine is the eastern white spruce, tall and straight, with rough bark and blue green needles. There are also a lot of other trees indigenous to the area: various birches and elms, poplars and oaks, maples and hickory. They like the cold climate, and grow tall and dense. Only the spruces and pines were green, of course; the rest looked like they might be thinking about throwing out buds but hadn't quite made the commitment yet, just in case we got another cold snap. The lack of growth made it easier to see where I was going as I shuffled along the narrow ribbon of beaten earth that led into the woods, surrounded by more trees than I'd ever seen in one place before in my life.

After a few minutes' walk, the path split: one branch going left, the other continuing more or less straight. Both new paths were even less defined than the one I'd used to get this far. I stopped at the fork, squinting through the pine needles and bare branches at the sun and trying to picture the layout of the island in my head. It started out wide and flat on the southern end, where Derek's and my house was. The other Colonial house was positioned on the western side. The little village, meanwhile, was situated at the back of a little cove on the northwestern shore, up where the terrain was higher. On the other side of the woods, and past more meadows. It would seem, then, that the path going straight led north to the village, and the one on the left went due west to Heyerdahl's house.

I struck out to the left, jumping over the muddy ruts left by the recently melted snow and skipping over gnarly tree roots and patches of dormant vegetation that bisected the skinny path, ruminating on my situation as I went.

A year ago, the idea that I'd own not just one, but two houses in Maine, in addition to a car and two cats, would have been laughable. The picture of me, wandering through the woods in worn-out jeans tucked into a pair of Wellies, would have made my eyes pop. My Wellies were pink with red lipstick kisses on them, admittedly, nothing traditional, but still. Amazing, the difference a year can make.

When I had first arrived in Waterfield, it had been early summer, and I'd planned to spend a weekend finding out what my aunt Inga wanted, and why she had summoned me, a relative she hadn't seen for twenty-six years, to spill the beans about family secrets and truths and lies. Only to discover, when I got here, that Aunt Inga was dead and I was her heir. But I still had no thoughts of staying. Renovating the house before putting it on the market was just to maximize return on the sale. I'd thought I'd stay a few months and then go back to my regular life in Manhattan. I had a boyfriend, a job I loved, good friends I enjoyed spending time with, and the hustle and bustle of the city around me felt essential.

Yet here I was, ten months later—house, car, cats, and

all—pretty much as happy as a clam. Sure, I still missed certain things. Like Balthazar coffee in the morning. Decent Thai food. And going to the grocery store at three A.M. The coffee wasn't too bad up here, even if it wasn't Balthazar, and the seafood was great. I can live without Thai. And Derek was a hell of a lot better than any other boyfriend I'd ever had. In fact, Derek made it all worthwhile.

Before Derek, I'd been—shall we say—unlucky in love. Or so determined to find Mr. Right that I saw him in every man I met. To my detriment. Over the years, I got involved with a string of guys I should have stayed away from, and that maybe I would have stayed away from, had I not been so eager to find my soul mate.

But this time, I'd found something real. Derek, who's sweet, and caring, and funny, and smart, not to mention good with his hands and good-looking, as well. At least if you're a sucker for tall, lean guys with dreamy blue eyes, the way I am.

While I'd been thinking about—all right, gloating over—my uncommon luck, I'd made my way through the woods covering the middle of Rowanberry Island, and now I could see the ocean blinking in the distance, between the trees. Another minute or two and I was out of the woods—literally—and standing in front of, or behind, the other Colonial.

From the back, it looked exactly like ours, except for the fact that this one was freshly painted, with no wood rot, and no blue tarp covering the roof.

It was a gleaming white, the windows shuttered for the winter, but I was willing to bet none of them were broken.

Sighing enviously, I picked my way around the side of the house. From this view, also, it looked exactly the same as ours, except for the condition. Four windows on each floor, plus an attic. No holes under the eaves for squirrels and birds to get into and build nests. (We'd be dealing with that little problem soon, hopefully in time to keep out the migratory sparrows and warblers that were, even now, I figured, on their way up from South America.)

The place looked deserted, although there was a boat tied up at the dock, a dock which, incidentally, was far superior to ours. Not only did it not droop into the water, but it had room for at least five boats in addition to the one that was there now. The extra berths were in case Gert Heyerdahl decided to throw a party for his friends, I imagined. There are a lot of writers who live in Maine. Maybe they got together for Algonquin-like roundtable discussions when Gert was in residence. Or debauchery and drink, at least.

I doubted Gert was in residence right now. Aside from the shuttered house, the boat didn't look like something a bestselling author would own. It was utilitarian, wooden rather than fiberglass. Not a fishing boat—I'd seen plenty of those in the harbor in Waterfield—but nothing like a yacht, either. There wasn't anything sleek or expensive about it; it was old, with a little deck house with curtained windows, and some coils of rope and things stowed on the deck. It reminded me of houseboats I'd seen in pictures, traveling the canals in England. Smaller, though. Too small to live on, but possibly big enough to spend a night or two in the cabin, if there was no other alternative. The name of it was *Calliope*, or so it said on the prow in red letters.

I wasn't really interested in the boat, though, other than as an indication that someone was here, so I turned to look at the facade of the house.

The Colonial looked just the way I hoped that ours would look one day. The white paint gleamed in the sunlight, all the windows were neatly shuttered, and it had a rather nice slab-stone stoop; not rickety wood, like ours. I made a mental note to ask Derek whether he thought such a stoop might be hidden underneath the little wooden porch outside our house; whether someone might have simply built the porch and wooden stairs right over it. Certainly worth looking into. I also wanted to figure out what lived underneath the porch. I'd seen the streak of blue gray fur a few more times in the past couple of days, but never close enough to identify. It had four legs and not much of a tail and it ran fast, but so far, that was all I'd been able to determine.

Colonial homes are pretty simple constructions, really. As Derek had told me, the style started out as your basic two-room cottage or cabin, then grew to a one-over-one and two-over-two as time went on. Three bays, a door and two windows, turned to five bays. A center chimney turned to matching chimneys, one on either end. The simplicity and symmetry continued to be a part of the design, though. The windows are on the small side, and unadorned; six-over-six panes, not much taller than they are wide. No six- or eight-foot windows here, like in Aunt Inga's Victorian. The only true ornamentation on the exterior of a Colonial home is usually the front door area. This one was no exception. The door itself was extra wide, made of vertical planks painted a pale sage green, same as the shutters, and held to the frame with black iron hinges. It sported a heavy black handle and separate deadbolt. Not very historical, that last one, but Gert probably had some nice stuff inside that he wanted to protect. Computer equipment, certainly, maybe even a home theater.

Above the door was a half-circular window, a fanlight, while beside the door on each side were sidelights. Outside that were pilasters, half columns, supporting a pediment that looked like the mantel on a fireplace. Heavy, black, iron carriage lamps hung on each side of the door, completing the picture.

I was gaping at the whole thing, so overcome with

door-envy that I didn't hear the footsteps behind me, until a voice asked me what I thought I was doing there, and then I realized I was no longer alone.

A skinny, middle-aged man with sunken cheeks and a ruddy complexion stood behind me. Or maybe he just appeared ruddy because he was outside in Maine in April. The wind off the ocean was brisk, even here on the lee side of the island. He was dressed for the elements in a pair of padded coveralls of the sort worn by construction workers. The fingers of a pair of black gloves stuck out of one pocket, and a ski cap was bunched on top of his head, ready to pull down once he got into open water.

His eyes were muddy brown, like pebbles, and suspicious. He repeated the question, and added, "Who are you?"

I extended a hand and my best smile. "Hi. I'm Avery Baker. My boyfriend and I just started fixing up the other Colonial. You know, the house across the island. The twin to this one."

He didn't take my hand, nor acknowledge that it was there, and after a few moments I lowered it, feeling awkward.

"I . . . uh . . . Someone told us this house is exactly the same as ours, so I thought I'd take a walk over to . . . um . . . look at it. To see if I could get some ideas, you know? I mean, it's so beautiful, and . . . eh . . . clearly very well maintained. Are you the . . . um . . . caretaker?"

He wasn't Gert Heyerdahl, whose hairy, considerably younger face I knew from the flaps of the dustcovers of his books. Derek had a few sitting around. Gert Heyerdahl is a man's man, writing a man's book, a hardcore thriller series about some former KGB agent or spy going around "solving problems" for people and ending up saving the world.

The man nodded.

"It's a beautiful place. You must work really hard to keep it looking like this."

He shrugged.

"I guess Mr. Heyerdahl isn't here at the moment, right? I mean, with the shuttered windows and all?" I glanced at them.

"Mr. Heyerdahl lives in Florida," his caretaker ground out, practically without moving his lips.

I nodded. "Right. Derek—my boyfriend—told me he has a place there. Good for him. Um . . . I don't suppose there's any chance you'd show me the inside of the place, is there? Since it's not occupied at the moment?" I fluttered my lashes and smiled my sweetest smile. Sometimes it works. This time it didn't.

"Sorry," the caretaker grunted, without making an effort to sound like he meant it. "Not without Mr. Heyerdahl's permission."

"Right." I nodded. "Of course. Sorry I asked. Um . . . when will Mr. Heyerdahl be here?"

His eyes maintained their flat lack of expression, but somehow he managed to look maliciously amused. "June."

Two months from now. "I see."

OK, then. I wondered if the caretaker lived here or just came out every day to work. From Waterfield or Boothbay Harbor or just around the island from the village?

"Um . . . I don't suppose you'd allow me to look through the sidelights before I go?"

He hesitated. For long enough that I thought for sure he'd say no. Then he shrugged. "Why not."

"Really?" Wow. I scurried up the two stone steps to the front door and leaned forward, straining, my nose practically pressed against the wavy glass. (Original 225-year-old glass!) The inside was dark, with no lights on and all the windows covered. After my eyes adjusted, I could just barely make out wide plank floors—like ours, but polished to a high gloss—and another tight run-around staircase.

The threads were polished hardwood, the risers painted white. The walls were paneled—225-year-old paneling; not 1970s—and also painted a light color. And that was all I could see. The doors to the left and right were closed, so I got no glimpse of furnishings or decor, and the hallway receded into darkness just a few feet in. I stepped back, fighting disappointment. "Thanks."

The caretaker nodded.

"I'll just be on my way, then. Back to my own house. Nice to meet you."

As I walked away, I turned to look over my shoulder. He was still standing in the same place, watching me. I guess he'd stand there until he was sure I was off Mr. Heyerdahl's property and not coming back.

In my hurry to get away from Gert Heyerdahl's house and back to my own, I guess I must have taken a wrong turn somewhere in the woods, because instead of ending up at our decrepit Colonial by the sea, I found myself on a path that ended at a little, old saltbox house instead.

They're called saltboxes because back in the time when they originated, in the late sixteen hundreds and throughout the seventeen hundreds, salt was kept in containers with that shape. A square box with a sloped lid, taller in the front than the back. Basically, the roof of a saltbox is much longer in the back than in the front, because it extends over a one-story addition called a lean-to. The saltbox style became popular after Queen Anne imposed taxation of houses with more than one story; because the two-story front of the house went down to just one story in the back, saltboxes were exempt from the tax.

With no other houses in sight, the place looked desolate and lonely, if also picturesque sitting there, half hidden in the brush. I walked around it but saw no sign of life. Like on Gert Heyerdahl's house, the tiny windows were covered with plain wooden shutters, and the door was locked up tight. (Yes, I tried the knob. Sue me.) The decrepit little dock, in worse shape even than ours, was boat-free.

• • •

"Probably another of the summer homes," Derek said when I had made my way back to our own place and had described the property to him. "It may even be the original van Duren house. Where Mr. van Duren lived. The guy who built our house. And Gert's."

"It looked old enough. Very small and primitive." I shrugged. "I don't care about that, though. The guy at Gert Heyerdahl's house—really seemed like a weirdo and he wasn't that friendly. . . ."

All right, I was the one who wanted to peek through someone else's windows, so maybe I was the weirdo, and he *had* let me . . . but he'd still freaked me out a little.

"I wouldn't worry about him, Avery," Derek said. "If he's responsible for keeping Gert's house maintained and protected while the great man is in Florida, it's understandable that he wouldn't want some dippy blonde wandering around inside."

"I'm not a dippy blonde!"

Derek grinned. "I know that, and you know that, but how's *he* supposed to know that? You're female, you're blond, and you're wearing pink rain boots with kisses on them. You probably batted your eyes at him, too, while you were trying to talk him into letting you in."

I made a face. So what if I had?

Derek chuckled.

I had found him standing with his hands on his hips contemplating the fireplace, his eyes serious. My story distracted him for a few minutes, but now his attention moved on. I turned to looked at what was so interesting.

As fireplaces go, this one was pretty basic. Nothing like Aunt Inga's intricately carved and mirrored mantels in dark wood and tile, taller even than the top of Derek's head. This was much shorter, barely coming up to my waist, and it didn't even really have a proper mantel; just a red-brick hearth and surround set into a paneled wall, like the ones I'd spied through the sidelight windows at Gert Heyerdahl's house. The paneling was intricate and lovely, with big rectangles over small rectangles, and crown molding ringing the room below the ceiling, as well as around the brick, but it looked pockmarked, not smooth. Holey and uneven.

"What's wrong with it?" I asked, brows wrinkled.

"Worms," Derek answered.

I took a step back, my wet rubber soles squeaking on the wood floor. "Worms?"

He glanced at me. "They're long gone. But at one time, there were wood-boring insects in that piece of paneling. They chewed tunnels through it."

"Yuck."

"It's no big deal. There are wood-boring insects in lots of wood. Old furniture, picture frames, even houses. And not only *old* houses, either. A lot of infestations are found in houses less than ten years old. It happens a lot around here, since the beetles like fir and spruce and other coniferous woods. The kind of wood we have a lot of in Maine."

"Beetles?" I repeated, wrinkling my nose. "I thought you said they were worms?"

Frankly, I like beetles even less than I like worms. It's the legs, I think. And the clicking noise they make when they move.

"Figure of speech," Derek said. "They're known as woodworms, but the tunnels are actually made by larva. Then the larva turn into beetles, which make the exit holes. But there aren't any here. This is old damage."

"Oh. Good." I took a relieved breath. "Will you be able to fix it? Or are we going to leave it? For verisimilitude, or something?"

Derek smiled and put an arm around my shoulders. "You know me; I'd love to leave it. It's part of the natural process. But I don't think whoever we sell this mansion to once we're finished with it will want wormholes in their paneling. We'll have to cut it out and replace it."

"That seems a shame." If it had been here for two hundred years already.

"I'll make it look good," Derek promised. "Just like it was always there."

"If anyone can do it, you can." I snuggled a little closer. He laughed and dropped a kiss on the top of my head before he let me go.

"C'mon, let's get busy. We'll have time for that later."

"That?" I tilted my face up at him.

"You know what." But he relented enough to give me another kiss, this one on the mouth. "*Now* can we get to work?"

"Sure," I said happily.

—3—

We were a little late setting out from Waterfield the next morning.

The weather had changed over the past couple of days from crisp blue skies and a brisk spring breeze on the day we started to gray and gloomy clouds full of stinging rain and wind that whipped across the ocean and stirred up choppy, foam-topped waves this morning. I huddled in the back of the boat, the hood of my raincoat—pink, to match the Wellies—up over my head, the color clashing rather pointedly with the orange life vest. Derek was at the wheel again, looking sort of like the Gorton's fisherman in his yellow slicker and hat, feet planted, squinting into the drizzle. Minus the beard, of course. And from the back.

Chilled and damp, I was focused on keeping my face down and my hood up, so I had no idea anything was wrong until Derek cut the engine.

"Are we there already?" I looked up, blinking as the rain hit my face.

"Not yet," Derek said over his shoulder, still steering the boat. The motor may have been cut off, but the boat was moving.

"Why did we stop?"

"There's something in the water." Derek's voice was muffled by the collar of the rain gear as well as the wind and rain. "Grab that hook, would you?" He waved a hand.

I looked around. Along the side of the boat lay an implement, a long pole that had a hook at the end, with a straight prong or spike behind it. "This?" I picked it up and extended it to him.

"Thanks. Could you to hold the boat steady?"

"Sure," I said, scrambling forward. "What's going on?"

I expected there to be a log or tree limb in the water, maybe, that he needed to push out of our way. I was wholly unprepared for what I did see when I followed the direction of his finger. All the color left my face and my breath caught in my throat. "That's a body!"

"Looks that way," Derek said. "Could just be a mannequin or a scarecrow, I suppose. Someone's idea of a joke."

"Not very funny, is it?"

He shook his head. "Not very, no. I think we're almost close enough. If you'll hold the boat steady, I'll try to hook her and pull her in."

I nodded, my hands wet on the steering wheel, my lips tight and my teeth clenched against the nausea rolling in my stomach.

The body was that of a girl or young woman, facedown in the water, and long, pale hair floated around her. She was dressed for summer, the small of her back exposed between low-riding jeans and a cropped top. Her skin, both on her back and arms, was pale and bluish, although not necessarily because it was her natural complexion.

"Don't look," Derek commanded, and I averted my eyes

as he used the hook to snag the corpse and bring it closer to the boat.

"Do you need help?" I asked, not looking at him.

There was nothing else to see in any direction. No other people, alive or dead; no debris from—for instance—a shipwreck. Nothing but choppy waves and rain. Where did she come from? Had she fallen off a boat, and no one had missed her? Had she been on a boat that sank?

"I got it," Derek said. "Would you go over to the other side of the boat, please. I'm gonna try to lift her in, and I need your weight on the other side so we won't capsize."

"Sure." I left the steering wheel—the boat was stationary now anyway, drifting on the swells—and headed for the port side. From the railing, I turned to watch Derek bend over the wale, straining. The small boat rocked, tilting almost flush with the water surface before he managed to haul the body, none too gently, into the boat.

I squeezed my eyes shut. I've read books describing bloated, drowned corpses fished from the water, nibbled by lobsters and fish, and I didn't think I'd like to experience one firsthand.

"It's OK, Avery," Derek said, his voice low. "She doesn't look bad."

"Just dead?" But I opened my eyes.

No, she didn't look bad, although she looked very dead. Pale and somehow empty.

She must have been a pretty woman, alive. Her features were regular, with wide cheekbones and a dimpled chin. Eyebrows and lashes were a few shades darker than the blond hair slicked back from her face by the salt water. Dry, it would probably be ash or wheat blond. At a guess, she was somewhere in her midtwenties, about my height, but with longer legs and a slim figure.

"Are you going to try mouth-to-mouth?" My voice was hushed.

Derek shook his head, his eyes on the still figure in the bottom of the boat. "It's too late. She's been in the water for hours. Probably since sometime last night."

"Poor thing. Drowning must be a horrible way to go."

"I don't think she drowned," Derek said. "She probably died from exposure. Hypothermia. The water is freezing this time of year, with all the snowmelt. Wearing just that"—he indicated the jeans and skimpy shirt—"she would have frozen to death long before she had time to drown."

"I'm not going to ask you how you can tell."

He turned back to the wheel. "We're gonna have to go back to Waterfield. Get your phone out, would you? There's not gonna be any reception out here, but once we get closer to land, you should be able to raise Wayne."

I nodded, digging in my pocket. Before I tried to call the Waterfield chief of police, though, I found a tarp under one of the seats and covered the dead girl with it. Both because I didn't want to look at her, and because I thought she could use that little bit of dignity.

By the time we were within sight of land, I had coverage, and I dialed Wayne's number. When he answered, I explained the situation. His first words were, "Not my jurisdiction," but then he said that he'd call the coast guard, although "it isn't their jurisdiction, either. They respond to incidents on the water, like shipwrecks, fires, and oil spills, but they don't investigate drowning deaths."

"So whose jurisdiction is it? The state police? Your friend Reece Tolliver?"

"Maybe," Wayne said. "I'll give him a call and find out. And I'll meet you at the harbor in ten minutes. Tell Derek to put in somewhere out of the way. When the ambulance shows up, I don't want a crowd gathering to see what's going on."

I relayed the instructions to Derek, and then I found

myself caught up in thoughts about the girl—the corpse—and wondering what had happened to her.

She wasn't dressed for being out on the water in early April in Maine. Or outside at all, for that matter. She should have been wearing an overcoat of some sort over the flimsy top, not to mention shoes and socks.

The soles of her feet were abraded, I'd noticed, as if she'd been walking barefoot over gravel or rough tree roots. But what kind of idiot goes outside barefoot in April, when the ground's only been thawed for a week or two?

• • •

"A drunk one," Wayne said when we had put in to shore and I had pointed out my observations. He'd been waiting for us at the far end of the harbor, as far away from any houses or businesses as he could get. "She's probably some girl from Barnham College, who had herself a good time last night, and now she's paid the ultimate price for it."

He looked at her, shaking his head sadly. I knew he was thinking of his son, Josh, and his stepdaughter, Shannon—Kate's daughter—both Barnham College students.

Our corpse would have to be one of the older students if she came from the college; she looked closer to twenty-five than twenty. Barnham was a four-year college, so barring the odd exception, the oldest students there were around twenty-three or so.

"If there were others involved, she probably scared them witless when she went in the water and disappeared," Wayne added, "and they were too worried to report it. May be drugs or something involved, that would get them into big trouble if they called us. The ME will figure that out. Toxicology will take a few days, but meanwhile I'll take a picture of her down to Barnham and see if anyone can identify her."

"*You* will?" Derek was watching as the ambulance crew approached. The ambulance itself was parked at the end of the road; the two paramedics were maneuvering their gurney across the rough planks of the pier.

Wayne grimaced, hands in the pockets of his tan uniform pants and shoulders hunched against the weather, his curly salt-and-pepper hair beaded with raindrops. "I talked to the coast guard. If there's a chance she's from Barnham, they want me to handle it. Even if she's not, I'm better equipped to deal with her than Reece, given the glut of dead bodies we've had since Avery moved to town."

"It's not my fault," I said. Several of those bodies had been dead before I even got to Waterfield. And I certainly hadn't had anything to do with killing the others.

"Of course not," Wayne agreed. "But you've gotten up to some trouble in the past year, Avery."

I shrugged, pouting. So what if I had? It still wasn't my fault. And I'd helped him solve several of those murders, let's not forget. Putting myself in grave personal danger along the way, too.

Well, this time there was no danger of that, anyway. I had no idea who the dead girl was, and apart from the fact that we'd found her, she had no connection to us. I had no reason in the world to concern myself in her death. In fact, once the paramedics had taken charge of the body, I intended to wash my hands of the whole thing—I'd make sure Derek gave his hands a good scrubbing, too—and then I intended to get back in the boat and go back to Rowanberry Island and back to work on the house, and I wasn't going to give the girl or her death a second thought. This time, it had nothing to do with me, and I was happy to keep it that way. It made for a nice change.

The two paramedics wheeled their gurney up to where we stood, with the corpse at our feet, still covered by the blue tarp. Wayne had blocked off the entire pier, so the paramedics had had to duck under several lengths of yellow crime scene tape strung from post to post down by the road. A very few people were hanging out down there, looking our way, but there were no crowds, per se. Maybe it was simply the unpleasant weather that was keeping most of the crowds at bay. Whatever the reason, I wasn't about to complain. I'd had my share of notoriety back in September, when news vans had been parked outside our house on Becklea Drive and Tony "the Tiger" Micelli from Portland's Channel Eight News had been hoping for another case like Chicago's John Wayne Gacy, with dozens of bodies buried in the yard and crawlspace. He hadn't gotten his wish, thank God, and the media onslaught had only lasted a couple of days, but I wasn't eager to repeat the experience.

It took only a few minutes for the paramedics to lift the drowning victim onto the gurney and confer with Wayne about where they were taking her and what they'd be doing once they got there. They were from the nearest fire department, doing chauffeur duty since it would have taken too long for a van to arrive from the medical examiner's office in Portland, the nearest big city to Waterfield. "Big" being relative; metropolitan Portland has about 230,000 inhabitants, versus my hometown of New York City's more than eight and a half million. Compared to Waterfield, though, it was a big place. Once again, I was aware of a feeling of displacement, my perceptions so radically different from what they used to be.

At any rate, the paramedics would be taking the victim to Portland, where they would deliver her to the morgue, where the ME would do whatever it is medical examiners do. I shut down that train of thought in time to hear what Derek was saying instead.

". . . don't need us, we'll just head back to work."

"Sure." Wayne nodded. "It's not like there's much you can tell me other than that you found her floating in the water somewhere between Rowanberry Island and the mainland at 8:42 A.M. or thereabouts. If you've never seen her before and there was nothing else out there with her . . ."

Derek shook his head. "Nothing we noticed. We didn't take the time to look around much, since we wanted to get her back here as quickly as possible."

"Don't worry about it," Wayne said. "The coast guard is having a trawl for anything unusual. Keep an eye out, just in case you notice something on your way back to Rowanberry Island, but other than that, I don't think there's anything more you can do. And no reason for you to concern yourselves further." His glance brushed mine.

OK, so perhaps a few times in the past I'd stumbled into one of Wayne's cases, where I didn't belong. Mostly because I'd found some kind of information that concerned someone I knew, and I felt compelled to figure out what was going on. And maybe he and Derek had had to come to my rescue a few times, when I'd gotten in over my head. Mostly because I didn't watch where I was going. But there was no need to worry about that this time.

"You don't have to warn me off," I said. "I'm sorry she drowned, or died of exposure or whatever, but I don't know her, and what happened to her is none of my business. I just want to go back to my house on the island and get back to work."

Wayne nodded.

"She's all yours. I won't even ask you later if you've figured out who she is and what happened to her."

"You don't have to go that far," Wayne said, while Derek's lips twitched. "I'll let you—both of you—know what I find out. Just as long as I don't have to worry about either of you interfering."

"I never interfere," Derek said.

"I never mean to interfere," I added.

Wayne shook his head, resigned. "Just go away," he said. "Let me know if you come across anything interesting. Like another body."

"Gah." I shuddered. "Please don't say that. One dead body is enough."

"More than enough," Wayne agreed, "but still, let me know if anything turns up."

Derek handed me back down into the boat and jumped in after me while Wayne followed the two paramedics and their sad burden toward the shore and the ambulance and police cruiser waiting there.

The return trip to the island was mostly quiet. The weather had gotten a little better in the past hour, the rain wasn't stinging my face so much as just settling like a damp, gray blanket over everything, but I guess neither of us really felt like talking. Derek steered the boat and I sat in the stern, huddled with my own depressing thoughts. I know I'd told Wayne—and myself—I couldn't care less, but it was hard not to be affected by what had happened. The girl in the water had been young and pretty, seemingly healthy; she had probably enjoyed life, and had expected it to go on for eternity, or at least for a long time to come. And now she was dead. She might have had a boyfriend, or even a husband. Young children, maybe. Certainly a mother and a father. Maybe siblings. Friends . . .

"Leave it alone, Avery," Derek said when he had pulled the boat up next to the leaning dock again and had hauled me out to stand next to him. We had seen no more bodies on the way here, and nothing else, either, with the exception of a coast guard boat off in the distance, slowly making its way between the islands scattered off the coast. Searching for clues, I guess.

I pulled my focus back in to look at him. "What?"

He shook me, gently. "Leave it alone. I know it sounds cold, but we didn't know her, and there's nothing we can do for her. Sometimes there just isn't. Even when they come to you still alive, sometimes there's nothing you can do."

"I know that. I'm just thinking about her family, you know? She's on her way to the morgue, and they have no idea. And she was so young. . . ."

"Accidents happen," Derek said, not unkindly. He let me go and started unfastening the straps on his life vest. "Especially here on the coast. There are a few drownings here every year. And a few people who die from exposure because they underestimate the temperature, either of the water or the air. I'm sorry about it, but it's life."

I nodded reluctantly, unbuckling my own life vest.

"Wayne will take care of her. They'll figure out who she is and notify her family, and that'll be it. In the meantime, let's just get back to work. It'll give you something else to think about."

I nodded. Sounded like a good idea.

We spent the rest of the day working on the house, which meant that Derek concentrated on getting the generator up and working while I walked around with pen and paper, counting the cracked window panes that needed to be replaced (fifty-six), and measuring the piece of worm-eaten paneling that needed to be matched (four feet by two and a half), and trying to come up with an accurate tally of missing bricks from the foundation and missing doorknobs from the interior doors. At some point, someone had done their level best to strip the house of anything not integral to the structure, so there were no light fixtures, just naked bulbs hanging from the ceilings, and no doorknobs or other hardware, either. Anything someone could walk off with was gone.

"There's a place up near Boothbay Harbor," Derek said when I mentioned it to him, "where they'll have what we need. A salvage yard."

"Old House Parts?" Everyone in Maine has heard of the Old House Parts Company. Except I had been under the impression that the famous architectural salvage company was located in the other direction.

"That's in Kennebunkport," Derek confirmed. "This place is smaller, and it's up the road apiece. The selection isn't as wide, but the prices tend to be a little better, and sometimes you can find some real treasures there. The competition isn't as stiff."

I nodded. "You want to go there now?"

"Probably not. Interior doorknobs aren't a priority. I'll give Ian a call, see what he can scrounge up and if he can hold some stuff for us until we can make it up there. He's usually good about that kind of thing, since he knows I'll get there eventually."

"What are we doing in the meantime, then?"

He grimaced. "Unfortunately, supplies probably take precedence right now. We should head back to town soon to make sure we can make it to the hardware store and the lumber depot before they close. I need lumber for the new paneling and the hardware store can cut the window glass we need."

"Do you know how to put them in?"

He smiled. "By tomorrow night, you'll know how to put them in, too. There's nothing to it."

"Until I slice my wrist open on a piece of glass and bleed out, you mean."

"Good thing I'm a doctor," Derek said lightly, and lifting my hand, he turned it over and kissed the inside of my wrist. My toes curled inside the pink rubber boots, and suddenly I couldn't wait to get back to shore.

Of course, once Derek had his pieces of wood for the new paneling, and we had ordered the fifty-six panes of glass we needed, and we were leaving the hardware store and we only had to walk around the building to the rear stairs and go up to Derek's loft and shut out the rest of the world for a while, the rest of the world interrupted.

"Yoo-hoo! Derek!"

"Oh, great!" I muttered.

Derek chuckled. "I don't think she did it on purpose, Avery."

I wouldn't bet on it. Personally, I think Melissa James, Derek's too perfect ex-wife, would be just delighted to screw up my prospects for a romantic tête-a-tête with her ex-husband. And not only because I think she wants him back, but because it's the sort of thing she'd do just because she could.

Melissa and Derek got married in their twenties, while he was in medical school and she was prowling for a husband. She stuck with him all through school and residency, and then moved back to Waterfield with him so he could join his dad, Dr. Ben Ellis, in the latter's medical practice. The Ellises have been physicians for generations. From what I gather, Melissa did it all with a pretty good attitude, too, probably envisioning herself becoming the gracious First Lady of Waterfield as time went by. That all changed about a year later, when Derek decided he wasn't happy being an MD, and he wanted to quit and start Waterfield Renovation and Restoration instead. Dr. Ben was disappointed but supportive, while Derek's other friends just wanted him to do whatever would make him happy. And, of course, Melissa had a fit. In the midst of all of this, she went out and got her real estate license, and then she hooked up with my cousin Ray Stenham, a local builder. As soon as she had him firmly wrapped around her finger, personally and professionally, she drop-kicked Derek to the curb.

Now that Ray was out of the picture, it seemed that she might want Derek's attention again.

"Derek! Over here!"

She was hanging halfway out of the window of a loft across the street, waving. Yes, once Ray and Melissa broke up, Melissa had moved out of the shared McMansion on the outskirts of Waterfield and sold it. Half the money went toward Ray's legal fees while the other half went toward a loft on Main Street, right across from Derek's and just up the block from Melissa's office at Waterfield Realty. She could probably look out her window straight into Derek's bedroom. I made a mental note to put up some curtains. Immediately.

"Derek!" Her voice was starting to become annoyed.

"I should go see what she wants," Derek muttered. Happily, he didn't seem thrilled at the prospect.

"Be my guest."

"You don't want to come?" He glanced down at me.

"You know me. I like Melissa better at a distance."

"Don't we all," Derek said. "You wanna go upstairs and wait for me?"

I shook my head. The rain had stopped, and although it wasn't precisely warm, I was all right, for the time being. "I'll just wait right here."

"It might take a while. She probably wants to talk about some new project she wants me to do."

"I don't doubt it at all," I said. "It's pitiful, how she can't come up with a better excuse than that. After spending six years ordering the Stenham Construction crews around, you'd think she'd know enough other plumbers and electricians and carpenters that she didn't have to cozy up to *you*."

"But I'm the best," Derek said with a grin.

I grinned back. "No argument here."

Melissa's lovely face had twisted into a pout by now, and she had crawled back into her apartment, where she was standing at the window, hands on her hips. As always, she was gorgeous: razor-cut, pale blond hair cupping her jaw, with a fuzzy, begging-to-be-touched V-necked sweater in the same violet blue color as her eyes hugging every curve.

"You better go," I added. "She's looking miffed."

He nodded. "The sooner I get it over with, the sooner I'll get back. Don't go anywhere." He dropped a kiss on my mouth before he turned and sauntered across the street, obviously in no hurry. I watched him stop under Melissa's window and call up to her. Wiggling my butt against the cold wetness, I made myself comfortable on a bench.

No sooner had I sat down than a black-and-white police cruiser pulled up to the curb and parked. The door opened and Wayne unfolded his lanky length. The chief of police is almost six foot four, so it's quite a production getting his legs in and out of a normal sedan. A truck suits him much better, and when he's off duty, he drives one, but he was still in uniform and on the job, looking grim and professional.

"Avery."

"Chief."

He made a face. "I need your help."

"And here I thought you were coming to arrest me for loitering. I'm waiting for Derek. He's right there." I pointed across the street to where Melissa was once again hanging halfway out of the window, creamy cleavage on display, while Derek had his head tilted back to look up at her. I'm sure she found the position fitting.

Wayne shot him a glance. "I don't need him. You'll do."

"Flattered, I'm sure. What can I do for you?"

He sat down next to me and fumbled in the pocket of his jacket. "What do you make of this?"

"This" was a ziplock baggie, sandwich sized, with condensation and a scrap of paper inside. The paper looked like it had been torn from the edge of something, and it also looked like it had been through the wringer, or at least through the washer. It was crinkly, and the letters written on it, in a crabbed pencil script, were pale and faded. I squinted, turning the baggie this way and that in an effort to make out the writing.

"I can read some of it," I said after a few seconds. "At least I think so. There's a small *g* here, with a period after it, and then I think it says *Waterfield*. Or something like it. Some of the letters are a little different. And then a lowercase *u* and a period before something funny that starts with a *b*. Or not exactly a *b* . . ." The letter looked like a cross between a lowercase and a capital *b*: Б. "And then the number fourteen." At least I recognized that.

"It's Russian," Wayne said.

I squinted at him. "Really? How do you know?"

"Took it to a professor of Cyrillic at Barnham College. The lowercase *g* denotes the town, and the lowercase *u* means street. In Russian, the street number comes after the address, not before like here."

"Interesting. But what's it got to do with me? I'm not Russian."

"The ME found it in the pocket of that young woman you brought to shore this morning," Wayne said. "That's why it looks like it's been submerged."

"Because it has." I nodded. "I appreciate your sharing it with me, but I still don't know what you want."

"It's an address," Wayne said. "On Becklea Drive."

He didn't have to add, "Where the two of you owned a house last year."

"No kidding? That's what those squiggles say? Wow." I thought for a moment before I added, "Number fourteen is Irina's house, I think."

Wayne nodded. "I know it is. This is her name, right here." He pointed to some of the squiggles—excuse me, Cyrillic letters—on the piece of paper. "I've already been there, but no one's home. You two work with her, don't you? Do you have a phone number?"

"Sure." I fished in my pocket for my cell phone just as Derek finished with Melissa and came back across the street again and stopped next to us.

"What's going on?"

"I need Irina Rozhdestvensky's telephone number," Wayne said, managing a reasonable approximation of the last name.

"Avery's got it." Derek turned to me. "Melissa says she has a leak in her bathroom. She wants me to come up and fix it."

"Right now?"

"Better right now than tomorrow morning," Derek said. "The hardware store is still open, so I can still get materials, and it won't cut into the time we have to work on our own house."

I shrugged. "Fine."

He grinned. "I'll charge her the going rate, plus fifteen percent for after-hours and a little for my suffering. I can meet you for dinner later, if you want. Melissa's paying."

"That's all right," I said, "I have to help Wayne track down Irina."

"Why?" Derek turned to Wayne, who shrugged.

"I'll tell you about it later," I said. "Just go look at Melissa's plumbing. I mean, Melissa's bathroom, and I'll call you."

"OK," Derek said. "See ya, Tink." He blew me a kiss and headed back across the street. Melissa was already downstairs at the door, ready to let him in. I turned to Wayne.

"I've got the number. What do you want me to tell her?"

Wayne sighed.

—4—

Irina was on her way back to Waterfield on the bus when I called, and Wayne arranged to meet her at the bus stop and drive her to her house on Becklea Drive, where they would "talk."

"Wait a second," I said when he got up from the bench without talking to me.

He turned to look at me. "What?"

"You're not leaving me here, are you? You need me!"

"Why?"

"Because if that girl we found in the water this morning is someone Irina knows, she's going to want someone there with her. *You*'re going to want someone there with her. I'm available. And between you and me, I don't think she's too fond of the police."

Wayne lowered his brows. "What do you mean?"

I hastened to assure him. "Oh, not that she's a criminal or anything. As far as I know, she's a perfectly nice, hardworking woman who gets by on very little. It's just an impression I got, back when we were dealing with that skeleton in the crawlspace."

Wayne's eyebrows were still tilted, so I continued, "She grew up in Russia. Or somewhere in what used to be the Soviet Union. And she's in her midthirties, so she probably remembers what it was like in the bad old days. The police weren't the good guys over there back then."

Wayne nodded. "I get it. In that case, maybe it would be best if you came along. Just don't interfere."

"When do I ever interfere?" I said, insulted.

Wayne didn't answer, just opened the passenger door of the police car for me and waited for me to get in.

Irina Rozhdestvensky is a few years older than me—thirty-five or thirty-six, maybe—and she's tall and severe, with dark hair pulled straight back from a broad face with a strong jaw and those high Slavic cheekbones. When she stepped off the bus, I saw she was wearing one of her tailored business suits, this one in navy blue with a yellow blouse underneath. When she came closer, I noticed that the blouse had small dots all over it. And when she stopped beside me, I realized that they weren't dots at all; they were tiny butterflies.

"Avery." She smiled when she saw me, her teeth crooked, but her smile genuine.

"Hi, Irina." I returned her smile. "This is Wayne. Police Chief Wayne Rasmussen. When he told me he was coming to talk to you, I invited myself along."

Irina's gray eyes turned wary. "Chief Rasmussen."

Wayne nodded. "Miss Rozhdestvensky."

Irina listened to him stumble over the name. "You may call me Irina, Chief Rasmussen. It will be easier for both of us."

I hid a smile. Wayne looked relieved. "Thank you, Miss . . . um . . . Irina. Why don't you get in the car"—he opened the passenger-side door for her; I was relegated to the backseat, behind the bulletproof glass—"and I'll drive you home. We can talk there."

Irina nodded, tucking her skirt around her knees as she got into the car. I crawled into the back and met her eyes in the mirror. She looked worried.

The drive from the bus stop to Irina's house on Becklea Drive was short, just a few minutes, and nothing much was said. Wayne pulled into the driveway outside Irina's mid-century brick ranch and cut the motor.

"How are Beatrice and Steve?" he asked me.

I glanced up the street to the house that Derek and I had renovated six months ago. Another low-slung brick ranch, it looked well maintained but empty. Derek's stepsister, Bea, and her husband, Steve, had ended up buying it and were moving here from Boston. Steve, a lawyer, was planning to open a general practice in Waterfield, just as soon as he got all his ducks in a row and took the Maine bar exam.

"As far as I know they're fine. They were here a couple of weeks ago, and they're coming back for Easter. I don't think they'll actually move in until the summer, though."

Wayne nodded. "And Miss Rudolph's house?"

The house next door to ours was also empty, since the owner had passed on in the fall.

"No idea," I said. "It belongs to her brother, I think. Derek and I thought about offering to buy it, but I don't know that I want to renovate two houses right next to each other. And there are some bad memories here."

Wayne nodded. Irina, meanwhile, had opened the door to her own house and was waiting for us to join her. We abandoned our discussion about the neighborhood and went inside.

The subdivision that Becklea Drive is part of—Primrose Acres—was built in the 1950s. Most of the houses looked and felt very similar. All were built of brick; some red brick, some yellow, some gray or rose. Some speckled. All of them had a big picture window in the front, where the living room was. Venetia Rudolph's house, right next to the one we had renovated, had the exact same footprint as what was now Bea and Steve's house, and the same interior layout. Irina's house was similar, with a living room–dining room combination up front, a kitchen beyond the dining room, and three bedrooms and two baths down the hall. The only difference was that everything was mirrored here; in our house and Venetia's, the dining room and kitchen were to the left, the bedrooms and baths to the right. In Irina's house, kitchen was right, bedrooms and baths left.

I say the *only* difference, but of course it wasn't. The house we had renovated was beautifully redone, with fresh paint, refinished wood floors, new light fixtures, maple kitchen cabinets . . . Venetia's house, when I'd been inside it, had been heavily carpeted and curtained, with draperies and wallpaper and *Gone with the Wind* tchotchkes everywhere. Not my taste, but it had been cared for and spotless; clearly a beloved home.

Irina had done her best with what she had, and it wasn't her fault her place didn't show to advantage. I pegged it for a rental, with bland off-white walls, stained, beige carpets, and thrift-store furniture. The kitchen, which I could see through the dining room, was basic: unpainted oak cabinets, off-white laminate countertop, chapped vinyl flooring, and appliances that had clearly seen better days. Basic scratch-and-dent floor models, they were unmatched and at least ten years out of date. The only attractive thing about the place was a collection of eggs on the fake-oak circa 1970 entertainment center along one wall, where Irina's small TV and old-fashioned VHS/DVD player were located.

There were roughly a dozen of them—the eggs—and they were in several sizes, from small chicken eggs to a huge specimen that must have come from an ostrich or dinosaur. All were painted in bright colors, some with geometric designs, others with stylized pictures of fauna—fish and fowl—or flora—flowers or wheat or what looked like oak leaves.

"*Pysanky*," Irina said.

"Bless you."

"That's what they are called. *Pysanky*. Ukrainian Easter eggs. Very famous."

"Can I touch them?"

"They are fragile," Irina warned. "There." She pointed to the coffee table, where another egg was lying amid pieces of paper, the Sunday comics, and a few store circulars. "That *pysanka* is made of stone."

I reached for it and felt my eyes widen when I tried to pick it up. She wasn't kidding; it was heavy and cool in my hands, a chunk of rock polished to eggshell smoothness and then painted with images of wheat and what looked like stylized deer and birds.

"Health," Irina said, pointing to the heads of grain. "Strength and prosperity." She indicated the deer. "Happiness." The birds.

"It's beautiful."

"It's a paperweight," Irina said. "Those"—she indicated the collection on the entertainment center—"are real eggs. I make some for Easter every year."

"Can you teach me? Sometime?"

"Sure." She shrugged. "It's easy. Like batik. You know about batik, right?"

I nodded. Batik is a traditional Asian method of dyeing fabric in which wax is applied to areas where you don't want the dye to take. In recent times, the word has come to mean any type of fabric with traditional batik prints, whether or not the actual batik technique was used to produce it.

While I turned the *pysanka* over in my hands, admiring the intricate design, Irina turned her attention to the furniture. “Please excuse the mess,” she muttered, moving books and magazines off the chair and sofa and onto the floor, indicating that Wayne should sit. There were books everywhere: on shelves along the wall, stacked on the coffee table, on the floor . . .

Wayne looked around, at the bodice-ripper romance novels rubbing elbows with teenage vampire sagas and recent thrillers. I recognized Gert Heyerdahl’s latest in a stack on the floor. “You must like to read.”

“The nights are long,” Irina said with a shrug. I wasn’t sure whether she was referring to the short winter days this far north or the fact that she lived alone and, as far as I knew, didn’t have a husband or boyfriend anywhere. “And I am trying to improve my English.”

“Your English is already fine.” I grabbed a stack of magazines and dumped them on the floor so I could curl up in a faded chintz armchair on the other side of the table, the *pysanka* still cradled in my hands.

Irina, meanwhile, sat next to Wayne on the sofa. She looked uncomfortable, perched on the edge of the pillows, knees together and hands folded—make that clenched—in her lap. Her jaw was tight, too.

“How long have you been living here?” Wayne wanted to know. “Where did you move from?”

Irina pried her lips apart. “Three years in Maine. I come from Kiev. In Ukraine.”

Wayne nodded. This was just preliminary information, intended to put her at ease. It didn’t seem to be working, but he kept on. “Do you have any family? Or did you come over alone?”

Irina had come over alone, she said. "My family is still in Ukraine. My brothers Alexi and Ivan, my sister Svetlana."

Wayne's ears pricked up, as did mine. "Oh, you have a sister? How old is she?"

"Younger," Irina said. "I am the oldest. Alexi is thirty-two; Ivan, thirty. Svetlana is the baby. Twenty-six."

I glanced at Wayne. He didn't meet my eyes. "And they're all still in the Ukraine?" he asked. "Even Svetlana?"

Irina nodded. "Especially Svetlana. She is a student at the *Natsional'nyi universytet Kyyevo-Mohylians'ka akademiya.*"

The Russian words rolled off her tongue. I thought I recognized a few of the sounds, and the translation didn't come as a total surprise. "The National University of Kiev, Mohyla Academy," Irina clarified.

"When was the last time you spoke to her?"

Irina had to think about it. "Six weeks. Maybe more."

So Svetlana could be the woman from the water. The age was right, and if Irina hadn't spoken to her for weeks, she could have left Kiev and arrived here, no problem.

"Does your sister look like you?" I asked.

Irina looked surprised, and maybe a little worried. She had to be wondering why we were so interested in her sister. However, she answered willingly enough. "She is ten years younger. And the last time I saw her, her hair was longer, almost to her waist. But it's brown, like mine."

Not the girl from the water, then. Not unless the long, blond hair was bleached, but I hadn't noticed any dark roots, and wet as it was, they ought to have been easy to spot. She was also considerably shorter and softer-looking than the severe Irina. That made things less complicated.

I glanced at Wayne. He nodded. Apparently he was thinking the same thing because some of the stress lines around his eyes disappeared.

"Do you know who this is?" he asked Irina.

Gone are the days of the instant Polaroids that you read about in crime novels. Wayne pulled his cell phone from his pocket and manipulated a few buttons before showing it to her. He must have snapped a picture of the body after we left him this morning. Or at the morgue, later.

Irina looked at the display. I watched her turn pale, but that could have been just because the girl so very obviously was dead. Her voice was steady, anyway. She shook her head. "I have never seen her before."

"Are you sure? Look again."

She looked again. And shook her head again. "I don't know her."

"It's not your sister?"

Now she looked shocked. "Of course not. I would know my own sister!"

"You haven't seen her for three years," I reminded her, gently. "She could have bleached her hair, maybe . . ."

Irina shook her head. "This is not Svetlana."

"Is she perhaps someone else you might know? Maybe from a long time ago?"

By now Irina was starting to look suspicious. "Why are you asking me all of these questions? Who is she? What happened to her? And why did you come to me?"

Wayne snapped his phone shut and fished in his pocket. Out came the ziplock baggie with the scrap of paper. "Do you know what this is?"

Irina shook her head. She didn't reach for it. I think I might have been tempted to snatch, had it been me. Again, I watched the color leach from her face as she looked at what Wayne held in front of her.

"Did you write it?" he asked.

She shook her head.

"But it's Russian?"

"Cyrillic. Yes."

"And it's your name and address." This time it wasn't a question.

Irina nodded, uneven teeth worrying her lower lip. Her hands were so tightly clasped that the knuckles showed white.

"Do a lot of people in the Ukraine know your address here?" I wanted to know.

Irina shook her head. "Just family and a few friends."

"What about the handwriting? Do you recognize it?"

But Irina said she didn't. Wayne put the Ziploc back in his pocket. "The woman in the picture," he said, "was found in the sea. Derek and Avery found her on their way to Rowanberry Island this morning."

Irina glanced up at me. I nodded.

"The piece of paper was in her pocket. It has your information on it. Are you sure you don't know who she is?"

Irina shook her head.

"Any idea who could have written the note?"

Irina said she didn't. I was watching, though, from the other side of the table, and as she said it, I thought I noticed a quick wash of color stain her cheekbones.

I suspect Wayne noticed, too. "I would like you to come to Portland with me," he said, "and have a look at the body. The picture is small. Maybe, if you see her, you'll recognize her."

Irina looked like she wanted to refuse but didn't dare. "Now?" she said instead, dismay clearly written on her face.

Wayne shook his head. "Tomorrow will be sufficient. Tonight is . . . inconvenient."

Inconvenient for the corpse, I gathered, more than for Wayne. The autopsy was probably under way, and the ME had to make the body presentable again before it could be viewed. Especially by someone who might know it. Her.

"Avery?" Irina had turned to me. I focused on her face. "Will you be there?"

I glanced at Wayne. He grimaced. More in resignation than refusal, I thought.

"I'll be happy to go with you," I said. "Derek can do without me for a few hours."

Irina smiled. She looked relieved.

• • •

"Wonder if I need to send Brandon to keep an eye on her house?" Wayne muttered, more to himself than to me, I thought, when we were back in the police cruiser. I had arranged to fetch Irina at nine the next morning to go to Portland. Wayne would be there, too, of course, but I didn't want to be dependent on him for my ride back to Waterfield after our visit to the morgue, so I thought I'd better drive myself. Plus, I never get tired of zipping around in the little spring green VW Beetle my mother and stepfather had given me for Christmas.

For the longest time I had resisted getting a car. I grew up in New York City, and although I made sure I had a license and knew how to drive, most people in the city rely on the subway and on cabs for transportation. I was no exception. After moving to Waterfield and realizing I really needed my own wheels, I still made excuses for why I couldn't buy a car. Too costly, couldn't find the right one, didn't know what I wanted. After nose-diving Derek's truck into a ditch when someone messed with the brakes, I'd gotten even more scared and resistant. I was amazed at how much I enjoyed driving my sassy little green Bug.

Now I watched Wayne maneuver the police cruiser out of Irina's driveway and head down the street to the corner. "Why would you put surveillance on her? Are you afraid she's going to run away overnight?"

"She did look nervy," Wayne said, looking both ways before taking a left on Primrose.

I couldn't argue with that. "I think that's just general nerves, though. Not a guilty conscience. If a dead body showed up with your name and address in its pocket, you'd be nervy, too. And if she was lying about recognizing the girl in the picture, she's the best liar in the world."

Wayne nodded, if reluctantly. "I'd tend to agree. That doesn't mean it isn't someone she knows, or knew once."

"But if she didn't recognize her, she wouldn't have any reason to run away. I guess you're hoping that she'll recognize the body tomorrow?"

"It's worth a shot," Wayne said, with a shrug.

—5—

I had had to tell Derek about the latest development over the phone because Melissa's plumbing problem had turned out to take all evening and half the night. I tried not to read too much into that.

No, I wasn't afraid that Derek was cheating on me. He's not the type. If he'd decided he wanted to go back to Melissa, and he wanted to end things with me, he'd end them, fair and square, before doing anything else. But I did feel a little miffed about the fact that he'd spent the evening with his ex-wife, even if it hadn't been by choice.

Not that I could complain about the company I'd kept myself; on my way up Main Street, I had run into Kate McGillicutty-Rasmussen, Wayne's wife, and had been invited to dinner.

Kate was my first friend when I moved to Waterfield. I'd spent the night at the Waterfield Inn, her bed-and-breakfast, after Aunt Inga sent me a letter saying she wanted to see me, and we had struck up a friendship. It was Kate who had insisted that I hire Derek to help me renovate the place; I still didn't know whether she'd been trying to matchmake, or whether she just wanted to do us both a good turn and throw some money his way while ensuring I had skilled help.

"Both," she said now, when I asked. "I knew you were going to need help with the house, and I knew Derek was the best person to help you. I figured you'd get along well once you got used to each other. And I thought he'd probably like you."

"What about me? Did you think I'd like him, too? Or didn't that really matter?"

"You're a woman," Kate said with a grin over her shoulder at me. "Have you ever met a woman who didn't like Derek?"

Now that she mentioned it, I hadn't.

"Here." She put a bowl of ziti on the table in front of me and sat down on the other side herself, with a bowl of her own. We were in the kitchenette of the carriage house, the one Derek and I had renovated over Christmas. "Dig in. So how are things going on the island?"

"Not too good today," I admitted between mouthfuls of food. "Did Wayne tell you about the dead girl in the water?"

She nodded. "He said he'd have to work late. They're still trying to identify her."

"Irina and I are going to the morgue tomorrow morning to see if Irina knows who she is. Apparently she had a piece of paper in her pocket with Irina's name and address on it."

"That's interesting," Kate said.

"I know. Wayne showed her a picture, though, and Irina said she didn't know the girl. Wayne's hoping that seeing her in person might make a difference."

"It might," Kate said. "Dead people don't always look like themselves."

"True." I glanced down. "Maybe we should talk about something else. I'm losing my appetite. And this is really good ziti."

"Glad you like it," Kate said, and smoothly turned the conversation to her special ziti recipe. Nothing more was said about Irina or the girl in the water, at least not until I'd left Kate's house and walked to my own and was on the phone with Derek.

He was sick and tired of tinkering with Melissa's pipes, and although he listened to my story about the scrap of paper with Irina's contact information on it, and Svetlana who was supposedly at university in Kiev, and the trip to the morgue I had promised to take the next morning, I could tell his mind wasn't on what I was saying. So I simplified things.

"I can't go to the island with you tomorrow. I have to drive to Portland in the morning. If it doesn't take too long, I'll take the ferry out later."

"That'll work," Derek said.

"Are you all right? You sound . . ." What he sounded was pissy, but he might not appreciate that word. ". . . annoyed."

"Melissa is annoying," Derek said.

"Wasn't there anything wrong with her plumbing? I mean, with her bathroom?"

"Oh, it was leaking. In the most inconvenient spot imaginable."

I thought for a second. I should know the answer to this. "Inside the wall?"

"You got it. So I had to cut through the drywall, replace the plumbing, replace the drywall, mud the drywall, and now I have to go back tomorrow night to sand the drywall, re-mud the drywall, and then re-sand the drywall and paint the damn wall the day after. I rue the day I ever met that woman."

"You could tell her no," I said.

"No, I can't. She asked me for help. I can't refuse to help her."

"What if she asked for something else? Would you do that, too?"

"Within reason," Derek said, his voice a little lighter. "But only up to a point. And I missed you. She doesn't stand by and hand me my tools the way you do."

Hopefully that meant she also didn't stand by and admire his rear view in the tight jeans, the way I was wont to do.

"On the upside," Derek added, "what I'm charging her is enough to pay for all the new window panes for the house on the island."

"That's good."

"And what's left will take a lot less time. We can have dinner together tomorrow night, if you want. My treat."

"That sounds nice," I said. "Anything but ziti. I had that tonight."

"I have to work for a few hours and you're already going out with someone else?" His voice was back to normal now, light with laughter. "Who'd you take up with while my back was turned?"

"Just Kate. Wayne was working late. She didn't want to eat alone."

"Can't blame her there. Much nicer to have company. So you're taking Irina to Portland in the morning?"

"She asked me to. She said her brothers and sister are still in the Ukraine, and if she has a boyfriend, I haven't seen him."

"Me, neither," Derek said. "I'm sure she's too busy trying to make a living. Real estate is a cutthroat business—just look at Melissa—and Irina has a few strikes against her. People are more suspicious of foreigners, and she's not from Waterfield, so she doesn't have a network of acquaintances already built up that can refer her business."

"Melissa isn't from Waterfield, either," I pointed out. Delaware or West Virginia or some such place, if I remembered correctly. Not the same as the Ukraine, but still, not a native Mainer.

"There have been Ellises in Waterfield for generations," Derek said, unconsciously arrogant. "The moment she was introduced as my wife, and as Dad's daughter-in-law, she belonged."

Figures. "Did she use your name? Or did she always keep her own?"

"She used mine," Derek said. "And went back to her own after the divorce." He paused, perhaps to wonder how we had gotten onto this subject.

"Anyway," I switched back to where we'd been before, "Irina asked me to go with her tomorrow. I couldn't really say no."

"So much for not getting involved this time," Derek said.

"I know. I was telling myself this morning that here's finally a dead body I have no connection to, and now look what's happened."

"Murphy's Law," Derek said. "Or something like it. OK. I'll go to the island without you in the morning, and if what you're doing doesn't take all day and you want to come out later, you can take the ferry."

"I'll wear comfy shoes for the walk across the island," I said. "And I can't imagine a trip to the morgue can take all day. I'll probably see you in the afternoon."

"I'll look forward to that," Derek said gallantly and hung up.

• • •

Irina and I got to the morgue just before ten the next morning. I was wearing my usual uniform of jeans and long-sleeved T-shirt; clothes I didn't mind ruining with paint, polyurethane, or power tools later on. Irina was wearing her usual uniform of staid business suit with starched blouse and high heels. Today's suit was black, and the blouse was gray; I wondered if she had dressed for the occasion or if it was just the outfit that was in the front of the closet this morning.

The choice of black clothing may or may not have been deliberate, but I couldn't see any signs of mourning on her face. She looked as she always did: composed and distant. Her eyes weren't red rimmed from crying, and she looked like she'd spent a perfectly pleasant night. If she had recognized the young woman in the picture, she wasn't someone Irina knew well. I thought I detected a sign of nerves when I turned the Beetle off outside the Portland City Morgue, though. When I opened the door and swung my legs out—for the occasion, I had replaced the pink lipstick boots with a pair of comfy, fur-lined clogs—Irina didn't follow suit. When I turned to look at her, she was staring straight ahead, her eyes fixed on nothing and her face pale. I nudged her.

"It's OK. She doesn't look bad." At least the corpse hadn't looked bad yesterday, when we fished her from the water. Now that the medical examiner had had a go that might have changed. But I thought he would be sensitive to what was a potential relative or acquaintance and make sure the body was presentable. I wasn't too sanguine about going into the morgue myself. I'd seen corpses before—more than my fair share—but I'd never been to the morgue, and I would have been happy to keep it that way.

I coaxed Irina out of the car and into the building. Wayne was waiting for us in the lobby and took us downstairs to the cold storage. He did give me the option of staying behind, but Irina looked like she was ready to bolt, and when I hesitated, wondering if maybe I could get away with waiting upstairs, she sent me such a desperate look that I couldn't in good conscience abandon her. So we all headed down to the basement in the elevator.

The first thing that struck me was the odor. That sickly sweet smell of death, not quite masked by the air fresheners and air-filtration system. For a few days last summer I hadn't been able to get it out of my nose.

"Avery?" Wayne shook my shoulder, gently. "The visiting room is this way."

I opened my eyes. The visiting room. Like we were stopping by to see an old friend in a nursing home or hospital. Or prison.

The visiting room was small, with just enough space for a gurney and a handful of people. A woman was already there: a tall and sturdy lady in her late fifties, with graying blond hair cut short. She was dressed in a white lab coat over green scrubs and was holding a clipboard. When Wayne ushered us in, she nodded a greeting. "Morning, Chief Rasmussen."

"Morning, Dr. Lawrence," Wayne returned. "This is Avery Baker and Irina . . . um . . ."

"Rozhdestvensky," Irina said faintly.

Dr. Lawrence bobbed her head at us both. "You're the one who found her," she said to me, tapping her clipboard. "I remember your name."

I nodded. "My boyfriend and I came across her in the ocean yesterday morning and brought her back to shore. Wayne took over from there."

Dr. Lawrence, who must be the medical examiner, turned to Irina. "And you're here to see if she's someone you know."

Irina hesitated. Her sideways glance at the covered gurney was agonized.

I had avoided looking at it myself so far. Not that there was much to see, really. A steel table with wheels, and a white sheet covering what could have been anything, but which was probably our girl from yesterday.

"Don't worry," Dr. Lawrence said reassuringly. "We've taken good care of her."

By way of proof, she folded the sheet gently back from the corpse's head. I averted my eyes automatically and had to force myself to look back.

Dr. Lawrence was right; from what I could see of the body—and that was just the head down to the very top of the shoulders—the medical examiner had been careful to be as respectful as possible. The blond hair was dry and combed, fanning out around the young woman's head. It still looked natural to me, not colored. I was certain Dr. Lawrence had sliced the body open and taken samples of all the innards, those incisions now decently hidden by the sheet, but if her examination had included opening the cranium and looking at the brain, I couldn't see any sign of it. Although I'll readily admit I didn't look closely. As far as the face went, it looked just like it had yesterday when Derek had lifted the young woman out of the ocean. Pale and wan, with sunken eyes and colorless lips.

"Her eyes are blue," Dr. Lawrence said softly, "and the hair color is her own. She was small, just five feet one inch tall and roughly one hundred and five pounds, and as far as I could determine, she was healthy. She had a broken leg sometime in childhood, but it healed completely, and in a way that wouldn't have given her any trouble. There are old fillings in some of her teeth"—she handed Wayne a dental chart—"but no untreated cavities, which leads me to believe she took care of her health."

He nodded.

"Other than a few bruises here and there, on her upper arms and one on her hip, there are no fresh injuries on her body other than some abrasions on the soles of her feet. From walking around barefoot recently, I gather. I removed a few small pebbles and pieces of vegetation." She took a small ziplock baggie off the clipboard and gave it to Wayne, who held it up to the light to peer at it.

"Looks like just regular sand and rock and maybe a pine needle?"

"Something very like that." Dr. Lawrence nodded. "Just what you'd expect if she'd been walking barefoot anywhere along the coast. I place time of death at some point between midnight and six A.M. yesterday morning. By the time you found her"—she nodded in my direction—"it was hours too late to do anything for her. She died from exposure, by the way. From being in the cold water. There was no water in her lungs."

I nodded. "I'll tell my boyfriend. He said all those things, too, and I'm sure he'll be happy to know he was right."

"Your boyfriend must know a lot about medicine," Dr. Lawrence remarked.

"Four years of medical school, four years of residency, and a year or so of practice before he decided he'd rather be a handyman." I shrugged.

"Ah." The doctor smiled. "I take it we're talking about young Mr. Ellis?"

"You know Derek?"

"Not well. I know his father. Doctors of pathology are doctors, too, you know."

"Right," I said. She and Dr. Ellis were colleagues. Of course. They probably had meetings or luncheons or Christmas parties they attended together.

While all this had been going on, Irina had been quiet, and now we all turned to her. She was standing next to me, her hands folded in front of her and her face impassive.

"Miss Rozhdestvensky?" Dr. Lawrence said gently from the other side of the gurney. "Do you know her?"

Irina's lips thinned before they parted. "No." She shook her head for emphasis.

"You're sure?"

Irina looked up, from Wayne to me to the doctor. "I have never seen her before. If I did know who she was, I would tell you. She's someone's daughter, or sister, or wife. Not my sister, not my parents' daughter, but someone's. I'm sorry I can't help you."

"That's all right," Wayne said. "It was worth a try. I don't suppose you have any idea how she ended up with your name and address in her pocket, either, then?"

Irina shook her head, her lips tightly pressed together now. "I have never seen her before. She didn't contact me. No one else has contacted me, either."

Wayne nodded. "I understand. If anyone does or you think of anything that might help, please let me know." He handed her his card.

Irina took it and put it in the pocket of her suit. She looked from Wayne to Dr. Lawrence. "May I go now?"

"Of course. And thanks for coming in."

Irina hesitated. "You're welcome" didn't quite suit the occasion, and "my pleasure" was even worse. Eventually, she settled for, "I'm sorry I wasn't able to help."

"Even negative information is information," Dr. Lawrence said with a nod. "Thank you for coming."

Irina headed for the door, and I excused myself to follow her, leaving Wayne and Dr. Lawrence together in the visiting room. We rode the elevator back upstairs in silence; it wasn't until we were outside, and could breathe fresh air again, that Irina opened her mouth. "Thank you for coming with me, Avery."

"My pleasure," I said. "I mean . . . I was happy to do it. It isn't easy being all alone in a new place, is it? Have you made any friends while you've been here?"

I hadn't done too badly in that department myself, in the months I'd been here, but I'd probably gotten lucky. If I hadn't met Kate, I wouldn't have met Derek, and if I hadn't met Derek, I wouldn't have met Dr. Ben and Cora and Beatrice, and then there were Shannon and Josh . . . If it hadn't been for Derek, I wouldn't have met Irina, for that matter. She, on the other hand, always seemed to be alone.

Irina made a face I took to mean, *no, not really.* "I have been busy. Real estate is a competitive business. But I have a partner I work with. We spend most days together. Her name is Ruth. She is waiting for me at the office so we can drive to South Portland to a house there that the owners want to sell."

"You use Ruth's car?" Irina didn't have one; that's why she took the bus to Portland every morning.

She nodded. "I meet her at the office every day. She lives in Kennebunk."

The other direction from Portland than Waterfield, then. I guess it made sense that she didn't want to drive all the way up the coast to pick up Irina.

"I'm sorry you had to come here first today. And for nothing, too. Although I guess it's good that the girl wasn't anyone you knew."

Irina nodded. "I almost wish she was. Somewhere, someone is looking for her."

If someone were, they were keeping quiet about it. By now, there ought to have been all-points bulletins all over down east Maine, TV and radio spots, front-page newspaper stories, or at least a missing-person report filed with a police department somewhere nearby. But even the Internet was quiet. I'd stopped by the down east Maine listserv last night to see if anyone was talking about anything related, and it had been quiet as the grave. Pun intended.

"I'm glad she's not your sister, anyway. Did you try to call Svetlana?"

I would have, just to make sure. Even if I knew it wasn't my sister—a sister I don't have; I'm an only child—I think I would have called anyway, just to hear her voice.

A shadow passed over Irina's face. It could just have been from one of the clouds in the sky. "I tried. She didn't answer."

If Svetlana wasn't the girl in the morgue, then surely that didn't matter. "I'm sorry you didn't get to talk to her. But at least that's not her, in there." I nodded to the building.

Irina shook her head and muttered something in Russian. I assumed it to be the equivalent of "Thank God!"

"How far is the real estate office from here? Do you want a ride?"

She shook her head, the tight bun at the nape of her neck bobbing. "I'd like to walk. Smell the fresh air." Get the smell of death out of her nose.

"You won't be cold?" She was just wearing the business suit with the blouse underneath, and high-heeled pumps.

Irina shook her head. "Ukraine is cool, too. And the jacket is wool. Nice and warm."

I nodded. "Well, walk carefully, then. And good luck on your appointment."

Irina returned the good wishes as far as Derek's and my renovations went and set off down the sidewalk in the direction of her office, her high heels clicking a rhythm against the pavement. I watched her round the nearest corner, and then I headed back inside the building.

Dr. Lawrence had walked Wayne upstairs, and I found them both standing in the lobby, still discussing the deceased.

". . . for toxicology," Dr. Lawrence was saying as I walked up. "Tomorrow, maybe longer. I'll ask the lab to put a rush on it."

Wayne nodded. "I'd appreciate that. What about food?"

"It's all in there." Dr. Lawrence nodded to the sheaf of papers Wayne was holding in his hand. "Dinner approximately nine hours before she died, a little chicken and rice with water to drink. Not much of either; maybe she was dieting."

"She didn't look like she needed to diet," Wayne remarked.

I shook my head; the young woman hadn't struck me as being overweight, either.

"Her clothes were slightly too big," Dr. Lawrence said. "I'd say she had perhaps lost five or ten pounds since she bought them. The tags were cut out, by the way."

"The tags in the clothes?"

Dr. Lawrence nodded.

"Interesting," Wayne said.

I cut in. "She was wearing Gloria Jeans. They're a Russian brand. You can get them in New York, though."

Wayne's eyebrows gyrated, and he turned back to Dr. Lawrence. "What about the shirt? Is that American made or foreign?"

"Isn't American made the same as foreign these days?" Dr. Lawrence didn't wait for an answer. "I'll go get her clothes and you can have a look. Both of you." Her eyes glanced off mine for a second.

"Textile designer," I said. "Fabric is kind of my thing."

"That explains it. Wait here. I'll be right back."

She headed down the hallway to the elevator, her rubber shoes squeaking against the polished tile floor.

"You didn't tell me that," Wayne said, reproach in his voice.

"What? About the jeans? I didn't think about it. That

was before you told me about the scrap of paper in the pocket. And it's not like they couldn't have been bought here, you know. Like I said, they're available in New York."

"But more readily available in Russia? Or the Ukraine?"

"Oh, sure. They're Russia's equivalent of Levi's. As a matter of fact, I think Levi Strauss invested in Gloria a year or two ago."

"So she's probably Russian. I mean, that plus the note she was carrying with Russian letters."

"Could be. An exchange student, maybe. Someone spending a semester at Barnham. Or even someone getting her whole education at Barnham. There are a couple of foreign students there. I had one of them in my Fabric through the Ages class last month."

"Anyone Russian?" Wayne wanted to know.

I shook my head. "Did you go down there yesterday?"

Wayne shook his head. "We found the scrap of paper in her pocket and focused on that. I was hoping that Irina could help us identify her. Now that it turns out she can't, I'll try other routes."

I nodded. "Do corpses still have fingerprints after they've been submerged in salt water?"

"Once she dried out, we were able to get them. Brandon was working on trying to identify her yesterday. I don't think he's had any luck. He would have called."

Brandon Thomas is Wayne's youngest and most gung ho deputy, a twenty-three-year-old Waterfield native who would really prefer focusing on crime scene investigation and evidence gathering, but who goes on patrol with a good attitude when he has to. In a small police department like Waterfield's, everyone goes on patrol, even the chief.

"So she's not a criminal."

Wayne shook his head. "She's not showing up in the criminal database, no. Neither for the police, nor for the

FBI or any other organizations we have access to. And she's not military, either."

"I didn't really think she was," I said.

"You never know," Wayne answered.

I changed the subject. "Irina said she tried to call her sister Svetlana, in Kiev, but she couldn't get hold of her. She seemed a little worried."

"Really? But this—who we have downstairs—isn't Svetlana, right?"

"She said it isn't. And if it was, why would she be worried about not being able to talk to her sister?"

"Damned if I know," Wayne said as the elevator doors opened down the hall and Dr. Lawrence came toward us, carrying a wrapped package. "But maybe I'll contact the police in Kiev and see if I can get hold of her. Someone wrote that information on that piece of paper and gave it to our victim, and it's possible it might have been Svetlana . . . um . . ."

"Rozhdestvensky," Dr. Lawrence said, stopping next to him. "Here you go. Everything our girl was wearing. Jeans, shirt, panties, and bra. Not a tag among them."

"Appreciate it." Wayne tucked the package under his arm. "Let me know when you hear from toxicology, OK?"

"And you let me know when you find out who she is. Meanwhile, I'll put her in storage. As Jane Doe." Dr. Lawrence made a face.

We took our leave of the doctor and the morgue and walked back out into the crisp spring air. It felt good, and I breathed deeply.

"Irina gone to work?" Wayne asked.

I nodded. "She'll be coming back home tonight."

"I'd like her to look at the clothes. You, too. Maybe one of you will recognize the make or brand."

"I'd be happy to," I said, "but I really don't think you'll

be doing Irina any favors if you show up at the real estate company to talk to her in full uniform. It's not urgent, so why don't you just wait until she comes back to Waterfield for the night. By then, maybe you can reassure her about her sister, as well."

Wayne agreed that this made sense, and then I called Irina and agreed to meet her at the police station at six P.M. so we could look at the clothes together. That done, Wayne got in his police cruiser and I got in my Beetle, and we both left the morgue parking lot and hit the road.

—6—

I didn't want to leave the Beetle in Portland, so even though I could catch the ferry to Rowanberry there, I still drove back to Waterfield and parked in the harbor parking lot. The ferry left at twelve fifteen sharp, and I made it to the dock just as the gangplank was hauled up. When the crew saw me coming, they held off long enough to let me skid across, and then they made tracks—or rather waves—out to sea. I dropped down on one of the dozen benches available and tried to catch my breath.

The ferry runs in a big circle from Waterfield to Moosehead Island to Rowanberry Island to Little Rock Island to Big Rock Island to Frog Island to Boothbay Harbor and back to Waterfield. The whole trip takes a couple of hours, and the ferry runs continually. Since Rowanberry Island was one of the first stops, I didn't have too long to wait, and I was able to sit back and relax and enjoy the weather, which was back to being partly sunny and not rainy at all today.

I did keep an eye out, though, just in case something interesting should happen to float by, but nothing did. As we left Moosehead Island and started heading across the sound to Rowanberry, I got up and wandered over to the young man who was guarding the gate and letting the gang-plank up and down every time we docked.

"This is Rowanberry Island coming up, right?"

He nodded. I placed him in his early twenties, with white blond hair and eyes of the same chlorinated blue as my own. He was chewing gum.

"First time?" he inquired between chews.

I shook my head. "My boyfriend and I are renovating a house on the other side of the island. But we have our own boat. I just couldn't go out with him this morning, so I'm taking the ferry."

The young man nodded. "I heard someone bought the old van Duren place. Is that what you're working on? You guys planning to move in?"

"We're just flipping it. Renovating and then selling."

The houses on Rowanberry Island were coming closer by the second. "Did you hear about the body in the water?" I asked, keeping my voice light.

The young man's face closed up. "The Waterfield cops stopped by the ferry yesterday to show me a picture. They asked me if I knew her or if I'd noticed anyone looking like that on the ferry recently."

"I guess you hadn't?" Since Wayne probably would have let me know if he had any leads.

He shook his head. "Never seen her before in my life. Would have remembered if I had; she looked hot." He paused a second, mulling the statement over, and then amended it. "Like she would have been, I mean. When she was alive. Not in the picture they showed me."

"Right." I'd figured that. "So do you ever see Gert Heyerdahl? The writer?"

"The guy in the other van Duren house? Nah. He has his own transportation. Doesn't take the ferry."

"Oh."

He relented just a little. "He's mostly here in the summers. Comes about June or so. The rest of the time he lives away. 'Scuse me."

The ferry driver cut the motor and the boat drifted toward the dock on Rowanberry Island. My new acquaintance busied himself with another boat hook, before tying off on a convenient pylon. Then he slapped down the gangplank and offered me his hand. "Here you go. Looks like it's just you getting off today."

He touched a finger to his forehead and jumped back on the boat. "You have a good day, ma'am." I grimaced. *Ma'am?* When did that happen?

The small ferry chugged away in the direction of Little Rock Island, and I looked around to get my bearings.

It wasn't the first time I'd been in the small Rowanberry Island village. Derek had dragged me out here in November to look at the house; this was while he was hankering to buy it. We'd come back a couple of months ago, just before we actually bought it, to make sure we still wanted to, and maybe to make sure it was still standing and hadn't deteriorated too much over the winter. The weather hadn't been cooperating either time: In November, it had been foggy and clammy, and in January, it had been freezing, with a foot of snow blanketing everything. This was the first time I'd been here when the sun was shining and I could actually see everything.

It wasn't a big place. Maybe a dozen houses along one main road, most of them private residences, but a few with commercial signs out front. There was a general store, which seemed to sell everything from bait to rubber boots to root beer and Moxie. It also served as the island's post office.

A little farther up was a little house with a sign in the window that said "Rooms for Rent." The sign was faded, and so were the curtains; I couldn't imagine that there'd be much demand for guest rooms in a place like this.

There were no bars or restaurants, nothing in the way of nightlife; I guess if the residents of Rowanberry Island wanted to kick up their heels, they'd take the ferry to the mainland and party there. And then they'd hop the ferry back again, with no danger of drinking and driving.

That thought brought me back to the young woman in the water. Dr. Lawrence had said it'd be a day or two before toxicology lab reports were ready. At that point, we'd know if the girl had been drunk when she went in the water. It didn't look like she'd been the victim of a crime—there were no injuries on the body save the scratches on the soles of her feet and the bruises the doctor had mentioned. No, she had died a natural death, if dying of exposure can be considered natural. But if she'd been drunk, that meant that someone had most likely been drinking with her that night, someone who hadn't reported her missing. And didn't being intoxicated make it more likely that she'd fallen off a boat? Was anyone out partying on a boat this time of year, though? Surely that'd happen in the summer, but in still-chilly April?

Could she have fallen off the ferry? Was it possible that my new acquaintance, the ferry conductor, had lied to me—and to the police—when he said he'd never seen her? If she'd been drunk, and he'd seen her come on board, and she had fallen out somewhere along the route without anyone noticing, might he lie to avoid trouble? To avoid a charge of being negligent?

He very well might, I decided. Although if she'd been on the ferry, unless she was the only person there, someone else would have seen her, too. The ferry had been practically empty just now, but even so, there had been three or four passengers on board, in addition to the captain and the conductor. As for the last ferry of the night, surely that'd be more populated, with stragglers trying to get home for the night?

Alas, speculation wasn't really getting me anywhere as I left civilization behind and followed the rutted track across the island toward our house on the other end.

So I turned my mind to other matters. Maybe I was being paranoid, because it was kind of hard to believe that Melissa would have sabotaged her own plumbing. Hard to imagine how she could have gotten into the wall to do it, too. But ever since she moved into the loft directly across from Derek, she had asked him for help with one damn thing after another, and it was getting on my nerves. First there were the locks; she didn't feel safe with the locks that were there, since someone else might have a key. Why she couldn't just hire a locksmith, I don't know, but no, she asked Derek to change them out for her. Then, a week later, there was the kitchen; she needed a vent fan installed for all the gourmet cooking she was planning to do for herself now that she was single again. She even fed him: little stuffed mushroom caps and oysters and things.

After the cooking vent and the aphrodisiac foods came the bedroom ceiling fan. He spent an hour standing on her king-sized bed, the one she'd be sleeping in alone from now on, to hang a new ceiling fan above it, because Melissa got so uncomfortably hot at night. If he caught the unsubtle implications of that statement, he didn't let on, but I sure did. I made a snide comment about hot flashes, and he laughed, and that was it. I wasn't worried. The whole situation didn't make me happy, either, though.

As a result of this train of thought, I arrived at the house flushed and riled, and no happier to find Miss Melly herself cuddling up to Derek in front of the fireplace in the living room.

I say cuddling, but I'm being a smidgeon unfair. He was kneeling on the floor in front of the fireplace, obliviously tucking new mortar between the old bricks. Melissa was standing over him, watching, close enough that she was practically rubbing up against him. I wondered if she'd been doing the same thing all last night as well.

When I closed the door behind me, she turned with her trademark smile. Melissa has more teeth than a crocodile, brilliantly white. "Hi, Avery," she cooed.

Derek pulled his head out of the fireplace to glance at me over his shoulder. "Morning, Tink. Everything OK?"

"Fine. What are you doing?"

"Tuck-pointing the fireplace. The old mortar has crumbled." He went back to work. Melissa stepped aside as I approached, politely giving the impression that she, in her magnanimity, was allowing me, the interloper, to come closer. I gritted my teeth.

What I wanted to say was, "What the hell are you doing here?!" She knew it, too, so I took a breath and moderated the statement, leaving off the expletive and the attitude. "I didn't expect to see you here, Melissa."

"Derek told me so much about this place," Melissa said, with a fond look at his bent head, "that I wanted to come see it for myself."

"And you walked all the way across the island? In those?" I glanced at her pristine suede boots with the three-inch heels.

Melissa tinkled a merry laugh. "Of course not. Tony ran me out here in his boat."

"Tony?"

"Micelli," Derek said from inside the fireplace.

"Oh. Right." Tony "the Tiger," reporter for Portland's Channel Eight News. The guy who had expressed hope for multiple dead bodies on our property on Becklea Drive. "Where is he?"

"He had to go back," Melissa said. "He just stopped in long enough to ask Derek a couple of questions."

"So we're stuck with you for the rest of the day?" fought with, "Questions? What about?" in my mind. The latter won. But just barely.

"About the girl," Derek said.

"The one in the water?" I looked from Derek to Melissa and back. "I thought you said people drown up here regularly."

"They do. I guess it's a slow news month." He shifted his shoulders in a shrug. Melissa mimicked the gesture, a pretty pout on her face.

"Hunh," I said.

"How did it go with Irina?" Derek asked, his voice hollow from inside the fireplace.

"Fine." And since I didn't think we should say anything more about the body in front of Melissa, who would probably report anything she heard back to Tony the Tiger, I added, "She went to work."

"I guess everything's all right, then?"

Melissa's delicate ears, with diamond studs in them, were almost visibly vibrating.

"Everything is wonderful," I said firmly. "I'm meeting her again at six. Is there any reason we can't be back in Waterfield by then?"

"None I can think of," Derek said.

Melissa sounded peeved. It was probably the mention of

Irina. A competing Realtor, and the one we gave our business to. "Are you buying something new?" she wanted to know.

Derek didn't answer.

"Not right now," I said. "We're plenty busy with this house at the moment. And for the next several months."

Melissa looked around, her perfect nose wrinkled. "It's rather rough," she said, in what was clearly the understatement of the year.

I looked around, too. Worm-eaten paneling, dull wood floors, stains on the ceiling from water intrusion. And I saw Gert Heyerdahl's gleaming white paint, polished floors, and perfect front door in my mind. "It'll be OK. We specialize in rough."

Derek sent me another grin. "If you say so," Melissa said, sounding doubtful. She could easily have turned the comment into a snide comparison between herself and me, so I should probably be grateful that she didn't.

We did end up being stuck with her for the rest of the day, and that may be why Derek agreed to leave the island earlier than usual. He just couldn't stand the company any longer. She was getting on my nerves, too; it wasn't like we could put her to work—not dressed in cashmere and silk—so she just stood there, arms folded under her breasts, watching what we did over our shoulders all afternoon. Occasionally she'd look at her watch, a dainty thing beset with diamonds, and sort of fidget.

By just after four o'clock Derek had had enough. If it had been just the two of us, I'm sure he would have insisted we get going on something else for a couple hours after the fireplace was finished and drying, but today he just straightened his back, stretched out the kinks, and said, "Ready to go home?"

Melissa nodded.

"Avery?"

I thought about giving him a hard time but decided against it. "Ready when you are."

"C'mere." He slung an arm around my shoulders and pulled me to him, totally disregarding the fact that Melissa was standing right there. "I didn't get a chance to say hello earlier."

"Hello," I said breathlessly, the smell of Ivory soap and shampoo, sawdust and paint thinner flooding my nose.

"I missed you this morning." He bent to drop a quick kiss on my mouth, his eyes warm.

"I missed you, too," I said when I'd gotten my breath back. Melissa rolled her eyes.

Derek glanced at her and grinned. "Let's get home," he said and steered me toward the door. Melissa brought up the rear, the clicking of her high heels sounding annoyed. Just as she stepped off the porch and onto the grass, a gray streak of fur shot across the grass directly in front of her. Melissa squealed and stumbled back, sitting down with a splat and an unladylike grunt.

"It's a kitten!" I told Derek excitedly. "A little gray blue kitten."

Lips twitching, he went to help Melissa up. "No kidding."

"I'm not. That's what it is. A kitten."

Melissa sent me a dirty look. She had a dirty spot on the back of her lovely, taupe-covered butt, too.

She managed to keep up through the pasture down to the boat, though, and got into the rocking vessel more easily than I did, in spite of her high heels and my clogs.

"Remember that boat trip we took just after we got here, Derek?" she asked when she had plunked her elegant—but dirty—posterior on one of the seats. "And that sweet little cabin we rented for the weekend."

Derek nodded. "Monhegan. It's another island," he explained for my benefit, "farther out into the ocean from here. Ten miles from the mainland."

"I've heard of Monhegan. Artist's colony, right? I wouldn't have thought it would be your kind of place, Melissa."

From what I knew, Monhegan was beautiful but wild. No cars or paved roads, and with a year-round population smaller even than Rowanberry's. And way out to sea.

Melissa smiled. Or showed teeth. "I'm not sure we left the cabin that whole weekend, Avery."

"Oh," I said, sinking my teeth into my lip, my cheeks flushing. Derek glanced at me and then at Melissa.

"Lay off her, Melly. She doesn't want to know about our sex life."

"Did I say anything about our sex life?" Melissa answered innocently.

"You said enough." He cranked the key in the engine and cut off anything else she might be thinking about saying. Melissa smiled, her expression that of a cat contemplating a big bowl of heavy cream as she looked at me under her lashes.

There's nothing wrong with the physical end of Derek's and my relationship. Or the other end, for that matter. I smiled back, a big toothy grin. She looked away.

We spent the boat ride in silence. The motor was humming loudly, the wind was blowing, and the water was misting. Derek and I exchanged the occasional smile, but other than that, no one spoke. I kept looking at the water to avoid looking at Melissa, but without seeing anything of interest.

"Here we are," Derek said when he had pulled the boat into the slip in Waterfield harbor and had tied off. He jumped up on the dock and extended a hand down. "Melissa?"

"Thank you." She held on to his hand a second or two longer than strictly necessary. "I'll see you later?"

If the flirtatious tone registered with Derek, he didn't show it. "As soon as Avery's settled. I have to put another coat of mud on that drywall patch in the wall." He turned to me. "Tink?"

"Thank you." I grabbed his hand and clambered out of the boat. "You don't have to wait for me. The sooner you finish the drywall, the sooner I'll see you."

"Right," Derek said, with a ghost of a grin.

"Plus, I left the Beetle right there." I pointed. The rounded, green top poked out of the sea of other cars a half block away in the harbor parking lot. "I'll give you a ride if you want."

"I forgot you drove yourself this morning. And no, we can walk. It's just two or three blocks. I'll finish the drywall repair and then I'll call you." He kissed me. Softly. For a long time. And then he winked. It was probably at least partly for Melissa's benefit, but I wasn't complaining.

"OK," I managed. Melissa rolled her eyes. Her suede boot was tapping impatiently on the pavement.

"Keep your hair on," Derek told her. "Big date tonight?"

Melissa's voice was stiff. "I'm meeting Tony for dinner at the Waymouth Tavern at eight."

We'll be sure not to go there, I thought.

"Don't worry," Derek said, "I'll be out of your apartment long before then. You can bring him home afterward with no worries that your ex-husband will still be hanging around."

"Jerk." Melissa sniffed.

I hid a smile. "Call me when you're finished. I'll go meet Irina now, and then we can hook up later."

Derek nodded and gave me a sort of salute. They headed off toward Main Street, while I veered right, toward the parking lot and the Beetle. When I turned to look at them over my shoulder, Melissa had hooked on to Derek's arm and was holding on as she minced up the street. Her butt was still dirty, too.

—7—

From what I've been told, the Waterfield PD used to be housed in one of the historic houses close to downtown. That was before my time, of course. About fifteen years ago or so, the town—and more importantly, nearby Portland—had grown big enough that the police in Waterfield needed more space for more officers, for parking, for technology; and at that point, they built a new police station on the west side of town, off the Portland Highway.

It's a typically utilitarian building, one-story tall and built of red brick, with a parking lot out front for a dozen cruisers and more visitors. I slotted the Beetle in between a parked black-and-white and a red truck with a gun rack in the back.

Inside in the lobby, behind a counter to the right, a middle-aged woman was fielding phone calls, a hands-free headset clamped over her gray-streaked black curls, and a tiny microphone arching in front of her mouth. ". . . will give Chief Rasmussen the message," she was saying into it when I walked in, "and we'll see what happens. Yes, ma'am, you're very welcome."

The call disconnected itself, and she looked up at me. "Can I help you?"

I introduced myself. "I'm here to see Wayne. Police Chief Rasmussen. About that body in the water."

"He told me you'd be coming." She ticked my name off on a list. "Have a seat on the couch there, and I'll tell him you're here."

"You must be Ramona Estrada," I said. The police secretary.

"That's right." She didn't ask me how I knew her name, just got on the horn with Wayne. Good thing, too, because I would have had to tell her that my boyfriend once strung me along for quite a while, making me believe that Ramona Estrada was some kind of super-hot Jennifer Lopez look-alike in a tight police uniform, instead of this fifty-something happily married grandmother in a flowered blouse and old-lady polyester pants.

I took my seat on the couch, and no sooner had I gotten comfortable than Wayne opened a door on the left. "C'mon down, Avery."

I jumped up again and hurried toward him. "Is Irina here?"

"She just arrived. Come into my office." He held the door open for me. I ducked under his arm—Wayne is six foot four—and inside.

The office wasn't any bigger than Aunt Inga's front parlor; nothing impressive for a chief of police. Most of it was taken up by a long row of filing cabinets against the back wall, with maps of Waterfield, of the rest of Maine, and of the islands off the coast tacked up above them. Irina was sitting in a straight-backed chair in front of the desk. Wayne waved me to a matching chair next to it and walked around the desk. I curled up on the gray fabric and nodded to Irina, who looked like she'd spent a rough day in the trenches. She nodded back and forced a smile that looked more like a grimace.

"Tough day?" Wayne inquired, stretching his long legs out under the desk. He looked from Irina to me. When Irina didn't answer, I felt I had to.

"When I got to Rowanberry Island this afternoon, Melissa was there. Hanging over Derek's shoulder. We were stuck with her for the rest of the day."

Wayne tried to suppress a smile but couldn't quite do it. "Where are they now?"

"Derek and Melissa?" And wasn't that weird, having to lump them together like that in the same sentence? "At her place. He's still working on her stupid bathroom. The leak is fixed, but he has to finish repairing the drywall. I'm meeting him for dinner when I'm finished here."

Wayne nodded. "Guess we'd better get on with it, then." He leaned down to open a cabinet in the desk and pull out the wrapped package Dr. Lawrence had given him that morning. Except now the paper was open, just lightly tucked around the contents. Wayne shoved a couple of things aside on his desk to make room for the package there. As we watched, he folded the waxed paper back.

A pitiful little collection of clothes lay there. A pair of blue jeans with frayed bottoms. A cropped top. A pair of underwear, plain cotton. A bra, ditto.

Wayne held them up, one at a time. "Either of you recognize these, or know where she might have bought them?"

Irina and I both shook our heads.

"All the tags are cut out. Even on the bra. Might mean that someone was afraid we'd be able to trace her that way. Avery, you said you recognized the brand of jeans?"

I nodded. "They're Gloria Jeans. I thought they were,

and now I'm sure of it. I recognize the stitching, and the pattern on the pockets."

"Irina?" Wayne turned to her. "Gloria is a Russian brand, is that right?"

"Yes." She hardly moved her lips to utter the single syllable.

"Are these popular in the Ukraine? Are they for sale there?"

Irina nodded stiffly.

"What about the rest of the clothes? Feel free to touch them; any evidence has been collected already."

Irina and I both reached out. I toward the top, she toward the bra. The shirt was stiff from the salt water. After fingering it for a minute, I swapped it for Irina's bra. Neither of us made a move toward the pair of panties. There's just something icky about other people's underwear, even when the person who used to wear it is dead. Perhaps *especially* when the person who used to wear it is dead.

"Honestly," I told Wayne when we had both finished our inspections and the clothes were back on the desk, "it's hard to tell. The jeans are clearly foreign. I recognize the brand. But like I told you, you can find them for sale in New York. As for the rest of it, like Dr. Lawrence said, even American-made clothes are made abroad these days, so there's not going to be much difference in the construction of American and foreign. Not if they're all made in the same place anyway."

Irina nodded.

"For what it's worth," I added, "I don't recognize the brands on any of these others. They're not designer originals. The bra isn't even Victoria's Secret. Just plain fare, probably bought off the rack at a Target or a Walmart. Or the Russian or Ukrainian equivalent. If there is a Russian or Ukrainian equivalent."

We looked at Irina. She shook her head.

"Anything you can add to what Avery's saying?" Wayne asked.

Irina shrugged. She had taken off her jacket inside Wayne's office, and her shoulders under the thin, gray fabric of the blouse were square. "I think Avery is right. They are probably foreign. Quite possibly Russian. The girl, she had a Russian look. And the note with the name and address was written in Cyrillic. But I still don't know her."

"Have you been able to get hold of your sister?" I asked.

Irina shook her head. "Alexi and Ivan haven't seen her since the beginning of the semester. Middle of January."

"Are they going to check on her?"

Another head shake. "They live too far. Hours from Kiev. And they are busy. Maybe in a week or two."

"I've contacted the Kiev police," Wayne said to me but with a wary look at Irina. "It took a while to find someone who could speak English and understood what I wanted, but he promised he'd send me information on all their missing persons, female, between fifteen and forty."

"That's broad." Especially since our dead girl was nowhere near either fifteen or forty.

Wayne shrugged. "I'd rather cast a wide net and catch something than not find what I'm looking for. I don't think she's under twenty or over thirty, but I'd rather be safe than sorry."

"I guess that makes sense. And Svetlana?"

"I asked them to see if they could track her down at the same time."

"Thank you," Irina said. I could see the worry in her eyes.

Wayne turned to her. "You're welcome. I'm not doing it just to set your mind at ease, though. I need to talk to her. Someone wrote your contact info on that scrap of paper, and if she didn't do it, she might know who did."

Irina nodded, but she didn't speak, her lips pressed together into a tight line.

We left shortly after that, and I used the Beetle to drive Irina home to Becklea Drive, with a short stop at Shaw's Supermarket on the way for Irina to pick up a few things for dinner.

Shaw's is the biggest supermarket chain in New England; there are stores all over down east Maine, and in Waterfield, it's the number one grocery store. Everyone I know shops at Shaw's. I wasn't surprised to see a few familiar faces in the aisles; I would have been more surprised had I not seen any.

Brandon Thomas, Wayne's young deputy, was wheeling a shopping cart through the produce section, and he was so busy smiling at the young woman walking alongside him that I practically had to play bumper-carts to get his attention.

"Oh." He flushed. "Hi, Avery."

"Hi, Brandon." I turned my attention to his companion. "Hi."

"You . . . um . . . remember Daphne, don't you? From the state police?" Brandon's fresh face managed to be sheepish, embarrassed, and proud, all at the same time. He's twenty-three, blond, blue-eyed, and strapping; the kind of young man who was a star quarterback in high school.

"Of course I do." I smiled at Daphne. She and I were old friends; we'd met during the Becklea Drive renovation, when she and her partner Hans had sniffed our yard for human remains. Hans is a regal German shepherd and the state police's cadaver dog. "How's Hans?"

She smiled back, a pretty girl with wide-set blue eyes and a turned-up nose framed by soft, brown hair. "He's fine. Taking the night off."

"And so are you, obviously."

"I'm cooking for Brandon and Phoebe," Daphne said, tossing her ponytail.

Phoebe Thomas is Brandon's mother. She's Wayne's age, late forties, and suffers from multiple sclerosis. Brandon lives in and takes care of her. He must be pretty serious about Daphne, I thought, if he'd introduced her to his mom and even let her prepare their dinner.

"You remember Irina, of course? From Becklea Drive?"

"Of course." Brandon nodded. "How are you?" His eyes were bright and speculative; he must be aware of the connection between Irina and the body in the water. Daphne didn't seem to have been filled in; she smiled and extended her hand.

"Nice to meet you. I don't think we spoke last fall."

"The pleasure is mine," Irina mumbled.

I turned to Brandon. "Any luck on those fingerprints? Wayne told me you've been putting them through all the databases."

Brandon shook his head. "I contacted ICE this afternoon. Their database isn't one I can access, so I e-mailed the prints over to one of their agents to see if they have any record of them. We'll hear back tomorrow."

"Who's ICE?"

"They used to be the INS, the Immigration and Naturalization Service. Now they're ICE, Immigration and Customs Enforcement."

"The border patrol?"

Brandon's lips twitched. "Sort of. If the girl is Russian, ICE should have a record of her. If she came here legally, that is."

I nodded, with a glance at Irina. She looked uncomfortable. "We should get going. Have a nice dinner. I'll see you around, Brandon. Daphne, nice to see you again."

"Likewise," Daphne said.

They pushed their cart off toward the deli. Irina and I wandered toward the tomatoes.

Next up was old Miss Barnes from the Historical Society, carrying a basket with a few things in it. I noticed a rather surprising box of double-stuffed Oreos, as well as a couple of cans of cat food.

Edith Barnes is Derek's old history teacher, a tall, skinny lady in her seventies, stiff-necked and straight-backed. After retiring from the school system, she went to work for the Fraser House historic home, where the Historical Society is located. I stop by there every so often to look something up, and I've always found her to be knowledgeable and helpful, if not precisely friendly. This was the first time I'd run into her outside of work. It was kind of surprising to realize she *had* a life outside of work.

"Evening, Miss Barnes." I gave her my best smile.

She blinked at me. "Miss Baker." And then she glanced over my shoulder.

"Derek isn't here," I said. All women adore Derek, and Miss Barnes adores him more than most. "He's helping his ex-wife with something."

Miss Barnes arched her brows.

"There was a leak in her bathroom."

"Ah," Miss Barnes said. Her eyes lit on Irina.

"This is Irina Rozhdestvensky. She's our Realtor. Irina, this is Miss Barnes from the Historical Society. She and I are old friends."

That was stretching the truth a little, but by rights we ought to be, as much time as I'd spent picking Miss Barnes's brain this past year. In fact, since I had her here . . . "Derek and I are renovating a house on one of the islands. Irina found it for us. Do you know anything about the islands?"

"I know a little," Miss Barnes allowed. "The Waterfield

Historical Society is limited to information about Waterfield history, but I've lived here for seventy years, and a few things have remained with me."

A whole lot more than a few things, from what I knew of the old bat. She has a brain like flypaper and could be counted on to know something about practically everything that had happened on the coast of Maine in the past several hundred years.

"Which island is it?" she wanted to know.

I told her it was Rowanberry and added, "The house is a 1783 center-chimney Colonial. One of two. The other belongs to Gert Heyerdahl, the writer. Irina told Derek they were built for two sisters." Irina nodded as I said this. "And a guy I met on the ferry this afternoon called it the old van Duren place."

"I'm familiar with it." Miss Barnes nodded. "What would you like to know?"

"Oh, nothing in particular. I just like to have the background on the houses we work on. When something's been around for two-hundred-plus years, there's usually a good story or two attached to it."

Miss Barnes agreed. "In fact, I think I may have some information in the archives."

"Really? Even though it's not in Waterfield?"

"There's a Waterfield connection," Miss Barnes said. "If you'll stop by in the next few days, I'll get the information together for you."

"That would be great. Derek keeps me pretty busy, but I'll try to find some time to get over there this week."

Miss Barnes inclined her head regally and moved on toward the dairy coolers. I turned to Irina. "I forgot to ask . . . you're the one who told Derek about the two sisters, right? Do you know anything more about the place, other than that?"

"Just the basic information," Irina said. "John van Duren owned a large part of Rowanberry Island several hundred years ago. He had two daughters. They did not get along. When they got married, their father built them each a house on the island, on opposite sides and facing away from each other."

"They must have *really* not gotten along."

"Families sometimes have problems," Irina said with a shrug. "Siblings don't always get along."

"I'll take your word for it." I'm an only child. My father died when I was thirteen, and for years it was just Mom and me. We've always gotten along splendidly. "What happened to them later? Did they make up?"

"No idea," Irina said with a shrug. "The other house has changed hands many times. The old man who owned your house refused to sell it, even when he couldn't live there anymore. He died in a nursing home last year, and that's when the house finally went on the market."

"Wow." I thought for a moment. "Do you and Svetlana get along?"

"Svetlana is ten years younger," Irina said. "When I moved out, she was nine. But we get along well."

"And your brothers? Do you get along with them, too?"

She shrugged. "They're boys. Men, now. They are different."

"No kidding," I said.

"They're married and have children. They're concentrating on providing for their families."

"What about you? Have you ever been married?" She was in her midthirties; it seemed a reasonable question. Not that I've ever been married. Most of my friends haven't, either, come to think of it.

Her face closed up. "When I was younger. It didn't last."

"In the Ukraine? Or here?"

"Ukraine. He died."

"Oh," I said. "Sorry. Is that when you came here?"

Irina nodded. Behind us, a voice rose, demanding to know if someone thought he was an idiot. The jar of tomato sauce Irina was holding slipped out of her hand and shattered on the floor. Tomato sauce splattered in every direction. I jumped back, straight into someone walking past.

"Oh! Oops. I'm sorry. Oh. *Hello,*" I said, recognizing the caretaker from Gert Heyerdahl's house. He was pushing a wagon with a couple of twelve-packs of Diet Coke, a few boxes of Special K cereal, two gallons of skim milk, a stack of Weight Watchers TV dinners, and a bag of apples. Plus a six-pack of light beer.

"How are you?" I added with my brightest smile.

He didn't answer, of course. Just glanced at Irina, squatting on the floor, her head still bent over the splattered mess of glass shards and tomato sauce, before pushing his wagon away.

"You shouldn't mess with that," I told Irina, "you could cut yourself. They'll be sending someone to clean it up."

In fact, the automated call of "cleanup on aisle seven" was already being broadcast over the speaker system.

"Who was that?" Irina said, looking after the man. Her cheeks were flushed, apparently over the gaffe with the tomato sauce. Some people don't like being the center of attention, and other customers were giving us a wide berth, stepping gingerly through the mess and shooting Irina annoyed looks.

I shrugged. "He's the caretaker at the other sister's house on Rowanberry Island, the one that belongs to Gert Heyerdahl. You know, the writer. I ran into him the other day when I walked over there to look at it."

"What is it like?" She started walking again, in the opposite direction, leaving the tomato mess behind. I followed.

"As far as I could tell, it's really nice. Very well maintained on the outside. There are shutters on all the windows—I guess in case there are storms during the winter—and he wouldn't let me go inside to look around. Not while Mr. Heyerdahl is away, he said. So all I was able to do was peek through the sidelights on the front door. I didn't see much."

Irina nodded. "Maybe when Mr. Heyerdahl comes back, he'll let you go inside. When will that be?"

"Probably May or June. Although I guess it depends on the weather. If it gets warm quickly, maybe he'll come sooner. Hi."

I nodded to the young ferry conductor I'd seen earlier in the day, pushing his way past us with a basket clutched to his chest. It had a few boxes of macaroni and cheese and cans of tuna in it. A man after my own heart; that's what I eat when I'm cooking for myself, too. He stared at me for a second, maybe trying to place me, before he nodded and moved on. Seemed like everyone in down east Maine was at Shaw's tonight. It was almost uncanny.

"Maybe," Irina agreed, with a thoughtful look in her eyes, still back on the subject of Gert Heyerdahl. "You and Derek will still be working on your house by June, won't you?"

"I'm sure we will. I'm not worried about it." I watched her grab a bag of frozen peas and one of frozen spinach from the freezer cabinet and put them in her basket. "That it?"

She nodded. "The sooner you take me home, the sooner you can get back to Derek."

"Works for me," I said happily.

—8—

Melissa and Tony the Tiger would be going to upscale Waymouth Tavern for dinner, so Derek and I decided to head in the opposite direction, geographically and economically, to Guido's Pizzeria.

It's a small cinderblock building not too far from Becklea Drive, which again isn't too far from Barnham College. As always, Guido's parking lot was full of beat-up trucks and economy cars with out-of-state license plates and college parking stickers, and the neon sign in the window flickered HOT-HOT-HOT, like a strip joint.

Inside, there was the usual hubbub. Floor-to-ceiling college kids, loud music, louder conversation, and a couple of waitresses in tight jeans and midriff-baring tops carrying pizzas over their heads through the throng.

As it often was, the big table in the back was occupied by people we knew: Shannon McGillicutty, Kate's daughter; Josh Rasmussen, Wayne's son; and their friends, Paige Thompson and Ricky Swanson.

Josh and Shannon have been best friends since Shannon moved to Waterfield seven years ago. Now, of course, they're step-siblings, as well. Add to that the fact that Josh is crazy about her while she seems totally oblivious, and you have the makings of a fine tragedy, comedy, or both.

Not that anything tragic seemed to be in the offing. All four of them greeted us with smiles and invitations to join them.

"So what's this about a body in the ocean?" Josh asked, scooting closer to Shannon. I slipped in beside him.

"Hasn't your dad told you?" Derek wanted to know, sliding in next to Ricky on the other side of the table.

"I don't see him as much now that we're not living together. Brandon came around with a photograph earlier today to see if anyone at Barnham knew her, but he didn't tell me much. Just that you'd found her in the water." Josh shrugged.

Josh is tall and lanky like his dad, with the same curly, dark hair, and bright eyes behind round glasses. Up until Wayne and Kate's wedding, he and his dad had shared a condo on the outskirts of Waterfield. Now he was living there alone. At one point, Shannon had been talking about moving in—to get away from the newlyweds and the B&B—but I guess once we'd turned the carriage house into a romantic retreat for two and Kate and Wayne had moved out there, Shannon decided just to stay in the Waterfield Inn.

"I don't know that there's a whole lot more to tell," Derek said. "She was floating in the water halfway between Moosehead Island and Rowanberry a couple mornings ago. Dead from exposure. The water's cold."

"She was young," I added. "Around twenty-five, maybe. Short, like Paige and me. Long, blond hair. She was dressed in a white summer top and a pair of Gloria Jeans."

"I've never heard of those," Shannon said, flipping her

black cherry hair over her shoulder. Shannon is gorgeous, with her mother's Playboy Bunny figure and her father's compelling dark eyes.

"They're Russian. You can find them in New York if you know where to look, but mostly they're for sale in Eastern Europe."

"So is the girl Russian, too, then?" This was Paige, her little-girl voice soft. She's a tiny thing, no taller than me and ethereal-looking. We're both short blondes, in other words, but where I'm sturdy, with rosy cheeks and bright hair, Paige is translucent; her hair is pale and her skin almost colorless, her body waiflike inside an oversized sweatshirt. She looks like a strong wind could knock her over.

"They're not sure yet," Derek said. "Brandon can't find any record of her."

I nodded. "I saw him at Shaw's Supermarket just now. He said he had sent her fingerprints to ICE, since he hadn't been able to find a match on his own.

"He was with Daphne," I added, "the canine handler from the state police in Augusta. You know, the one who brought her dog down to sniff the yard on Becklea Drive this fall. And who came down to sniff Peter Cortino's auto shop in December."

Derek nodded. "Hans. I remember. And Brandon told you he sent the fingerprints to Immigration and Customs?"

"He did. I guess they're going on the assumption that if she was wearing Russian clothes, she might be Russian. Are there any Russian girls going to Barnham College?" I looked around the table.

The four students exchanged glances.

"None I know of," Shannon said.

"We didn't recognize the photograph," Paige added.

"If she's twenty-five, she's too old for Barnham, anyway," Josh contributed.

Ricky nodded. He doesn't usually say a whole lot. But at least these days he looks you straight in the eye, instead of peering furtively out through curtains of dark hair, the way he used to do. Or usually he does; now I thought he might be avoiding my eyes.

Before I could pursue the thought, Derek had continued. "Brandon probably asked you if you knew of any party-hardy students who may have had something to do with this, right? Like, a boat party with alcohol a few days ago?"

"Barnham isn't really a party school," Josh offered. "I'm sure there are people here who have a few drinks, or a few bottles of beer, on the weekend, but campus security almost never has to break up loud frat parties or anything like that."

"And I haven't noticed anyone acting strangely," Shannon added. "You'd think if someone knew something, even if it was an accident and she just fell off a boat, whoever was with her would be freaking out."

"You'd think." I turned to Ricky. "What about you? Have you noticed anyone acting weird?" The girl would be closer to Ricky's age than the others', since he was a couple of years older than they were.

Ricky hesitated before replying. "I don't know who she is—or was—and I haven't noticed anyone acting weird, but there's a guy in my class—his name is Calvin—who was going on about Russian women before Christmas. Russian-bride websites and all that. You know, how women from Eastern Europe are dying to come to the U.S.?"

The obvious pun didn't seem to strike him, and I didn't have the heart to point it out.

"Really?" I said instead. "Did you tell Brandon?"

Ricky shook his head. "I had no idea about the Russian thing until now. Brandon didn't mention it."

"You should tell Dad," Josh said, fumbling for his cell

phone. "I'll call him." He pulled the phone from his pocket. But before he could dial, the waitress appeared next to our table, the same girl who usually waited on us when we were here.

"What can I get you?" She looked from me to Derek, where recognition seemed to strike. "Oh, it's you again." She dimpled.

"Hi, Candy." Derek dimpled back. He gets a kick out of the fact that at thirty-five he's still got what it takes to charm the co-eds. What he doesn't seem to realize is that it isn't just the co-eds, it's every woman between the ages of three and ninety-three. He's just a charming sort of guy.

"What can I get you to drink?"

Derek ordered a beer, I ordered a Diet Coke, and we all ordered pizzas to share. Candy was just about to tuck the order pad into the waistband of her skintight jeans and swish off, when Ricky spoke up.

"Is Calvin here tonight, Candy?"

"Calvin?" Candy wrinkled her adorable nose. "That nerdy guy in computer science, you mean?"

Ricky and Josh, both of them computer science or information technology majors, nodded. Ricky kept a straight face, but Josh smirked. Candy tossed her ponytail.

"I think he's over there by the door. You want me to go get him?"

Ricky and Josh looked at me. I shrugged. I wouldn't mind meeting Calvin and hearing what he had to say. Normally it wouldn't occur to me to encroach on Wayne's turf, and I definitely thought Josh should call his dad and tell him what Ricky had said, but . . . well, we were here, after all.

"Please," Josh said. "Tell him Josh and Ricky have a question."

Candy nodded and sashayed off, popping a pink bubblegum bubble as she went.

Derek looked resigned. "You're gonna get involved," he said, "aren't you, Tink?"

"Surely it can't hurt to talk to him. In case he knows something. He might be more forthcoming with us than he would be with the police. And I'll tell Wayne what he says. Plus, I'm already sort of involved. Because of Irina."

Derek shook his head, but he didn't argue.

"Is Calvin really a nerd?" I turned to Shannon and Paige.

They exchanged a look, amused. "I don't know if I'd call him a nerd," Shannon said, "but he's different."

"He grew up on one of the islands," Paige added. "Without a lot of people around. I think he must have been in high school before he started associating with other people on a regular basis."

"He's not a bad guy, though," Shannon added. "Just a little socially backward."

"And he's a good programmer," Josh said. "Here he is now." He waved.

I followed the direction of the wave and saw a young man make his way toward us, twisting his body through the teeming masses, making apologies left and right as he bumped his way through the overpopulated room.

He was on the tall side, if not as tall as Josh, and almost painfully thin, with big feet and a pointy nose, soft, light brown hair flopping over his forehead, and the beginnings of a fuzzy mustache on his upper lip. He looked a little bit like a stork, or maybe a heron. When he saw the girls, he flushed to the roots of his hair, and after that, he kept his attention firmly on Josh and Ricky. "What?"

"Question," Josh said.

"Ah-yup?"

"This is Derek Ellis and Avery Baker. And you know Shannon and Paige?"

Calvin nodded. "What's up?"

Josh indicated Ricky. Calvin shifted his attention to the other side of the table. "Rick?"

Ricky was silent for a few seconds, probably trying to decide how to form the query, out of the blue like this. "A couple of months ago," he said slowly, "I heard you talking about Russian women. What was that about?"

Calvin flushed an even more painful shade of crimson, all the way to the tips of his (large) ears. "Nothing," he muttered, looking down, shuffling those big feet.

"You sure?"

"Sure I'm sure. I was just talking." At this point, Calvin's ears were burning so bright I could practically feel the heat coming off him in waves. When nobody at the table said anything, he must have felt compelled to continue. "I heard somebody saying how it's easy to find Russian women who want to come to the U.S., and I was just thinking, you know, that some of those Russian women are pretty hot. Sorry." He glanced around the table.

"Who was talking about Russian women who want to come to the U.S.?" I asked.

Calvin shrugged, avoiding my eyes. "Just a couple guys on the ferry dock."

"Which ferry dock? Here in Waterfield?"

He shook his head. "Boothbay Harbor."

"Do you know who they are? Where they're from? Had you seen them before?"

But Calvin couldn't help me. "They were just guys, you know. And it was January, so they were wearing parkas and hats and scarves and suchlike. I didn't get to see 'em real well."

We couldn't even get a good description of body type, since heavy winter parkas can make even the skinniest guy look like he's packing on weight. Nor would it help me to ask him to describe the parkas, hats, and scarves, since they were surely in storage somewhere by now. When the snow melts and the ground thaws, Mainers can't wait to shed their winter clothes and get into something lighter.

I thanked Calvin for the information, and he slunk away, without another word.

"That's interesting," Josh said when Calvin was gone.

I nodded. "Wayne definitely needs to know about that. I don't know how much good it'll do, when Calvin doesn't know who the men are. But at least Wayne will know that someone on one of the islands has been discussing Russian women."

Derek nodded. "Josh'll let him know. Let's talk about something else for a while, OK? Pretend that we haven't landed in the middle of yet another criminal investigation."

"Fine with me," I said happily. "What do you want to talk about?"

"I don't care, as long as it doesn't have to do with dead bodies. Or Russian women. Or the weather."

Josh grinned. "Tell us about this house you're renovating, then. What's it like? Can we come see it?"

"If you want to brave the elements. You'd have to walk across the island from the ferry dock to get there. Unless you can get your hands on a boat. But you're welcome to come check it out sometime, if you'd like."

I didn't doubt they'd all end up coming to visit. All four of them had stopped by the house on Becklea Drive while we were renovating it, and Josh and Shannon had been frequent guests in Kate and Wayne's carriage house cum romantic retreat while it was under construction. Not surprisingly, since it was where their parents would be living after the wedding.

Soon Candy appeared with the pizzas and with Derek's and my drinks, and we got busy stuffing ourselves. The conversation wandered off into innocuous territory and didn't return to the girl in the water or the men on the ferry dock. I wasn't worried that Josh would forget to call his dad and tell him about Calvin and the conversation the latter had overheard, though. Josh is not only very intelligent with a good memory, but he sees himself joining the police someday, too, once he's finished college. According to Kate, he wants to become Waterfield's first cyber detective, thus relieving Brandon of the task of matching fingerprints and searching databases for missing people. That would leave Brandon free to become Waterfield's first bona fide forensic tech. Nothing would make Brandon happier than to be able to mess with his blood spatter, DNA, and fibers without interruption.

On the way home in the car, I told Derek about my brief conversation with Miss Barnes in the produce section at Shaw's. "Apparently she snacks on overstuffed Oreos. And she said she might have some information about our house. Seems there's a connection to Waterfield."

"We'll have to stop by the Fraser House sometime to see what she's got," Derek said calmly, steering the truck down the dark road toward downtown and the Village. "Not tomorrow, though. We didn't get much done today, between you being gone all morning and Melissa breathing down our necks all afternoon. We'll have to try to do better tomorrow."

"How did it go at her place earlier? Did you get the drywall done? Was she hanging over your shoulder then, too?"

He shook his head. "She was getting ready for her date with Tony Micelli. Pulling out all the stops. I hardly saw her at all."

This was excellent news. Maybe Melissa had her eye on Tony the Tiger instead of Derek. What a relief that would be. And really, I couldn't think of two people who deserved one another more. I sat back and smiled, watching the streetlights go by outside.

Once we got to Aunt Inga's house on Bayberry Lane, Derek turned to me. "See you tomorrow, right?"

"Absolutely. Bright and early. On the dock by seven."

"Good girl," Derek said.

I looked at the house over my shoulder. It's a Second Empire Victorian, with tall, arched windows and a square tower with a mansard roof. In bright sunshine, it looks like a fairy-tale cottage. Now, with none of the lights on and no moon in the sky, it was dark and a little forbidding. And quite empty. "Sure you don't want to come in?"

He smiled. "I'd love to come in. Just not tonight. It's been a long couple of days."

"Right." I couldn't exactly argue with that.

"I'll wait until you're safely inside."

"I don't think you have to worry," I said. "Nobody's out to get me these days. I haven't had anyone sneaking around my house for six months, at least."

"Just about time for someone to start again, don't you think?"

"Surely not," I said. If I was bothering anyone, or I was a threat to someone, that'd be different. Like, when a certain someone wanted me out of Aunt Inga's house so he could have it, he'd broken in and sabotaged the basement stairs. Or when we'd just found the skeleton in the crawlspace of the house on Becklea Drive, and I was trying to figure out who it was, the killer had snuck around my house as well as tampered with the brakes on Derek's truck to try to get rid of me. But at the moment I wasn't a threat or a bother to anyone. Except . . . "You don't think Melissa would want to get me out of the way so she could have you back, do you?"

Derek put his head back and laughed. "I doubt it, Tink. Seriously, she's no more interested in getting back together than I am."

"And you're not?"

His eyes were warm. “Why would I want Melissa when I have you?”

“About a million reasons I can think of,” I said. Beginning with that beautiful face and gorgeous body and ending with the happy times they must have spent together before things turned sour between them. Including that weekend in bed on Monhegan.

“You must have a more vivid imagination than me.” His voice was warm, too. “I love you, Avery. I may not be ready to remarry right now, but when I am, you’ll be the first to know.” He put the truck in gear. “Go to sleep. Sweet dreams.”

“You, too.” I wandered up to the door and let myself in. He didn’t pull away from the curb until I had turned on the hall light and had waved the all clear.

—9—

I share my house with Jemmy and Inky, two Maine coon cats I inherited from my aunt Inga along with the house itself. The house has turned out to be an easier inheritance than the cats. Once Derek and I went through it last summer and replaced all the old knob-and-tube wiring and galvanized plumbing, and got rid of Aunt Inga's hideous wallpaper and ugly 1970s teak furniture—and once I decided to stay in Waterfield instead of going back to New York and my textile design career—the house itself became my home. Jemmy and Inky were not so easy to win over. They were grown cats, settled in their ways, and used to my ninety-eight-year-old aunt and her quiet life. They'd loved her, and they clearly felt I was an inferior substitute.

It wasn't that we didn't get along. They were intelligent creatures, who realized I was the one putting kibble in their bowls and keeping the cat flap open in the back door. They knew they had to stay on my good side. And they did; they were polite and well mannered, but not friendly. After almost a year together, they didn't let me pet them for more than a second or two, they didn't seek me out unless I'd forgotten to feed and water them, and as long as they had what they needed, they didn't seem to care much whether I was there or not. When I walked through the door, Jemmy—striped in shades of brown and tan, with tufted ears and that distinctive bushy, ringed tail—opened a yellow eye to look at me, before closing it again. Inky, black as her name, was curled up next to him on Aunt Inga's love seat in the parlor and merely twitched her ears and whiskers. She had heard me come in, but I didn't merit so much as a look. And this from the cat that had once helped me fend off a murderer.

My mother raised me right, though, so I ignored the snub to greet them properly. "Good evening, Jemmy. Good evening, Inky. I hope you're well?"

Inky opened her eyes to look at me. They're a pale green, startling in her dark face. Jemmy yawned, his little pink tongue showing, and meowed. I don't speak cat, so I'm not sure exactly what he tried to say, but it was clearly a complaint. Maybe he objected to my disturbing his nap.

"Sorry," I said. "You stay right where you are, OK? I'm just going to turn on the computer"—it was on the desk in front of the gray velvet love seat the cats considered "their" spot—"and look for something."

Inky stretched, curled up the other way, and closed her eyes again. Jemmy sighed. I sat down at the desk and prepared to get to work.

Ricky had mentioned Russian-bride websites. Calvin hadn't, and I hadn't wanted to push too much—I was cautious that he not get his back up so Wayne or Brandon might be able to get a little more information out of him—but I thought the idea was worth following up on. Just in case the girl from the water was a Russian bride—someone who had developed an online relationship with an American man, and who had come to the United States to get married. Maybe the relationship hadn't worked out, maybe the guy was abusive, or ancient, or had no plans of marrying her, and she had run away, and that was how she had ended up in the water. If the guy lived on one of the islands, for instance. Maybe she'd thought she could swim to shore and get help to get back home to Russia.

Typing the search term "Russian women" into Google brought up a slew of other suggestions, some of them quite disturbing. "Russian women for marriage" was one of them. So was "Russian women for sale." Along with "Russian women personals." And then there was "Russian brides for sale," and "Russian brides for free." As well as "Russian girls for marriage" and "for sale."

One of the terms was "Russian brides photos," and I decided to start there. Maybe I'd luck out and find our dead girl's face among the offerings.

I spent the next hour surfing and scrolling through hundreds of images. The experience left me feeling dirty, disgusted, appalled, and angry, as well as a lot of other emotions. Pity was high on the list; sympathy both for those among the women who seemed to be genuinely looking for love—as opposed to the airbrushed ones who were probably models hired to make the site look good—as well as embarrassment for the poor suckers who believed the glossy model types were really available and who put their hard-earned money into paying for introductions and e-mails.

All in all, the whole thing may not have been much worse than the personals on any American dating or classified site. Once upon a time, I had occasionally visited those. They—the sites—all made it clear that in spite of the website addresses and search terms I had used to get there, the women were not actually for sale; they were looking for their one true love. I wished them luck with that. And I meant it sincerely. True love is hard to find. Whether such a thing is likely to be found through an Internet dating site, I'm not sure, but I suppose stranger things have happened. Several of the websites had "success stories" listed, anyway: Russian women who were now safely settled in the United States, Australia, and Western Europe with bald, paunchy men they wouldn't have looked twice at had they seen them on the street at home. If that's true love, then I guess they did find it.

Yes, I sound cynical. It's hard to spend a long time looking at this stuff and not be affected by it.

The faces started to blur after a while, and too many of the women had long, straight, blond hair. None of them jumped out at me specifically as being the girl from the water, but several of them might have been. I bookmarked a few to draw Brandon's attention to, to see if he could pinpoint any of these women as being our girl.

It was getting late and I was getting tired. I was just about to close out the webpage and turn in for the night when a face jumped out at me.

No, it wasn't a small blonde with blue eyes. This was a brunette, with long, straight hair and heavy bangs highlighting steady eyes, straight brows, and those high, Slavic cheekbones. She looked a little like Paulina Porizkova in her modeling heyday, fifteen or twenty years ago. Her name and age were listed under the photo: Svetlana, twenty-six.

• • •

"Look," I told Wayne the next morning, waving the page I had printed out under his nose. "Look at her. She looks exactly like Irina, doesn't she?"

Wayne squinted at the paper moving in front of him and

then grabbed my wrist to hold my hand steady. "Let me see that. Hmmm."

I bounced on my toes next to him. "Doesn't it? Look like Irina? It's her sister, don't you think?"

Wayne didn't answer, just inspected the paper.

It was early—just after seven—and I had knocked on his and Kate's front door on my way down to the harbor to meet Derek. Kate was already up and inside the B&B kitchen feeding her guests, but Wayne was still getting ready for the day, bleary-eyed and half dressed. His uniform shirt was hanging out, and he was unshaven, a shadow of salt and pepper outlining his jaw.

"Sorry," I added, "looks like I dragged you out of bed."

"Not quite. But I spent a late night. Josh called to tell me about this friend of his, Calvin, who had overheard someone talking about Russian women."

I nodded. "That's what made me look up Russian brides on the Internet."

"I also spent some time on the phone with the local director of ICE to see if I could convince them to assign a field agent to look into things."

"And?"

He grimaced. "They're sending someone. Some hotshot rookie with less than two years' experience."

"It's better than nothing. And maybe he or she will have a fresh eye."

"One can hope," Wayne said, but without sounding like he meant it. "Then, in the middle of the night, I got a call from my contact in the Kiev police—there's a time difference I guess he forgot—to tell me that they can't find Svetlana Rozhdes . . . um . . . Irina's sister anywhere."

"You're kidding."

"I wish I were. Apparently, she didn't return to the . . . um . . . Kiev University for the semester that started in

January. Her apartment is occupied by someone else, and so far, no one seems to know where she is. Not her brothers, nor her professors, nor her fellow students."

"That's a little creepy."

Wayne nodded. He looked down at the paper in his hand. "What makes you think this is her?"

"They look alike. Same dark hair, same eyes, same face shape."

Wayne nodded. "I have to go see Irina anyway. Tell her what the Kiev police said. See if she has any suggestions for where else her sister might be. I'll show her this picture at the same time. But even if it is Irina's sister, I'm not sure what it proves, Avery. Other than that she's looking for Mr. Right and is willing to advertise herself to find him."

"I'm not sure it proves anything beyond that, either," I admitted. "It just seems very coincidental. We find a dead girl in the ocean, with Irina's contact info in her pocket, written in Russian. Or Cyrillic or whatever. Then Ricky mentions that someone has been talking about Russian brides. And now we've found a girl who looks like Irina's sister on a Russian-bride website. There has to be a connection."

"You'd think," Wayne said. "The dead girl isn't Svetlana, though. And these bride websites aren't illegal, you know. Unless they're fraudulent, of course. Which some of them may very well be, but that's out of my jurisdiction. There are organizations who deal with that sort of thing. But for two people to meet on the Internet, and then meet in person and decide to get married, isn't illegal. Even if one of them is American and the other Russian. And that's all this seems to be. An introduction service."

I nodded. "That's what they all seemed to be. All the sites I looked at yesterday; and I looked at a bunch. Full of single Russian women seeking wealthy American—or

Australian or European—husbands. But there's no law against marrying for money."

"Right." Wayne glanced at the paper in his hand with Svetlana's vital statistics. She was five foot seven, 137 pounds, with brown hair and gray eyes, and she liked long walks on the beach, candlelit suppers, and snuggling in front of a fireplace. All the usual stuff that men expect women to like.

"I should get going," Wayne said. "If I hurry, maybe I can catch Irina at home before she heads out to Portland for the day. I can give her the news about her sister, ask her about the picture, and let her know to expect a call from the ICE agent, all at the same time. And after that, I'll swing by Barnham College and see if Calvin might remember any additional details about the conversation he overheard or the people having it when it's the police asking."

"It's worth a shot." I stepped off the welcome mat. "I'll be on Rowanberry Island with Derek all day. If you need me for anything, you know where to find me."

Wayne nodded. "I don't think I will, but if I do, I'll call."

"You can't call. There's no cell phone service. But if you're desperate, there's a ferry."

"If I get desperate," Wayne said, "there's the coast guard. But I doubt it'll come to that."

"Glad to hear it. I'll give you a call tonight, OK? Just to see what Irina says."

Wayne nodded. I guess he'd realized the futility of trying to stop me from meddling. Or rather, from "taking an interest."

He closed the door, and I hoofed it back out of the yard and down the hill toward the harbor to where Derek was waiting with the boat.

Forty-five minutes later we were on Rowanberry Island, in our house, working on replacing worm-eaten paneling. There hadn't been anything even remotely interesting in the water today—thank God, because I really didn't want to come across another body; I just couldn't keep myself from looking—although Derek thought the discovery of Russian-bride Svetlana was interesting. I had printed out a second copy of the personal ad to show Derek. He agreed with me that this Svetlana did look a lot like Irina, and that it was quite likely, if not certain, that she was Irina's sister.

And then he went to work recreating two-hundred-plus-year-old paneling.

If you're thinking of 1970s paneling, which comes in flimsy sheets, you couldn't be further from the truth. If you're picturing 1940s knotty pine, you're a little closer to the mark, but only a little.

Colonial-era paneling is thick and made from sections of eastern pine put together into a pattern, with grooves and raised panels of various shapes and sizes. Squares, rectangles, skinny strips.

"These are the stiles," Derek explained as he laid things out for me, his finger on one of the vertical pieces. "The horizontal pieces are called rails. The big pieces in the middle are panels. All of them have grooves on the sides so they fit together neatly."

"And then they get glued?"

"They can be." He was working as he talked, and we had to raise our voices over the whine of the saw. "In Colonial times, they weren't. That was part of the point of having lots of panels."

"How so?" I wanted to know. I mean, wasn't the point of having lots of panels to make it look intricate and pretty?

He squinted at me. "You know that wood breathes, right? It can expand and contract with the weather and humidity."

I nodded. "You're talking about how doors sometimes stick in the summer, right?"

Derek nodded. "A door that sticks has picked up moisture

and expanded, so it doesn't fit into the frame anymore. But if you cut it down, when it contracts again in the cold weather, you'll have a gap."

"OK." This made sense, as far as it went.

"The settlers wanted their houses to be able to breathe. The panels would expand and contract with the weather, and the grooves would let them do it. Any kind of ornamentation would hopefully mask the fact that here and there, now and then, there might be a gap."

"Interesting," I said.

"Have you given any thought to color? Usually the paneling was painted."

"I hadn't really thought about it," I said, perking right up, "but I guess I should. Do you think the hardware store has a good selection of Colonial colors?"

"I'm sure they do."

"If they're open when we get back to town, I'll stop by and pick up a brochure," I promised. "Meanwhile, can I do anything for you?"

Derek thought for a moment. "You can stand by and hand me my tools and wipe my sweaty brow once in a while."

"Or?"

He grinned. "You could find something useful to do."

"Like?"

"I'm finished with the palm sander. Why don't you take it out to the hallway and start sanding the stairs?"

"I could do that," I said.

"And then we'll have to decide whether to poly the steps and paint the risers, or whether you want a poor man's runner."

"A what?"

"Poor man's runner. It's when you paint the steps in two

different colors; one on the edges and one in the middle, so it looks like there's a carpet runner going up the stairs."

"Why do they call that a poor man's runner?"

"Back in those days, most people couldn't afford floor coverings, so they lived with bare plank floors. That's if they were lucky; in many places, people had dirt floors. Some of the big houses painted their stairs to look like there was carpeting going up."

"That's interesting. I thought they had sailcloth rugs, though."

Derek looked up and quirked his brows at me. "How come you know about sailcloth rugs but not about poor man's runners? Oh, wait. Textile designer. I forgot."

"And I've seen some sailcloth rugs in museums. There's one at the Fraser House, I think."

For those of you who aren't textile designers, let me explain: As Derek had mentioned, up until the seventeen hundreds, flooring generally consisted of unfinished wood or earth, tamped hard by walking. Most Americans were too poor to afford woven floor coverings, i.e., carpets. At some point, someone came up with the idea of using worn canvas sailcloth off the ships as a substitute. They'd take a piece of sailcloth roughly the size of a room and cover both sides of it with several layers of oil-based paint to prevent shrinking and make the fabric waterproof. The exposed upper surface would be painted a base color, and then in a pattern; often a black-and-white check or a diamond pattern with embellishments. Little flowers or such in the squares. Sailcloth rugs, interestingly, often look and feel a lot like 1950s linoleum. They were durable, easy to clean, insect resistant, and pretty to look at, and they were cool underfoot in the summer and blocked cold drafts from below in the winter.

As I plumped my butt down on the tight runaround staircase and ran the small, handheld sander over the steps, I thought about sailcloth rugs and poor man's runners, and whether I should paint one, or both, for the house. The runner, for sure. It would look cool and authentic. The sailcloth rug . . . it might be fun, I decided. If whoever ended up buying the house didn't like it, then they could get rid of it. Or maybe I'd just take it out of the house before closing and bring it back to Aunt Inga's house. Or put it in Derek's loft, or something. But painting a sailcloth rug was something I'd never tried, and really, there was no time like the present. I'd probably never renovate another Colonial home, so I'd never have a better excuse. And I could use up all the leftover paint after we had finished painting the walls. That'd make it easier to get the paint cans back to the mainland, too. And to dispose of them later.

I could see it now: a big, square sailcloth rug with a yellow ochre background and black squares along the edges, a few rows deep in a checkerboard pattern. After that, maybe a row of little silhouettes holding hands, like the ones children cut out of folded papers. And in the center, maybe a primitive house scene: the house we were renovating, perhaps, painted white, with a stylized dog or a couple of cats, and some apple trees and the ocean with a boat with white sails . . . sort of like an old-fashioned sampler that someone might have embroidered a few hundred years ago.

In such happy contemplation, with the accompaniment of Derek's hammering and sawing and occasional swearword from the living room, the day went by pretty quickly. We stopped for a picnic lunch in the middle—I made sure to bring a basket every day; Derek's no good unless he has food in him—and today I had even thought to bring a little bowl with some kitty kibble I had skimmed off the top of Jemmy and Inky's bag. I added a pinch of tuna from my sandwich on top and carried it outside, where I put it next to the porch. By the time we left for the day, the bowl was empty. Not only empty, but licked clean. Inside the house, the stairs were lovely and the paneling exquisite, except for the fact that it hadn't been painted yet. But we got back to Waterfield in time to stop by the hardware store and pick up a brochure with historic paint colors.

"I need to go across the street and finish Melissa's drywall," Derek said when we stood outside on the sidewalk again. He didn't sound happy.

"That's a shame."

"I know. The good thing is, it won't take long. And after tonight, I'm done." He grinned.

"Until she comes up with something else she wants you to do."

"How much more can she want? I've done practically everything already."

"She'll figure something out," I said darkly. In spite of Melissa's presumably hot date with Tony the Tiger Micelli, I wasn't entirely convinced that she wouldn't gladly have Derek back if she could. Maybe she was hedging her bets. Or maybe she was trying to make Derek jealous by hanging out with Tony. Or vice versa.

My head was starting to hurt, so I stopped thinking about it. "I can wait for you," I said. "Or come upstairs and hang out while you work."

"Stake your claim?" He smiled. "That isn't necessary, Avery. This'll take less than an hour. How about I come get you after that, and we'll go grab some dinner?"

"You want me to cook instead?"

"After working hard all day? Of course not. We'll go to the Waymouth Tavern. If Miss Melly was there yesterday, she probably won't be back tonight. We can have a romantic dinner, just the two of us." He winked.

"Works for me." I smiled back.

"Can you be ready by six thirty?"

An hour and a half? "Sure."

"See ya, Tink." He bent and kissed me. I kissed him back. And then I wound my arms around his neck and hung on.

The status quo lasted until a window opened across the street and Miss Melly's mellifluous voice floated down to us. "Yoo-hoo! Derek!"

Derek muttered a bad word against my mouth. I giggled. He smiled sheepishly and dropped his arms from around my waist. "Let's continue this later."

I nodded. That'd be nice.

—10—

The Waymouth Tavern is perched on the cliffs overlooking the ocean, off the coast road in the direction of Boothbay Harbor. It's built out of old timber, with fishing nets and old lobster pots on the walls, and imitation Tiffany lamps above the tables. Very dark and cozy. If you squint, you can see Rowanberry Island from the windows, but you can't see our house, since it's on the other side of the island. You can see the lights in the village, though, on the northeastern tip, but that's about it.

The night was clear, with a quarter moon and a sprinkling of stars, and some lights bobbing here and there on the water. One of them looked like it was chugging determinedly straight for Rowanberry Island. The southern tip, where our house was.

"Look," I told Derek, "isn't that boat heading for our house?"

Derek squinted out the window. "Looks more like it's heading for Gert Heyerdahl's house."

"What would the caretaker be doing out there this time of night?"

"Maybe he sleeps there."

"Maybe. Although it can't be much fun, with all the windows shuttered."

"They may not be shuttered all the time. Maybe he came to unshutter them the day you saw him." He dipped a french fry in ketchup and popped it in his mouth.

"Maybe so," I admitted, picking at my own crab cakes. "Do you know Gert Heyerdahl?"

"Personally? Not really. I've met him once or twice."

"Is he a nice guy?"

"He's a writer," Derek said. "They're weird, you know? In their heads a lot. And they see things differently than normal people. Especially the ones who write crime thrillers."

"Like, I'll notice the nice, new-car smell in the Beetle, and he'll wonder how many bodies he could stack in the trunk?"

Derek nodded. "Exactly. But apart from that, he struck me as a nice-enough guy. Quiet. Maybe a little shy. Unless he just likes to sit back and watch people instead of interacting with them."

"Could very well be that he likes to watch. That's what writers do, isn't it? Observe life, and then write about it. And suddenly you find yourself playing the killer or the dead body in a murder mystery."

Derek grinned. "I guess maybe so."

"So how did things go with Miss Melly?"

He shrugged. "Oh, fine. Drywall is patched. Paint is drying as we speak. I won't have to go back again."

Great. If only I could believe it. Unfortunately, I was willing to bet that within the week she would have decided on another project she needed his help with.

I didn't say it out loud, though. I don't think I would have even if we hadn't been interrupted. Didn't want to sound jealous.

"Well, look who's here!" a voice said, and Kate McGillicutty-Rasmussen nudged Derek with her hip so she could slide onto the seat next to him.

I smiled at her. "Hi, Kate. Wayne. You want to sit down?"

"We don't want to interrupt anything. . . ." Wayne began, although clearly Kate had already taken it upon herself to do just that. She was shaking her copper-colored curls at Derek, who was giving her his usual half-amused, half-exasperated look. The two of them dated briefly just after Melissa dumped Derek six years ago, but things didn't work out, and they defaulted to being friendly in an older sister, younger brother sort of way. And then Kate hooked up with the chief of police, and eventually Derek ended up with me.

"You're not," I said, scooting over. "We're just sitting here talking about Gert Heyerdahl."

Wayne folded his long legs under the table next to me. "Why?"

"No particular reason. We saw a boat that looked like it was headed for his house and got on the subject."

Wayne nodded. "I don't know him well, but I think Reece does. Mr. Heyerdahl contacted him for some information once, I think. Background for a book he was writing."

"Derek doesn't know him, either, but he says they've met once or twice. And that Mr. Heyerdahl is weird."

"He's a writer," Wayne said. "They're all weird."

"Right." I hid a smile. "Any news since this morning? On the dead girl?"

He grimaced. "Nothing good. The toxicology report came back and showed that she had tranquilizers in her system. That wouldn't have helped at all when she got in the water. And I spoke to Irina, and the Russian bride you found *is* her sister Svetlana. Who is still missing, or at least gone. She's not where she's supposed to be, and no one can get hold of her. Irina has been trying all day."

"She must be frantic," I said at the same time as Kate seemed to realize she was missing something.

"What?" She looked from Wayne to me, her hazel eyes round.

I turned to Wayne. "You haven't told her?"

His tone was curt. "It's an open investigation. One that doesn't involve her."

"Oh. Right." I bit my lip. I'm so used to talking to Wayne about his cases, the ones I inveigle my way into, that it's just automatic to think that everyone else knows as much about them as I do. Especially Wayne's wife. "Can I tell her?"

"Can I stop you?" Wayne retorted.

"If it's about the girl in the water," Kate said, "I know all about her already. Avery told me about finding her, and Shannon told me about Brandon coming around with a picture of her, and Josh told me about a friend of theirs who had heard someone talking about Russian women."

Wayne rolled his eyes. "Figures."

"Who's Svetlana, though?" She turned to me.

I told her about Irina's sister and the entry for Svetlana I had found on the Russian-bride website. "Apparently no one has seen her or heard from her for weeks."

"And no one's reported her missing?"

"I guess no one realized she wasn't where she was supposed to be."

"And by now she could be anywhere." Kate looked around, as if she expected to see Svetlana materialize next to the table. Instead, it was the waiter who appeared, with two glasses of water and the menus. Wayne ordered a beer and Kate a glass of Chablis, and the waiter departed again.

"I don't think she's at the Waymouth Tavern," Wayne

responded to Kate's look around the restaurant. "I'm more concerned that she might be dead."

"But that wasn't her in the water, right?"

We all shook our heads.

"We still haven't identified the girl from the water," Wayne said. "I spoke to the agent from ICE—she stopped by to introduce herself earlier today—and they have no record of her."

"What was the ICE agent like? This was the hotshot rookie you were telling me about this morning, right?"

Wayne nodded. "She's less than thirty and gung ho, although she seemed competent enough. Her name is Lori Trent. I gave her Irina's contact information and sent her on her way." He smiled.

"Passed the buck, eh?" Derek leaned back and lifted both arms above his head to stretch. Muscles moved smoothly in his shoulders and arms under the blue shirt. Kate caught my eye and winked. I blushed, sheepishly.

"I don't really know much," Wayne answered calmly. "And I have a feeling Irina knows more than she's told us."

I looked away from Derek—he was lowering his arms again anyway, so the show was over—and twisted sideways to stare at Wayne. "You don't think she lied about the girl from the water, do you? She really didn't seem to know her."

Wayne shook his head. "I didn't get the impression that she did, no. But I think she knows, or suspects, something about that note the girl had in her pocket. Most likely who wrote it. There's something she's not telling me. And she wasn't happy when I mentioned that ICE had been called in."

Silence reigned for a few seconds while we all chewed on this.

"Is she illegal?" Kate suggested.

"I don't see how she could be. She's working. I assume she's paying taxes."

We all sank back into silence. In the middle of it, the waiter came back to take Kate and Wayne's food orders and menus, and Derek's and my plates and dessert order.

"Whoopie pie?" my beloved inquired, blue eyes on me across the table.

"You know me. I'm always up for whoopie . . . pie."

He grinned. "One chocolate whoopie pie with two forks, please. And the check."

"Yessah." The waiter grinned, too. I blushed. Derek laughed, and Kate smiled indulgently, but only until Derek turned to her, maliciously.

"So how's married life treating you? You're looking a little haggard. Not getting enough sleep?"

"And by the way," I muttered, "do you still beat your wife?"

Kate ignored him to address me. "I beg your pardon?"

"It's one of those 'damned if you do, damned if you don't' questions. If you're getting enough sleep, you're not having enough sex, but if you admit you're not getting enough sleep, you also admit you're having too much sex."

"There's no such thing as too much sex," Kate said. And blushed. Derek chuckled.

Our whoopie pie arrived shortly—it's a Maine delicacy, consisting of two soft chocolate cakes with whipped vanilla topping between them; sort of like a dessert hamburger in a bun—and we gobbled it up while Kate and Wayne were still waiting for their dinner to arrive. And then we scooted out of the booth and headed home, both so the newlywed Rasmussens could enjoy what had probably been intended to be a romantic evening for two, and to enjoy a romantic evening of our own.

I won't go into details on that score, but the result was another late morning. And since it was late anyway, I prevailed upon Derek to let me stop into the Fraser House to see Miss Barnes and whatever information she had dug up about the house on the island. That allowed us an extra half hour in bed, too, since we had to wait for the museum to open before we could head out.

The Fraser House is one of Waterfield's historic properties, a Greek Revival house built between 1839 and 1842 by Jeremiah Fraser, a Waterfield captain engaged in the China trade. It's a lovely place, full of antique furniture and paintings, including a bergère, a small armchair which supposedly belonged to Marie Antoinette.

Edith Barnes holds court behind the counter in the entry, a forest of brochures in Plexiglas stands in front of her and a wall of filing cabinets behind. She was thrilled to see Derek and was so busy simpering under his practiced and old-fashioned flirtation that she completely forgot why we were there. I had to remind her.

"You said you'd get some information together about the house on Rowanberry Island for us, remember? The other night, when I met you at the store."

"Of course." She put hands on a skimpy folder waiting somewhere on the surface behind the counter. "Sign here, please." She brought out a big book, the same book I'd signed over the summer, when I wanted to take some of the information about Aunt Inga's family, the Mortons, home with me. Then, I had seen the name of Aunt Inga's murderer in the records. This time, the name on the previous line was a horrible scrawl, absolutely impossible to decipher.

"Who had this before me?" I wanted to know.

Derek leaned in to peer over my shoulder. "Ouch," he said, "that's even worse than my handwriting."

"Well, you know what they say about doctors."

"Doctors do it on call?" He turned his head to grin at me, so close I could almost kiss him. "I'm not a doctor anymore. And Dad has beautiful handwriting."

"That's true," I admitted. Dr. Ben spends his free time painting lovely little watercolors of Waterfield landmarks, and he has a gentle hand, both with a paintbrush and a pen as well as with a patient.

Meanwhile, Miss Barnes was examining the entry. "That's Mr. Heyerdahl's signature," she said after a few seconds. "I remember now. He came in last summer to do research for his next book."

"He's writing about our house?"

"Probably just writing about *his* house," Derek said, leafing through the slim folder. "There's information on both in here."

"Actually," Miss Barnes said primly, her arms folded across her scrawny chest, "I believe Mr. Heyerdahl is writing about smuggling."

Smuggling?

"O-ho!" Derek said, eyes still on the folder. "Listen to this, Tink: John van Duren made his fortune as a smuggler before the Revolutionary War."

"You're kidding?"

He shook his head. "Remember we talked about smuggling once, soon after you moved here? About William King, Maine's first governor, and how he traded with both the British and the Americans during the War of 1812?"

I nodded. "We were talking about Alexander Cooper and the house on the cliffs outside Waterfield. Where I got stuck in the tunnels with Philippe and the dead body."

Derek nodded, his lips tight. I've been in tough spots since, with and without him, but that first one was scary, and he doesn't like to be reminded of it. I don't, either, for that matter.

"So are there tunnels under our house, too?" I couldn't help the quiver in my voice. Those hours I spent underground, with my terrified ex-boyfriend and a reeking corpse, were forever etched in my memory. Every once in a while, a nightmare will bring me bolt upright in bed, shaking, with the smell of death in my nose, and I'm still not too happy about being alone in the dark.

Derek shook his head. "No room for tunnels under our house. Too close to sea level. No need for tunnels, either. A ship could anchor out on the ocean and a small boat could sneak in under cover of darkness, straight up to the beach."

"Right." I breathed a secret sigh of relief.

He turned his attention back to the folder. "It says here that the house was used for rum-running during the prohibition, as well."

"Rum-running being liquor smuggling?"

"Exactly. Big business around here. And everywhere with a coastline. Do you know what the rum line was? Or Rum Row?"

I shook my head.

"U.S. jurisdiction ends three miles off the coast. That was the rum line. Rum Row was the line of ships that would anchor there, just outside the rum line, and wait for small local boats to come out and buy their wares. It was unsafe for the smugglers to go into U.S. waters and easier for the smaller boats to outrun the coast guard. They could disappear up small rivers and inlets where the coast guard couldn't follow. You ever hear the expression 'the real McCoy'?"

"Of course," I said. It means the real thing or the genuine article. "Why?"

"In the early 1920s, there was a rumrunner called William Frederick McCoy. Some say he inspired the expression, because he refused to water down his liquor to make it go further. Bill McCoy is credited with coming up with the idea of Rum Row."

"Did Bill McCoy have anything to do with our house?"

"I doubt it," Derek said. "It's just a fun story." He closed the folder. "Can we take this with us?"

Miss Barnes nodded. "Miss Baker signed for it. Don't lose any of the contents, if you please."

"Would I do that?" Derek asked, favoring the old bat with his most charming smile. She blushed but held her ground.

"I do remember a time or two when your homework went missing, young man."

"That was because Ray and Randy Stenham waylaid me before class and took it," Derek answered. "That won't happen this time."

Miss Barnes let us walk out with the folder, and we headed for the harbor.

"Do you think there's a secret storage room somewhere in our house?" I asked Derek as we walked down Main Street. "If they didn't need tunnels, they might at least have needed somewhere to store their goods. It wasn't just tunnels under Alexander Cooper's house, you know; there were rooms, too. Where the smugglers kept their stuff, and probably where they could hide themselves if they had to."

"We'll have to look," Derek answered, "although I can't imagine where a secret room might be, if there is one. Cliff House was . . . well, it was on the cliffs, wasn't it? There was plenty of room below for tunnels and rooms and all sorts of things. The island is a lot flatter, at least down on that end. Up on the north side, where the village is, they may have basements, but we don't. There'd be constant water intrusion."

"Unless John van Duren built a secret room into the house itself."

He glanced down at me, eyebrows tilted. "Why would he do that?"

"You said he made his fortune smuggling in the years before the Revolution, didn't you? Tea, I guess?"

"And molasses and sugar and wool, among other things."

"But he didn't build the houses until after the Revolutionary War. Don't you think he might have wanted to make sure there was somewhere safe to store stuff, just in case he'd have to go back to smuggling? Or one of his descendants might?"

Derek shrugged, putting an arm around my back to guide me across the street and onto the pier. "It's worth looking into, I guess. Where would you start?"

"No idea," I said cheerfully. "Look for trap doors in the floors and secret panels in the . . . um . . . paneling, I guess."

"Shades of Scooby-Doo," Derek said with a grin. He kept his arm around me as we navigated the uneven and slippery boards of the pier, where the paramedics had wheeled their gurney with its grisly burden just a few days ago. The air smelled salty and briny. Boats bobbed in the water on either side of us, thick ropes groaning as they stretched, and underlying it all was the sound of the water lapping against the piles holding the walkway up, and in the distance, seagulls squawking and boats chugging.

The sun was breaking through the haze, the day looked like it would turn out to be crisp and clear, and everything was lovely. Until Derek stopped dead, dropped his arm from around me, and breathed a very bad word.

I stopped, too, a step or two ahead, where my momentum had carried me, and turned to him. "What? Did you forget something?"

He shook his head, his face grim. "In the water."

"What?" I looked around. It took a few seconds, and a nod from Derek, to see what he'd seen. And then I breathed the same bad word myself. "Not another one?"

"I'm afraid so," Derek said, looking around. "Call Wayne. I'll get a boat hook and see if I can snag her. I'm afraid you'll have to help me get her up on the pier."

"No problem." I swallowed and reached for my phone.

—11—

It took Wayne a moment to respond to the announcement that we'd just discovered the body of another woman floating in the water. I imagined him pinching the bridge of his nose to ward off what was surely an oncoming headache. Then he said he would be with us in five minutes and so would the ambulance crew. I closed my cell phone and rejoined Derek, who had managed to find a boat hook, and who was in the process of dragging the body toward a ladder halfway down the pier, where he'd be able to climb down and get to her.

"Wayne says to leave her in the water until he gets here," I told him. "He or the paramedics will help you get her out."

He glanced at me. "I want to make sure she's really dead first."

"Is there a chance she might not be?"

He shook his head, grimly. "Not much of one, no. The ME will have to make the final determination, but it looks like her head is bashed in."

"Yow." My stomach swooped. Derek gave me a narrow look but seemed to determine that I was OK on my own and that the corpse needed him more.

"Here," he said, "hold her still."

He grabbed my hand and wrapped it around the end of the boat hook. I followed with the other; not because I wanted to, but because I had to, to keep the body steady. I could feel it—or more likely the tide—pulling on the hook, and it took both hands to resist. I planted my feet and held on.

Meanwhile, Derek swung himself over the side of the pier and fumbled for a foothold on the slippery ladder. I leaned over the railing, watching the top of his ruffled head descend.

Below in the water floated the young woman. Derek had hooked one of the belt loops of her jeans—Lee, not Gloria—and she was just bobbing there, like one of the boats. Swallowing, I forced myself to take a closer look.

Like the other woman, she was floating facedown, but unlike our previous victim, she was dressed for the weather this time of year. She wore stout shoes with thick soles, and above the snug jeans was what looked like a corduroy jacket. Her hair was short and dark, not long and fair, and I could see what Derek had been talking about: the back of her head wasn't smooth and round, but kind of caved in. That thought gave me the heebie-jeebies, so I averted my eyes to watch what Derek was doing instead.

"Move a couple steps to your left, Avery," he said. "I can't reach a pulse point."

I obeyed, stepping sideways and towing the body along. One of her hands hit against the ladder where Derek was perched, and he reached down and grabbed it, wrapping his fingers around the pale wrist. I counted along with him. Silently. Ten seconds. Twenty.

"Nothing." He dropped the hand back in the water and

wiped the water off his own hand on his jeans. "Damn. I feel guilty leaving her there."

"It's not for long," I reminded him, gripping the pole. My knuckles were white, I noticed, not so much from the strain of holding the hook and the body as from the whole situation. "And if there's nothing you can do for her . . ."

"I can get her out of the water!"

"Right. Well, Wayne will be here soon. In fact"—I risked a glance over my shoulder—"here's the ambulance now. The paramedics will be on top of us in a minute. Maybe you'd better come back up on the pier. This pole is a little heavy for me."

It wasn't, really, but the suggestion that I needed him brought him back up the ladder, just as I intended. He really is incapable of turning down anyone who asks for his help.

The paramedics arrived, the same two guys as last time, and while Derek held the body steady and I watched, wincing, they were able to get the woman up out of the water and onto the gurney. By then, Wayne had also arrived, and he let out an expletive when he got a good look at her.

From the front, I could tell she was a little older than our other victim, although she was still a year or two younger than me, I thought. Right around thirty, at a guess. Her short, dark hair started curling as soon as it got out of the water, and her eyes were dark brown and startled. It was Derek who reached out and closed them. I shuddered but continued looking.

She was tallish and lean and looked like she'd have been in pretty good physical shape. Under the black corduroy jacket, she was wearing a turtleneck in the same color. There were small silver hoops in her ears, and the water hadn't completely managed to eradicate what had to be waterproof eye makeup. It was smeared but still there. Before Wayne let loose with his four-letter word, I already suspected we were not dealing with the same sort of situation as last time, and the crack on the head was only one of the clues.

"Who is she?" Derek asked, his voice soft. He must have come to the same conclusion I had.

Wayne glanced at him, his face grim. "This is Lori Trent."

"The ICE agent?" I turned back to her, my eyes wide.

"Afraid so. Damn." He reached for his phone.

Derek put his arm around me, and I realized I was shaking. "I'm OK," I tried, but he didn't let go, and I was glad. The warmth of his body through the wool sweater felt good. I snuggled in closer, slipping a hand into the back pocket of his jeans.

"What happened?" Wayne asked when he had completed his phone calls; one to Brandon asking for backup, and one to Dr. Lawrence the medical examiner, telling her to expect a new delivery. I guessed he would wait to make the unpleasant call to ICE until he was on his own.

We went over the story again. Not that there was much to tell; we'd just been on our way to our boat when we'd noticed the body in the water below.

"Getting a late start this morning, aren't you? Any particular reason?"

"The whoopie pie from yesterday," Derek said.

The tight set of Wayne's lips loosened a little. "Right."

"And then we stopped by the Fraser House on the way. To pick up some information about our house on the island. Where's the folder?" I looked around for it.

"You must have put it down somewhere," Derek said, "when I asked you to take the pole. Over there." He pointed. I could see the pale square of the manila folder on the worn planks of the pier a few yards away. We'd only planned to work a half day today—it was Saturday—so there was no lunch basket beside it.

"Can't lose that. Miss Barnes will have my head." I didn't make a move toward it, though. Didn't want to miss anything Wayne might say.

"Did she contact either one of you yesterday?"

Derek and I exchanged a glance. "Agent Trent? Of course not." And especially not after nine P.M., which was when we'd left Kate and Wayne at the restaurant. If we'd heard from the ICE agent before then, we would have mentioned it last night.

"Why?" I added. "What would she want to talk to us about?"

"Can't imagine." Wayne grunted. He turned away to give the paramedics instructions for the body; the same instructions as last time. I watched them wheel the gurney down the pier toward the ambulance with an unpleasant sense of déjà vu.

"What happened?" I said, more to myself than to the two men. Both of them looked at me.

"Guessing," Derek said, "she discovered something she shouldn't have."

"Or something someone didn't want her to discover," Wayne added.

Obviously. That wasn't really what I'd meant, though. "Does this have to do with the other body? The probably Russian girl? Or something else?"

The two men exchanged a glance. "Could be either," Wayne said. "She was in Waterfield to look into that, but she could have stumbled onto something else while she was here. Or into someone she knew from before."

"Could even be personal," Derek added. "You never know."

The chief of police nodded.

"I suppose you'll have to talk to Irina about what the two of them discussed yesterday." I made it something of a question, although it wasn't really.

Wayne nodded. "Guess I'd better. See if I can track Miss Trent's movements yesterday. I'm sure I'll have help in that." He grimaced.

"The ICE?"

"They'll be crawling all over everything in a couple hours, I'm sure. And that reminds me . . . you two are free to go. I know where to find you if I need you. I'm gonna wait here for Brandon and make my phone call to ICE."

"Good luck with that." I left the comfort of Derek's arm to go pick up my manila folder. Derek gave Wayne a sympathetic clap on the shoulder before he followed. By the time we were in the boat and chugging out to sea, Brandon's squad car had arrived at the entrance to the pier, tires squealing, and Brandon was on his way out to meet Wayne at a good clip.

"I'm not sure I can concentrate on working today," I told Derek. We'd both been quiet so far; this second discovery had been an unpleasant surprise for both of us. I mean, what are the chances?

Then again, the two situations were totally different, really. The young Russian woman had died accidentally, either from going or falling in the water and getting hypothermia before she could get back out. Agent Trent had been deliberately killed, or so it seemed to me. But maybe I was wrong.

"Could it have been an accident, do you think?"

Derek glanced at me over his shoulder. As usual, he was steering the boat and I was sitting on one of the seats farther back, after cranking up the outboard motor. "The knock on the back of the head, you mean?"

I nodded.

"Anything's possible."

"But maybe not likely?"

Derek shrugged. "I didn't have a chance to examine

her," he said, his words coming back to me on the wind. "I just saw the back of her head from a few feet away. It looked like she was hit with something smooth and round, not too big around."

"Broom handle?"

"Not big enough. A boom, maybe. Although I don't quite understand . . ."

"What's a boom?"

Another flash of blue eyes. "The beam that holds the bottom edge of a sail on a sailboat. It swings. Sometimes people get knocked overboard when the wind shifts."

"And that could have cracked her skull that way?" My stomach was objecting to the subject matter, but I pushed on.

"It oughtn't to have hit her on the head at all, unless she was kneeling. Would have gotten her in the middle of the back instead, and sort of swooped her into the water."

"So that's something that might have happened to the other dead girl. The Russian. Or the one we think is Russian. She could have been on a sailboat and been hit by the boom and swept overboard. If she were alone, no one may have realized it."

Derek nodded. "Someone would have noticed the boat adrift, though, probably."

"That's true. What about Agent Trent? She could have been kneeling, couldn't she? And the boom hit her on the back of the head? And then she lost consciousness and fell in the water?"

"But again, either she was with someone, who ought to have reported her missing, or she was alone, and we would have found the boat."

We traveled in silence another few minutes.

"Are you serious about not wanting to work today?" Derek asked. "Do you want me to turn around?"

I gnawed on my bottom lip. "Would you mind? I'm a little worried about Irina, to be honest. You don't think Wayne suspects her of anything, do you?"

Derek pondered. While he did, he slowed the boat to a crawl. "He might," he admitted, finally.

"Do you think we should go look for her? Give her the news?"

"I think," Derek said, "we should leave that to Wayne."

"He probably wouldn't like it if we did, would he?"

"No," Derek said, "he wouldn't."

"I'm concerned, though. That he'll think she had something to do with it."

"Why would she have something to do with it? And why would he think so?"

"I'm not sure," I admitted. "But remember yesterday, he said she was unhappy when he told her about the ICE agent? Maybe she really is illegal. And if she is, even if she didn't do anything to Agent Trent, she had a motive."

Derek didn't answer. After a minute, though, he turned the boat around and headed back to the harbor.

By the time we reached the pier, it was empty. Wayne had left, and so had Brandon. Probably because the pier and the water below wasn't much of a crime scene, really. There was debris floating in the water—empty soda bottles, beer cans, scraps of newspaper, last autumn's dead leaves—but nothing that looked like it would have anything to do with a dead Immigration and Customs Enforcement agent. And there was no telling how she'd gotten into the water, anyway; whether she'd been pushed off the pier right there or had been dumped off a boat. She might even have floated in on the tide, for all I knew.

"Are you coming with me?" I asked Derek when we were walking up Main Street again, toward the hardware store and the truck parked in the lot behind it. "Or do you want me to go home and get the Beetle?"

"D'you think I'd trust you on your own?" He glanced down at me.

"I think you'd better. What are you afraid I'm gonna do? Tell Irina to make a run for it because the law is on her tail?"

He didn't answer.

"I just want to know what's going on," I said.

"That's fine," Derek answered, "but what if she did have something to do with it? What if she bashed Agent Trent over the head with a rock or something?"

I looked at him sideways. "You don't think she did, do you?"

"If she's illegal, and Lori Trent threatened to have her deported? I think she might."

"How would she have gotten the body into the water?"

"She's a big woman," Derek said. "Tall and strong-looking. I imagine she might have managed."

"She doesn't own a car, though. How would she have gotten the body from her house on Becklea Drive and down to the harbor?"

It was his turn to give me a sideways look. "How do you know they met at Irina's house on Becklea Drive? They could have arranged to meet somewhere in town. Irina may not have wanted Agent Trent to know where she lives."

Damn. I bit my lip. He was right about that.

Derek had been watching my face, and now his voice softened. "I'm not saying she had anything to do with it, Avery. I don't want to believe it, either. I like Irina. But you've had a couple of close calls this year, and you're not always careful. I just don't want anything to happen to you."

"You're worried about me? And you're coming along to protect me? My hero."

"Whatever," Derek said, a flush of color creeping onto his cheekbones. I giggled. He looked down at me, and then he bent and tossed me up over his shoulder, the way he used to do when we'd just met and I was exasperating him. I squealed and giggled and hung on as he strode around the corner of the hardware store and across the parking lot to the truck.

• • •

"It's been a while since you did that," I remarked a couple of minutes later, when we were rolling sedately down Main Street and I had gotten my breath back. "We're not becoming set in our ways and boring, are we?"

He shot me a glance out of the corner of his eye. "You can ask that, after last night? And this morning?"

"Oh . . . um . . ." I flushed, remembering our breathless session between the sheets before rolling out of bed this morning. "I guess not."

"I should hope not." He grinned, but after a block or two he added, seriously, "It's different when you're in a relationship. Last summer we were just getting to know each other. Now we've been together awhile. Things are quieter."

I nodded. "This is the longest I've ever managed to last in a relationship. That's a little scary, isn't it?"

"Not that scary. Means I've beaten all the other guys." He winked.

"I've still a ways to go." He and Melissa had been married for five years. They'd probably dated for a while before that, too. I'd never asked how long, and I didn't now.

"Don't worry about it. You've already beaten all the other girls, too."

"How so?"

His voice was easy. "After Melissa, I thought I'd always break out in a cold sweat at the thought of commitment. And then I met you."

"And I don't make you break out in a cold sweat? Awww! That's so sweet!"

"Except when you do stupid stuff," Derek said.

"Good thing you're around to rescue me."

He smiled back. "Good thing." And then he leaned over to drop a kiss on the top of my head before he concentrated on driving.

Becklea Drive lay quiet and peaceful when we turned the corner from Primrose Drive. Arthur Mattson, who lives two doors down from Irina with his shih tzu, Stella, was in the front yard working on one of his flower beds. I waved when we drove by, but he didn't wave back. Maybe he didn't recognize me. It was almost six months since I'd spoken to him, so he might have forgotten me. People do when they reach a certain age. Not that Arthur is old; just around sixty. But maybe he couldn't see me clearly; the truck had tinted windows. He ought to be able to recognize the truck itself, though, with its Waterfield R&R sticker: Derek Ellis, Proprietor; Avery Baker, Designer. He'd seen it every single day six months ago.

Whatever. Derek pulled into the driveway two doors up, and we got out. Arthur shaded his eyes and peered at us. I waved again. After a second, he waved back. Stella yipped.

There was no sign of life at Irina's house and no answer when I knocked on the door.

"She's probably out showing houses," Derek remarked. "Weekends are busy for real estate agents. It's not a nine-to-five job. Nor is home renovation."

I nodded. He had that right. When we're working on a house—and that's most of the time—every day is pretty much the same, unless something specific is going on that we have to take time off for. But if not, we're just as likely to work on a Saturday or Sunday as we are on a weekday. When you're in business for yourself, the faster you work, the sooner you see a payoff. And when you're dealing with other people, who often work nine to five, and whose only opportunity to go look at houses is Saturday and Sunday, weekends become even more important. Someone in Irina's position, eager to get a foothold in a competitive business, would make herself available whenever someone wanted her.

She didn't answer her phone, though, when I tried to call.

"She may not," Derek said, "if she's with a client. She might think it would be rude."

"That's true." I bit my lip.

I knew he was right about everything he'd said. But something about this still didn't feel right. Or maybe it was just my imagination. If I'd gone to Irina's house any other time and hadn't found her at home, I would have assumed she was working. Now her absence worried me.

Something else was missing, too, I noticed: that big, heavy *pysanka* she'd had on her living room table yesterday. When I peered through the window, it wasn't there. Not where I'd put it, and not where it had been when I first saw it.

"Why don't you go ask Arthur if he's seen her," Derek suggested, interrupting my train of thought. "Meanwhile, I'm gonna check around back."

"You don't want me to come with you?"

He shook his head. "Just go talk to Arthur. I'll let you know if I find anything."

"OK." I walked with him to the corner of the house and watched him go into the backyard before I cut across the neighbor's lawn and hailed Arthur Mattson.

Stella the shih tzu went crazy as soon as I set foot on

Arthur's property, but because she's only about fifteen pounds—roughly the size of Inky the cat—and not all that brave, she barked at me from behind Arthur's khaki-clad legs. I'd long since given up on making friends with the little mutt; she growled and snapped every time I came near her.

Arthur was friendlier. "Haven't seen you two for a while," he remarked, showing me his dirty hands and making a face to explain why he couldn't shake my hand.

"The house up the street is finished, and we're on to the next project," I explained.

"Where are you working now?"

I filled him in on the house on Rowanberry Island, and Arthur nodded. "Nice out there."

"You've been there?"

"Not to your house. To Rowanberry. Got a friend who owns a house on the island."

"Really? In the little village where the ferry docks?"

Arthur shook his head. "One of the summer homes. He retired to Florida and only comes up when it's warm."

"It isn't Gert Heyerdahl, is it?"

"Oh, no." Arthur gave another decisive shake of his head. "Name's Lon Wilson. Gert Heyerdahl's house makes Lonnie's look like a shack. Lots of people around here are snowbirds. Spend their winters where it's warm and only come back to Maine in the summer."

I nodded. Derek's grandfather, Willie, had retired to Florida, too. Except he hadn't been back since. Too busy playing bocce ball and driving a golf cart through the sand dunes, I guess.

"You looking for Irina?" Arthur changed the subject.

I glanced over my shoulder. Derek was still behind the house and out of sight. "That's right. Have you seen her today?"

Arthur shook his head. "Not since yesterday," he said. "She came home in the late afternoon and then left again around six. Haven't seen her since."

"Any idea where she went?"

"Camping," Arthur said.

"I beg your pardon?"

"She had on jeans and a sweater, and she was carrying a big backpack with a sleeping bag attached."

"Wow." I had a hard time picturing Irina in jeans and a sweater; every time I'd seen her, she'd been dressed in a severe business suit, with her hair so tightly scraped back from her face that her eyebrows were elevated. Then again, I'd pretty much only seen her when she was working. It stood to reason that she had to have a personal life, too. Maybe she spent every weekend tramping around in nature.

"Oh, no," Arthur said when I suggested this, shaking his head. "Not at all. I've never seen her do it before. Usually she works on the weekends. She works all the time."

"I don't suppose she told you where she was going?"

But she hadn't. Of course not.

Behind me, Derek came toward us across the grass, his approach accompanied by growls and tiny yips from Stella. He stopped next to me and put a hand out. "Arthur."

Arthur shook it, of course. Apparently it was OK to shake Derek's hand when his own was dirty; just not mine.

"Anything?" Derek asked me.

I repeated what Arthur had said. "What about you?"

His shook his head, a floppy lock of hair falling across his forehead. "Nothing. The place is locked up tight. No way to know whether she talked to Agent Trent or not."

"Agent Trent?" Arthur repeated.

"Lori Trent, special agent with Immigration and Customs Enforcement. She was up from Boston to talk to Irina about the body of a young Russian woman who was found in the sea earlier this week." Derek's voice was bland, giving no hint that we knew anything more about the body than anyone else would.

"I met Agent Trent." Arthur dug in the pocket of his khakis and came up with a battered business card. It had the logo of ICE on it, Lori Trent's name, and an address and phone number in Boston. "She stopped by yesterday afternoon."

"Before or after Irina left?"

Arthur thought back. "Before. About one o'clock or so. Irina came back around five and left again around six."

Derek and I exchanged a look. So there was still time for Agent Trent to have pinned Irina down in Portland or downtown Waterfield in the hours between one and five. There was probably time for Irina to have bashed her over the head with something and to have tipped her into the water, too. That kind of thing is a lot harder to do in broad daylight, but not impossible. And it would explain why Irina had grabbed a backpack and her sleeping bag and disappeared.

Down at the corner, a car appeared. It was black and white and had the logo of the Waterfield PD on the door.

"Here we go," Derek said.

"Did you call them? Him?" I recognized Wayne's profile as the cruiser pulled up to the curb.

Derek shook his head. "Great minds, I guess. I figured it was just a matter of time before he got here. If Irina isn't answering her phone, this is the logical place to start."

I nodded. Wayne had gotten out of the car and was scowling. I braced myself.

—12—

"That went rather well, I thought," Derek said judiciously thirty minutes later, after Wayne had finished chewing both of us out for interfering with his investigation. Never mind the fact that we hadn't done anything wrong, and if it hadn't been for us talking to Arthur, and Arthur saying that Irina had gone camping, we'd have no idea what had happened to her. Wayne was still upset that we'd beaten him here.

"I thought you were headed for Rowanberry Island!"

"We changed our minds," I said.

"Avery was worried about Irina," Derek added, throwing me to the wolves. I shot him a betrayed glance. He shrugged, and not apologetically.

"And so she should be," Wayne snarled. "You realize how this looks, don't you?"

I made a face. Of course we did: like Irina had met with Lori Trent, had been spooked by something the ICE agent had said or done, and had bashed her over the head with something—like the missing *pysanka*. And then she had dumped it, and the body, in the water in the harbor.

Except . . . the backpack may have been big, but was it big enough to hide the body? Probably not. Or—if they'd met near the harbor, as Derek had suggested—why would Irina be carrying the paperweight? Unless she had brought it specifically to bash in the head of Agent Trent. But that would make it premeditated murder. . . .

"Yes, Wayne," Derek said, watching the thoughts chase each other across my face, "we realize exactly how it looks. Unfortunately."

Wayne snarled something before turning to Arthur. "We have to talk."

Arthur nodded.

"What about us?" I asked, a little diffidently.

Wayne scowled at me. "You two can go. I know where to find you. And no more interfering with my investigation!"

"I wouldn't dream of it," I said.

Wayne growled and waved us away, as if we were annoying midges buzzing around his head.

And that was what prompted Derek's remark when we were back in the truck and on our way back to Waterfield proper.

"You mean, because he didn't arrest us for impeding his investigation?"

"We're not impeding his investigation. It's not like we held anything back."

"There was nothing to hold back," I pointed out.

"That, too. But we wouldn't have held anything back even if we'd learned something interesting."

I didn't answer. "I don't think he wants us to keep looking for Irina, though. Did you get that impression?"

Derek glanced at me. "Are you thinking of looking for Irina? Because I'm not sure I want you to do that, either."

"Why not? You don't really think she killed Lori Trent, do you?"

Derek didn't respond. My voice rose and became shrill.

"Are you crazy? Can you imagine Irina bashing someone over the head with a paperweight and pushing them into the harbor? Irina!"

"Paperweight?" Derek repeated, without actually answering my questions.

I squirmed. "She had this big, egg-shaped paperweight in her living room the other day, when I was there with Wayne. A *pysanka*. Ukrainian Easter egg. Painted in bright colors. I picked it up, and it weighted a ton."

"Really?" Derek said.

I nodded. "I looked for it through the living room window earlier, but I couldn't see it. Wayne will probably go inside, don't you think? And see if it's still there?"

"I'm sure he will," Derek said. "Do you want me to call and remind him?"

I shook my head. "He was there the other day, too. We talked about it. The *pysanka*. He'll remember." And if he didn't, and it wasn't there, it wasn't my job to remind him.

"Right," Derek said, but he didn't say anything else. He knows me well, though, so I'm sure he knew what I was thinking.

"So what now?" he asked instead.

I glanced at the clock on the dashboard. "Almost lunchtime. I guess we should find some food and something useful to do for the rest of the day."

"Want to run up to Boothbay Harbor and see what Ian has come up with for us?"

"Your friend at the salvage store?"

Derek nodded. "I called him a couple of days ago and told him to gather doorknobs and old fireplace tiles and anything else he has that might be Colonial or Federal."

"You think he's had time to put anything together?"

"He'd better," Derek said, turning the truck onto the ocean road. "He knows every piece of junk in the place, so I don't see why he won't have. And there's a little clam shack up that way where we can have lunch, too." He took his hands off the wheel for a second to rub them together in anticipation.

"With Ian?"

Hands back on the wheel now, Derek glanced over at me. "If he wants to. Though I don't think he will."

"Why not? Can't he leave the business in the middle of the day?"

"That's part of it. It's just him since his dad retired, so he usually eats his meals at the counter and sleeps under it. Good man, knows a lot about a lot of things. But he isn't real comfortable around women."

"How come?"

"No idea. We've never talked about it. But I took Melissa up to the salvage yard once, and it wasn't pretty."

"What happened?"

Derek rolled his eyes. "You know what she's like."

I did, indeed. Gorgeous, elegant, confident, and condescending. I couldn't imagine she'd have enjoyed waiting while her husband crawled around a dirty, dusty junkyard full of other people's castoffs. Especially since she'd thought she'd be married to a doctor and not a glorified handyman. "She probably wasn't very nice, was she?"

"No," Derek said, "she wasn't. Don't get me wrong; Ian's a nice guy. But you should probably just ignore him. Pretend he isn't there unless he talks to you."

"I can do that," I said, and sat back to enjoy the drive and the occasional glimpses of the waters of the Atlantic through the window. After almost a year in Maine, I still hadn't gotten tired of looking at the ocean.

Boothbay Harbor is about the same distance from Waterfield as Portland, but in the other direction, up the ocean road to the northeast. We got there a little before one and stopped for lunch at the clam shack Derek had mentioned, where the food was every bit as good as he'd intimated. By the time we got to Ian's place, on the north side of town, it was closer to two.

Boothbay Harbor is another gorgeous little Maine town. Like Waterfield, it started life as a shipbuilding and fishing village, and those industries are still alive and well, but during the tourist season, tourism trumps everything. At the moment, it was still too early in the year for many out-of-towners, and the streets were mostly quiet, while many of the tourist traps were closed for the winter.

"What do these people do all winter?" I asked Derek as we passed another little souvenir shop with a sign in the window: Back at Half Past April.

Derek grinned, reading it. "Snowbirds," he said, "most likely. Folks who spend the summers working around the clock, and who take the winters off and go to warmer climates."

"Florida?" Like Gert Heyerdahl and Arthur Mattson's friend Lon Wilson and Derek's paw-paw Willie.

He nodded. "Mostly Florida. Although some go to Arizona or Alabama or Texas, too."

"Do they all go away? Everyone whose store is closed?" If so, the permanent population of this place must halve in the winter.

He shook his head. "Some just close up shop and do other things. Sometimes the tourism businesses are sidelines, and they have other jobs as well. Sometimes they take temporary jobs over the winter to keep money coming in until they can open the business again. Some make enough during the season that they just sit back and wait it out."

I nodded. "Is that Ian's place?"

It looked like a junkyard: a big, ramshackle, shedlike building with a smaller building next to it; the smaller building actually had both walls, windows, and a door, as opposed to the bigger structure, which had a wall in the front and the back, but nothing on the sides. The whole thing was surrounded by a tall chain-link fence topped with barbed wire. Beyond the chain link, I could see an ocean of toilets, sinks, and old-fashioned claw-footed and pedestal bathtubs. Under the roof of the shed were stacks and rows of windows and doors, sidelights and shutters, with light fixtures suspended from the ceiling beams above. The sign on the front said Burns Salvage.

Derek nodded. "This is it. Ian's last name is Burns."

His eyes had turned soft and dreamy, the way they always do when he sees something appealing. And I'm not talking about when he's looking at me. No, this is the look Derek reserves for architectural elements that get his blood pumping. The first time I saw it, he was looking at my aunt Inga's kitchen, with its peeling linoleum floor, rusty half-circular wall sink, and driftwood cabinets. I've seen it many times since, in every house we've ever renovated. Now I saw it again, as Derek took in the many possibilities inherent in the cast-off bathroom fixtures, old wooden doors, and many-paned windows stretched out before him.

"Are you ready?" I nudged him.

His eyes came back in focus and he grinned. "Sure."

"Then let's go. You can turn the place upside down after we see what Ian has found for us."

Derek nodded, and I could see that he did, indeed, plan to do just that.

He held the door into the office open for me. I passed through first and looked around.

The space was small and old. The walls were paneled—not nicely paneled, like our Colonial, but paneled in ugly 1970s sheet paneling, speckled green—and there was an old counter taking up most of the room, with two ratty office chairs up against the wall under the window. They were orange and dirty, and the stuffing was coming out in places where years of wear had worn away the fabric. Behind the counter hung a dog-eared calendar with pictures of lighthouses, and a notice saying, "I can only please one person per day. Today is not your day. Tomorrow doesn't look good, either." I wondered whether this was Ian's philosophy or whether it was a joke. It could be taken either way, I thought.

The man behind the counter, reading a copy of *Hunting & Fishing*, must be Ian.

Now, Derek is no shrimp, height-wise or in any other way. He's six feet tall, give or take an inch, and there's nothing wrong with the rest of him, either. A guy doesn't haul lumber and heavy tools around all day and fail to build some muscle. But next to Ian, he looked downright puny.

Ian looked like Paul Bunyan, in a black and red checkered flannel shirt with the sleeves rolled up to the elbows. And his lower arms were as big around as my thighs, furry with dark hair. He had shoulder-length, black hair, a big beard, ruddy cheeks—what I could see of them behind the growth—and different-colored eyes under bushy brows. One bright blue, one hazel, like an Australian shepherd. Although it was hard to tell with all the hair, I placed him at a few years older than Derek; maybe forty, maybe a year or two over or under. He blushed when he saw me, but the beard split in a grin when he spied Derek behind me.

"Hey, man!" His voice was raspy, as if he had a pack-a-day habit, or laryngitis. The smile made him look younger. Getting up made him look bigger; he towered over me as he leaned across the counter to clasp Derek's hand. If he didn't exactly tower over Derek, it was a near thing. Ian must stand almost seven feet tall, and correspondingly broad.

I stood politely aside as the two of them exchanged pleasantries. Eventually, Derek turned to introduce me. "This is Avery. We're in business together." The look he gave me was a reminder to be nice to poor, delicate Ian. I made a face.

Ian's dual-colored eyes wandered over me. "Just business?"

Derek shrugged, smiling. Ian smiled, too. He didn't offer to shake my hand. I didn't mind. He looked like he could break a few of my bones without even trying.

"I like her better than the other one," Ian said. I wasn't sure that I liked being talked about like I wasn't here and couldn't hear every word they said, but on the other hand, he liked me better than Melissa, so that had to be a good thing.

"I do, too." Derek winked at me.

Ian grinned. "I got something to show you, too." He turned away, then bellowed, loud enough that I was worried the windows would break, "Angie!"

"Angie?" Derek repeated, giving his head a shake. He was probably trying to stop his ears from ringing. I know mine were.

Ian nodded. "Just wait."

We waited. After a minute, a door opened somewhere, and we heard light footsteps in the back room, somewhere behind the office. A figure appeared in the doorway. "Yes?"

Derek straightened up. I blinked. And Ian's beard broke open in a beaming, adoring smile.

The woman in the doorway couldn't be much over twenty. She was only a fraction of an inch taller than me, and slender. Everywhere except for the stomach, which looked like she had swallowed a basketball. She was wearing a pair of black leggings and a long-sleeved, pink T-shirt with black lettering, like those signs you see in station wagon windows: Baby on Board. The "sign" was positioned directly on the belly. Her hair was soft and brown, curling around her ears. Her eyes were huge and melting brown, like chocolate, and surrounded by gorgeous, long, curving lashes.

"This," Ian said, walking to her and wrapping a meaty arm around her slight body; her head didn't even reach the top of his shoulder, "is Angela. My wife."

A beat of silence followed, while we stood there speechless. Then I pulled myself together. "Congratulations."

I elbowed Derek, who was still gaping. He closed his mouth and opened it again. "Guess it's been longer than I realized since I was up here."

"We met just before Christmas," Ian explained, gazing fondly down—way down—on his wife.

Derek finally got it together. He turned on the charm and took a couple of steps forward, holding his hand out. "Nice to meet you, Angie. Congratulations."

When Derek comes toward them, smiling, most women smile back. Angie shrank into Ian's side while her eyes got even bigger.

"It's OK," Ian rasped. "This is Derek Ellis. He's been coming here for years, buying stuff."

Angie nodded, a jerky little movement of her head. She still didn't look comfortable, but she extended a small hand and shook, forcing a smile.

"This is my girlfriend, Avery." Derek put his arm around me and pulled me forward.

I smiled and waved across the counter. "Hi, Angie. It's nice to meet you." If she didn't want to shake hands, I certainly wasn't going to force her. Maybe she was worried about catching cold or something. Pregnant women can be weird sometimes. Or so I hear.

"Nice to meet you, too," Angie murmured. She had an accent much like Irina's.

"Are you from the Ukraine?" I asked impulsively.

She jerked, like I had slapped her. Her cheeks flushed and her eyes widened, and I don't think I imagined the panic with which she looked up—way up—at her husband.

"Why do you ask?" Ian said.

I looked from one to the other of them. Huh. "No reason. We have a friend in Waterfield who's Ukrainian. You sound like her."

Angie bit her lip. At this rate, she'd gnaw a hole in herself.

"Her name is Irina Rozhdestvensky," Derek added, doing a credible job with the sneezy syllables that made up Irina's surname. "Maybe you know her?"

Angie shook her head.

"Angie doesn't get out much," Ian said. "Difficult pregnancy."

Right. That's why she was bouncing around here, her cheeks rosy, the very picture of health.

We stood in awkward silence for another few seconds, and then Derek broke it. "Have you had a chance to look for anything Colonial for me? Doorknobs? Latches?"

"Sure." Ian dropped his arm from around his wife's shoulders with a murmured assurance. "Through here." He disappeared into the back of the building, where Angie had come from, waving Derek to follow.

"Be right back," Derek said, letting me go.

I nodded. "I'll be right here."

The two of them disappeared. Angie and I were left

alone. She looked uncomfortable and seemed to wish she were somewhere else. Anywhere else. I smiled. "When are you due?"

"Pardon?"

"The baby? When is the baby coming?"

"Oh." She put a hand on her stomach. "End of May."

"Congratulations. Do you know if it's a boy or a girl?"

Usually women who are expecting are happy and excited to talk about their pregnancies and soon-to-be offspring and their delivery dates and all the rest of it. Not Angie. She shook her head without a word.

"Want to be surprised?" I offered. That's the usual reason why people don't find out the sex of the baby ahead of time, isn't it? Personally, I've always thought it would be useful to know—for decorating purposes, you know—but then I've never been pregnant, so maybe I just don't understand the whole suspense thing.

Something about the question must have bothered Angie, anyway, because she turned a shade paler before she nodded.

It was obvious that talking about the baby wasn't the way to her heart. "So how long have you lived in Maine?" I tried instead.

Angie had been in Maine just over a year.

"Why did you decide to come to Boothbay Harbor? Are there a lot of Ukrainians around here?"

Angie shook her head, her enormous eyes darting from side to side.

"Where did you and Ian meet?" Of course, I was jumping to the immediate conclusion that perhaps it was through one of the Russian-bride websites.

At this question, Angie turned pale all the way to the tips of her lips and put a hand on her belly. I watched, worried, as she sank down on the chair behind the counter that Ian had vacated earlier.

Of course, he chose this exact moment to come back into the office, and when he saw his wife's expression, he fell to his knees next to her chair with a worried bellow. She smiled shakily and patted his shoulder.

"What happened?" He turned to me, scowling. If he'd been intimidating when he was happy to see us, he was doubly intimidating now, even kneeling. I took a step back, straight into Derek, who had swung around the counter to come up behind me. He tucked his arm around my waist.

"Nothing happened," I said. "We were just talking. About the baby and how long Angie has been in Boothbay Harbor and where the two of you met."

Ian didn't answer. "I think Angie needs to lie down," he said, gently helping her up from the chair. "I'll be right back to ring up the doorknobs."

Derek nodded. We watched Ian half support, half carry his tiny wife out the door in the back wall.

"Is it me," I said softly, tilting my head back to look up into Derek's face, "or is something weird going on?"

"No idea. Look at this, though." He grabbed my arm and pulled me after him, toward the door he'd passed through earlier. Just before he got there, he stopped in front of a bulletin board hanging on the wall. "Look at that."

I looked at where his finger had landed. "That" was a business card, identical to the one I'd seen three hours earlier in Arthur Mattson's hand.

"That's interesting."

Derek nodded. "Wonder when Agent Trent was here?"

I wondered, too. And not only about that. If Ian and Angie hadn't met until this winter, who was the father of her baby?

—13—

"It was last month sometime," Ian said when he came back into the office and Derek asked him about the business card. "March. Just after Angie and I tied the knot."

"Did she come to talk to Angie?"

He shot me a look. "Yeah. Why?"

I shrugged. "No reason. Just curious. Have you seen her since? Lori Trent?"

"No," Ian said. "That'll be two hundred and three dollars." He held out an oversized paw. Derek put his credit card in it.

"Spoken to her?" I suggested.

Ian shook his head, eyes on the credit card and on the old-fashioned machine he used to take an imprint of it.

"You sure?" Derek pushed.

Ian tossed the too-long hair out of his face. "Sure I'm sure. What's with the third degree?"

"Agent Trent is dead," Derek said.

For a second, Ian looked like he was reeling; a mighty

redwood in a storm. I inched back, just in case he fell. Then he bit down on the shock. "That's too bad."

"It happened last night. We found her in Waterfield harbor this morning."

"Drowned?" Ian handed the credit card and sales slip back to Derek.

Derek shook his head. "Bashed over the head with something."

"What?" It wasn't an exclamation, but a question.

"Could have been anything. A boom. A baseball bat." One was leaned up against the wall in the corner behind the counter. Ian didn't glance toward it, but I did. "A Ukrainian Easter egg paperweight."

Derek finished signing the credit card slip and pushed it back across the counter at Ian. The latter picked it up and shoved it in the cash drawer.

"What?" he said, bushy brows wrinkling.

"I saw one yesterday," I explained. "Polished stone, painted to look like a Ukrainian Easter egg. A *pysanka*. It had ears of corn and deer and birds on it, and it weighed a ton."

Ian looked blank. Maybe Angie hadn't told him about that particular Ukrainian custom.

"I guess you guys don't have any," I added. "*Pysanky*, I mean."

He shook his head. "Never heard of them."

"What did Lori Trent want? Back in March, when she was here?"

"It was just after we got married," Ian said. "She was doing an at-home visit. They do that when Americans marry foreign nationals. Especially when one of 'em looks like Angie and the other one looks like me."

"Agent Trent thought yours was a marriage of convenience? Pro forma?"

This was something else I'd read up on the other night, the sometimes horrendously difficult process a foreign spouse has to go through to get legal residency in the United States. Not that I'm saying it should be easy, just that I'd come across some real horror stories about wives and husbands being torn out of their spouses' arms and sent back to their native countries because they couldn't prove that they'd married for the right reasons. On the other hand, it's no good when bad people get onto American soil and do bad things. Although if Angie Burns was a spy, I'd eat that fricking paperweight.

Ian nodded. He looked from me to Derek and back. "If you'll excuse me, I should go check on my wife. Make sure she's feeling all right."

Derek nodded. "I'll give you a call next time I need something."

He bent and hoisted the cardboard box. It contained a jumble of old doorknobs, plates, latches, and the like, in black, hammered iron.

"And let us know when the baby comes," I added.

Ian said he would, and we walked out of there. Derek put the box into the back of the truck and me into the front seat before he loped around the hood and opened the driver's side door. I waited until he was inside with the door closed and the engine running before I opened my mouth.

"Did that sound a little cagey to you?"

"About Lori Trent?" He put the car into gear and backed out of the parking space and onto the road. "Maybe a little."

I glanced back at the office, just in time to see Ian turn the sign in the window from Open to Closed.

"He just closed up shop."

"It *is* Saturday," Derek said.

"I know, but it's also only twenty minutes after two in the afternoon."

"So maybe he's worried about his wife."

We rolled down the road, picking up speed, leaving the salvage yard behind. I gnawed on my lower lip, pensively.

"She did look like she was about to faint, didn't she? And all I did was ask her where they'd met."

Derek glanced at me. "Where did they?"

"No idea. She just looked like she was about to pass out. I was wondering if maybe it was one of those Russian-bride websites."

Derek nodded. "Would have explained a lot if so. It's just the sort of thing Ian would do. Try to find a wife online. He's not good with people."

He'd seemed to deal with Angie just fine. If Agent Trent really had stopped by for an impromptu at-home visit, surely five minutes with the two of them would have convinced her that their marriage was legit. The girl was practically bursting at the seams with fertility, while Ian was hovering just as anxiously as any dad-to-be.

Unless Agent Trent had also figured out the time issue inherent in the pregnancy, of course, and then she might have had questions.

"How long have you known him?" I wanted to know.

Derek shrugged. "Five or six years now. Since just after I started doing renovations. I was looking for something—some prisms to complete a crystal chandelier, I think it was—and he had 'em. We've never been close friends, though. Never hung out or anything. Ian's a bit of a loner."

I nodded. "Makes you wonder how he managed to snag a girl like Angie, doesn't it? I mean, I'm sure he's a nice guy and all, but she's gorgeous. And much younger than him."

"He *is* a nice guy," Derek said, "and maybe that's what she was looking for."

"Maybe."

We drove in silence for a few minutes as the outskirts of Boothbay Harbor flashed by outside the window.

"Do you think he told the truth?" I ventured. "About Agent Trent? That they hadn't spoken to her since March?"

"No idea. Why would he lie?"

"Because he killed her? You did see the baseball bat, didn't you?"

"A lot of shop owners keep weapons behind the counter, Avery," Derek said.

"Yeah, but . . . Ian looks like he could take a robber apart with his bare hands. I mean, who would be stupid enough to try to rob *him*?"

And why would anyone bother? It wasn't like a salvage store on the outer edge of the back-beyond would be taking in a ton of money. There were easier targets elsewhere, for someone who wanted a quick buck. A liquor store, a video game store, a convenience market with a teenage girl behind the counter . . . No one in their right minds would take on Ian Burns if they didn't have to.

Derek shrugged, conceding the point. "He's not stupid, though, Tink. If he'd used that baseball bat to kill someone, he wouldn't put it back behind the counter. He'd get rid of it."

"Where?"

"In the water, when he got rid of Agent Trent's body? Or in a Dumpster somewhere in Boothbay Harbor? It's not like anyone would be looking for it there."

He was probably right about that, since no one would have realized that there was a connection between ICE agent Lori Trent and Ian and Angela Burns. Until now, that is.

"We're gonna have to sic Wayne on him, aren't we?"

Derek's face was reluctant. "I guess we'll have to. Mention the business card, at least." He grimaced. "Man, I hate to tattle on people."

"If he didn't do anything wrong, he shouldn't have anything to worry about."

"I know." But he didn't look happy. He hesitated for a moment before he added, reluctantly, "Maybe she came here yesterday to talk to Angie. After Arthur Mattson saw her in the afternoon. She knew Angie from when she was here in March. Maybe she thought Angie might know who the dead girl was."

"Huh." That was a scenario I hadn't thought of. "Why would Ian kill her, though?"

"Maybe Agent Trent wanted to take her in for questioning."

"Maybe." That seemed far-fetched, though. I know people kill for a variety of stupid reasons, from pairs of sneakers to imaginary insults, but would Ian really resort to murder just because an ICE agent wanted to interview his wife?

"Do you have a better idea?" Derek inquired.

"I don't know about better. But what if Agent Trent didn't believe Ian and Angie when they said that Ian's the father of the baby—I mean, how could he be, if they only met this winter?—and she was trying to deport Angie? Any idiot can see that Ian's crazy about her. If Agent Trent threatened to send her back to the Ukraine, he might have snapped. And if the baseball bat was right there . . ."

Derek nodded. "That's a possibility. It seems like quite the coincidence, though, Avery. That Agent Trent is killed on the same day that Wayne calls her to look into the body in the water, but she's killed for a different reason."

True.

"So maybe it's all related. Agent Trent came up here to talk to Angie about the body, and she discovered that there was a connection between them. Maybe Angie wrote Irina's name and address on that piece of paper, or maybe they were together the other day, when the girl fell in the water, and Angie didn't report it. Maybe Agent Trent tried to arrest Angie, and then Ian snapped and whacked her with the baseball bat."

"That would do it."

We drove in silence for a minute before I told Derek to change direction.

"Why?" He did it, though, without waiting for me to explain.

"That kid from Barnham, the one who overheard someone talking about Russian women? He said it was on the ferry dock in Boothbay Harbor. We're here, so why don't we stop and see if there's anyone there who remembers?"

Derek headed for the ferry dock, although he still felt he had to issue a warning. "You probably won't find anyone, Avery. It's a long time ago, and there are no guarantees that anyone who's there now was there then. Or that they'll remember."

I realized that. "I'm hoping that there's a ticket taker or something, someone who works there, who might be able to give us a description of the two men."

"Maybe one of them was Ian," Derek suggested, "and he was telling a friend about Angie."

"That's possible. You'd think Calvin would have been able to describe Ian, though. He's almost seven feet tall."

Derek nodded and cut the engine.

Down at the end of the dock, the ferry was waiting for passengers. The young blond conductor I'd met before was hanging out on the dock, manipulating the buttons on an iPhone. He squinted at me as I came closer, sort of like he thought he ought to know who I was, but he couldn't quite place me. I smiled.

"Hi. We met earlier this week. On the ferry. I was going to Rowanberry Island."

Those bright blue eyes cleared. "Yeah. Sure. I remember you. The van Duren house, right?"

I nodded. "This is my boyfriend, Derek."

Derek and the young man shook hands. His name turned out to be Ned Schachenger. "You riding?" He nodded toward the ferry. "Going back to the island?"

I glanced at Derek. "We weren't planning to."

"What are you doing here, then?"

"I just had a question. Another question."

"About that dead girl?" Ned said.

I hesitated. "Yes and no. I wondered if you'd ever heard anyone talking about Russian women on the ferry or on the ferry dock?"

"People talk about lots of stuff," Ned said.

"This would have been sometime this winter. January, maybe. Two men."

"How do you know that they were here? And talked about Russian women?"

"A guy named Calvin told me," I said. "He's a student at Barnham College. He said he'd overheard them."

"Calvin Harris? Guy with big ears, big nose, big feet, who looks like some kind of bird?"

"That's him."

"I know Calvin. We went to high school together."

"Here?" I looked around Boothbay Harbor, at the quaint houses, the narrow streets, the little marina with the boats.

Ned nodded. "Boothbay Harbor High School has kids from some of the islands, too. Calvin came in on the ferry every morning."

I nodded. "Which island is Calvin from?"

"Rowanberry," Ned said.

"That's quite a coincidence." Although it did explain what he was doing on the ferry dock. "Does he live in the village?"

"I imagine he does. I've never been to his house, though. We're not tight. But most of the other houses are for the summer people. Closed off in the winter."

I nodded.

"I never heard anyone talk about Russian women," Ned added, "but I remember Calvin asking me about a couple of people once. It could have been January, but I think it was more recent. Everyone was wearing rain gear. It's usually too cold for rain in January."

No kidding. January had been bitterly cold. Calvin probably just had a bad memory; instead of not being able to describe the people because of winter parkas and scarves, it was because of raincoats and umbrellas. "Which two people?"

"One of 'em was Ian Burns. He owns a salvage business on the north side of town. You can't mistake Mr. Burns; ain't nobody else as tall."

"We just came from Burns Salvage," Derek said. "Looking for doorknobs for the house."

"What about the other person?" I asked. "Was it someone Ian was talking to?"

Ned nodded. "Woman," he said. "Hard to tell under the umbrella, but I think she had short, dark hair. Curly. She was pretty. And preggo."

Definitely Angie. "What did Calvin want to know?"

Ned shrugged. "Just who they were." The ferry tooted, and he had to raise his voice to continue. "I told him that the guy was Ian Burns, but that I'd never seen the woman before. He said thanks and got on the ferry. Just like I have to do."

He turned away.

"Thanks for the help," I called after him. He waved a hand in acknowledgment.

I turned to Derek. "What about you? Want to take a pleasure trip in the nice weather?"

"I think I'll pass. Don't want to get stuck on Rowanberry Island for the night."

"The ferry runs a couple more times today, doesn't it?"

Derek admitted that it did. "But not for hours."

"I'm a little concerned about my kitten," I said.

Derek's eyebrows arched. "Your kitten?"

"You know, the little blue one that lives under the porch."

"When did it become yours?"

Oh. Um . . . "I guess when I brought some of Jemmy and Inky's food out for it."

"Uh-huh," Derek said, unimpressed. "Are you planning to take it back to Waterfield with you?"

"I don't know about that. I can't imagine Jemmy and Inky taking kindly to an interloper, can you?"

The idea had a certain appeal, though. It'd be nice to have a soft, purring kitten around the house. One that actually liked me and that would curl up in my lap and allow itself to be petted; not a full-grown cat set in its ways which couldn't care less whether I was there or not. Not that this particular kitten seemed inclined to be friendly and let itself be petted, although that might change, given time.

"No," Derek said, "I can't. And if you're not adopting it, you're better off leaving it alone. If it gets dependent on handouts from you, it won't be able to take care of itself when you leave."

"But I can't leave it there. That would be cruel. Maybe I can give it to someone else. *You* don't have a cat."

"I don't want a cat," Derek said. "I see enough of yours."

"Maybe Kate would like a cat. Or maybe not. She cat-sat Jemmy and Inky just after Aunt Inga died and I was in New York getting things organized, and she said that people were canceling their reservations because of allergies. I guess a cat probably wouldn't be a good thing in a bed-and-breakfast."

Derek shook his head. “C’mon,” he said, resigned, “let’s just go. There’s probably somewhere on the island we can buy a can of cat food, don’t you think? Or at least a can of tuna?”

“There’s a little grocery store. I’m sure they’ll have something.” I skipped toward the ferry. Derek turned around to point his car keys at the truck and set the alarm, before he followed.

—14—

The little village on Rowanberry Island looked just like it had last time I was there. Deserted and desolate, like an outpost on the edge of nowhere. As the ferry chugged away, a sleek blue gray adult cat disappeared around the corner of the general store.

"Look," I said to Derek, pointing, "it looks like my kitten."

The only other person to disembark on Rowanberry Island was a middle-aged woman in a worn coat, with a scarf over her head—to protect her permed hair from the ocean breeze, I assumed—and half a dozen shopping bags clutched in her hands. "That's Pepper," she said, her voice hoarse. "She's a Russian blue."

"Is that a breed?"

The woman nodded. "She belongs to Gert Heyerdahl. You know, the writer. Usually he takes her south for the winter, but maybe she tucked herself away somewhere and he couldn't find her when it was time to leave last fall."

"I think she must have had kittens recently," I volunteered. "At least there's a kitten living under our porch that looks a lot like that. Maybe Mr. Heyerdahl left her with the caretaker for the winter."

The man I'd met probably lived in the village. Maybe he had taken Pepper back to his house with him instead of leaving her at Mr. Heyerdahl's house. If not, she was a long way from home.

"Where is your house?" The woman fastened hazel eyes on me.

"I'm sorry." I introduced myself and Derek. "We live in Waterfield. But we're renovating the old van Duren place on the other side of the island. You know, the twin to Gert Heyerdahl's house."

The woman nodded. "I'm Glenda Harris. I live there." She indicated the house that had had the Rooms for Rent sign in the window. It was gone now.

"Nice to meet you," I said politely, shaking her hand. A stray thought scurried through my brain, but I wasn't able to hold on to it. "Have you always lived on Rowanberry Island?"

Glenda nodded. "I was born here. I'll probably die here." She said it calmly, looking around at the peeling paint and the general desolation of the small village. "Every year, people leave, move to the mainland, where things are easier and more convenient. But this is my place. Where would I go?"

"How long has your family lived here?" Derek wanted to know.

Glenda turned to him. "I'm descended from one of the van Duren girls. Daisy. She lived in Sunrise two hundred and twenty years ago."

"Sunrise?"

"That's the name of your house. The houses were named Sunrise and Sunset."

"Because they're on opposite sides of the island?" Our house was facing east, toward the ocean and the sunrise, while Gert Heyerdahl's was facing west.

"That, plus Daisy's husband was a patriot. Clara's husband—the two of them lived in Sunset, Mr. Heyerdahl's house—was a loyalist."

"Really?" I spared a thought for the folder from the Waterfield Historic Society we had left inside the truck in the parking lot in Boothbay Harbor. I had looked it over at lunch while waiting for the food we had ordered to arrive, but I hadn't had time for any in-depth examination. And while Irina had told me that the two van Duren girls hadn't gotten along, and that was why their father had built them houses on opposite sides of the island, I hadn't known about the patriot versus loyalist angle. In 1783, just after the Revolution ended, that must have been a pretty big deal. No wonder they didn't get along.

Glenda nodded when I said as much.

"What about Mr. van Duren?" Derek wanted to know. "Which side was he on? Didn't he have a problem with one of his daughters marrying someone from the other side?"

Glenda grinned. "John van Duren didn't care. He was playing both sides against the middle."

"Meaning?"

"He was an opportunist. A smuggler. Before the Revolution, he imported tea and sugar and molasses and all the other things the British government had levied a tax on. During the war, he smuggled goods to the army at Long Island, and after the Revolution, he brought British goods into the new United States under the nose of the new government."

"Equal opportunity," Derek said with a grin. "Although if he intended Sunrise to be a reflection on the new day, and a new beginning for a new country, that says a little about his sympathies right there. Maybe?"

"Maybe so," Glenda admitted.

"Where did Mr. van Duren live?" I asked. "Somewhere in the village?"

Glenda shook her head. "He owned the southern part of the island, where Sunrise and Sunset are. His house was down there, as well. The village wasn't built until much later."

"I guess it isn't there anymore, is it? Mr. van Duren's house?" More than two hundred and thirty years old and exposed to the elements . . . it wasn't likely.

"Actually, the last I heard, it still was. It's rather primitive and rough, as I recall, but Lonnie doesn't seem to mind for the couple weeks a year that he's here. My second cousin a few times removed. We're all related in one way or another." She thought for a second and then added, judiciously, "Or maybe he does mind; I don't think he was here last summer."

"I think I may have seen it," I said. "I took a wrong turn on my way back from Gert Heyerdahl's house a week ago and ended up at the end of this little path where there was a very small saltbox. It looked quite old."

"That sounds like old John's house," Glenda nodded.

"All the windows were shuttered. Gert Heyerdahl's windows were shuttered, too, when I tried to stop by his house."

Glenda gestured with a package-laden arm. "There are shutters on every house in the village. We need them during the winter. We don't keep them closed all the time, since we have to live inside, but the snowbirds close their shutters when they leave in the autumn and open them when they come back in the spring. It cuts down on broken windows."

"I can imagine." If someone would have just made sure to shutter our windows, maybe we wouldn't have had to replace fifty-six window panes.

Derek was shifting impatiently beside me—I guess he

was worried that I'd talk so long that we wouldn't have time to walk to the house, feed the kitten, walk back, and still catch the next ferry—so I added, "We should probably go. It was nice to meet you, Mrs. Harris."

Mrs. Harris reciprocated before she trudged up the cobblestoned street and into her peeling little house. Derek and I ducked into the small grocery store cum post office to look for cat food.

The interior of the store looked like something out of a 1930s movie: dingy and dark, low-ceilinged, and overflowing with weird and wonderful things I never would have expected to see in a place that sold food. Snow shoes were rubbing elbows with fishing lures and bird shot, while old-fashioned galoshes sat next to bags of chicken feed and souvenir snow globes. A thin layer of dust covered everything, with circles here and there where something had been removed since the last time the place was dusted. A snow globe must have been sold recently, sometime in the past week or so, and someone obviously had a fondness for canned vegetables, since there were circles all over the shelf with the green peas and corn. In comparison, the floor was sparkling clean, so clean it glimmered where the light hit it.

A man about Glenda Harris's age was perched on a stool behind the counter, an unlit cigarette hanging from the corner of his mouth. He looked up when the bell above the door clanged, deep-set eyes tracking us as we piled inside and spread out to look around.

"Afternoon," I said perkily as I headed for the snow globes.

The man grunted. He didn't take the cigarette from his mouth. "Do for you?"

"Oh. Um . . ." I aligned the snow globe I'd picked up with the circle I'd plucked it from and watched as the sparkling snow settled on the ground around the little scene inside. "Greetings from Rowanberry Island," it said in curly script on the base, and I guess the green blob inside was supposed to be the island. There wasn't much resemblance that I could see, but the trinket was well made and surprisingly heavy. "We're looking for cat food. Or if you don't have cat food, a can of tuna fish."

He pointed. "Shelf." He was jowly and unshaven, with pouches under his eyes and unhealthy skin color. Probably from the smoking. Or maybe he'd quit, or was trying to quit, and all he was allowed to do was chew on the filters.

I looked around. "Where . . . ? Oh, I see it. Thank you."

Derek had already reached the shelf, only a few feet away, and was plucking down a couple of cans of cat food in different flavors. The tops of the cans were dusty.

"Check the expiration dates," I said under my breath. "Some of this stuff looks like it's been sitting here for years."

He nodded. "It's still good." He raised his voice. "So how's business?"

"Slow," the shop owner grunted. He rang up the three cans of cat food and bag of crunchy bits and told me what I owed him. I went to look in my purse for my wallet and money and realized it wasn't there. The purse, I mean. For a panicked second I thought I must have left it on the ferry, by now halfway to Big and Little Rock Island, and then I realized I'd left it sitting on the seat of the truck in the parking lot in Boothbay Harbor. I'd been telling myself that we'd only spend a minute or two talking to Ned before getting back in the truck and going home, and the bag would be OK. And then I'd forgotten to go get it in my hurry to get on the boat. But at least Derek had set the alarm before we boarded the ferry; I distinctly remembered him turning toward the car and pushing the button.

I turned to him. "I left my purse and my wallet in the car in Boothbay Harbor. Can you pay for the cat food?"

He pulled out his wallet. Men have it so easy.

"I'll pay you back," I added.

He rolled his eyes. "It's cat food, Avery. I think I can support the expense."

"I'm sure you can, but . . . it's *my* cat food."

"And your kitten. I know." He tucked the five-pound bag of cat food under his arm and left me to grab the brown paper bag with the three cans. "Thank you, sir."

The man behind the counter nodded. He had already looked down at the newspaper he kept folded behind the counter when Derek added, "I guess there aren't many visitors this time of year."

"Ain't seen a stranger in here since August." The unlit cigarette bopped up and down when he spoke.

"The police have probably asked you about the three missing women, right?"

The cigarette stopped moving. After a moment, he took it out of his mouth and put it in an ashtray behind the counter. "Missing women? Three of 'em?"

"I guess I shouldn't say missing," Derek admitted. "Only one of them is missing. The other two are dead."

The man blinked. "Dead?" he said cautiously. "I heard about that young lady last week that they found in the ocean. Is someone else dead now, too?"

"The police found another body this morning." Derek skipped lightly over the fact that we, not the police, had found her first. "In the water in the harbor. And a third woman might be missing. Another Russian. Irina Rozhdestvensky."

The shopkeeper didn't answer. His face was a careful blank. "What's she look like?" he asked after a moment.

"Irina? She's tall and dark haired, in her late thirties."

The shopkeeper nodded.

"Have you seen her?"

"Should I have?"

"Not that I know of." If I'd had any sense, I would have questioned Ned while we were on the boat. Not that I had any reason to think Irina had taken the ferry to one of the islands. If for some reason she was trying to get away from the police, she'd be better off going the other way, into the interior of the state, away from the ocean. Easier to get lost there. On an island, she'd be stuck until the next ferry came, and there was no way on or off the island without someone seeing her.

"Must be hard to get by out here during the winter," Derek remarked. "With fewer and fewer people living on the island full time, and no tourists."

"We're making do," the man said.

"Glad to hear it." Derek turned to me. "C'mon, Avery. The sooner we get there and can feed your kitten, the sooner we can go back home."

I nodded. "Thanks for your help."

The shopkeeper grunted a good-bye. Derek held the door for me and we passed out into the afternoon sun again. Down the street, Pepper the kitty slunk around another corner. Whatever arrangements Gert Heyerdahl had made for her while he was in Florida—whether she'd gotten away from him or he'd left her in someone else's care—she didn't seem to be suffering. Her fur was sleek and shiny, and she looked neither too thin nor like her belly was bloated from eating out of garbage cans. Someone was taking care of Pepper the Russian blue.

"Do you think that's a coincidence?" I said.

Derek glanced down at me. "What?"

"That there are Russian women dead and missing and that Gert Heyerdahl owns a Russian blue cat."

Derek blinked. "I don't see how it can be anything but a coincidence," he said after a second. "I mean, they're women and that's a cat. Or are you suggesting that Mr. Heyerdahl has some kind of obsession with anything Russian? Not that the women are even Russian, really. Ukraine isn't Russia."

"That's true, I guess. It just seems like it ought to mean something. I mean, he writes about a Russian, doesn't he? Some kind of KGB agent or spy?"

"He does," Derek said. "And you have a great imagination, Avery. But I really don't see how a Russian blue cat, two Ukrainian women, and a reclusive American writer who spends the winter in Florida fit together."

"I don't, either," I admitted. "Not when you put it like that. Unless . . . Gert Heyerdahl isn't married, is he? Maybe he really does have an obsession with all things Russian. Or Slavic. Maybe he went looking for a Russian girlfriend. Maybe he found that cute little Angie on one of the Russian-bride websites and talked her into coming to Maine, and then he kept her locked up in his house all summer long. As his sex slave, or something. Then, when he left for Florida in the fall, she got away from him and hooked up with Ian. Maybe that's why she's so skittish. Maybe she's having Gert Heyerdahl's baby!"

"Interesting theory," Derek said, his lips twitching. "What about the second Russian girl? The dead one? How do you account for her? Another of Gert's sex slaves? And what about Agent Trent? And Irina? If Gert has been in Florida since the fall, he can't have had anything to do with any of what's been going on here this week."

"Maybe he's paying someone to take care of things for him. Like that guy I met. And not just around the house, you know? He's a writer; he must be loaded. And his cat is here. Someone is feeding her. Maybe that same person is going around killing people at Gert's command."

"That's true," Derek admitted. "About the cat, I mean. I think you're jumping to conclusions about the rest of it, though, Avery. You've found him guilty based on nothing but the fact that he owns a cat called a Russian blue. I'm sure a lot of people own Russian blues. You're about to acquire one yourself, from what I understand."

I made a face. "OK, so maybe I'm way off base. I probably am. It just seems very coincidental. Russian cats and Russian women. And a guy who writes about a Russian spy."

We had left the village behind and were walking through last year's dry grass now, on our way to the woods that covered much of the southern tip of the island.

"Can we at least mention it to Wayne?" I continued. "Just in case?"

Derek shifted the bag of cat food from one arm to the other. "I guess it can't hurt."

"And can we maybe go over to Gert's house again—together—and you can see if the caretaker will let *you* in?"

"Not a chance," Derek answered, ignoring my disappointed pout. "First, we don't have time today. Not if we want to catch the next ferry back to Boothbay Harbor. And second, if you're right and I'm crazy, instead of *me* being right and *you* being crazy, I don't want you anywhere near that guy. When we get back to Waterfield, we'll tell Wayne about the cat and let him deal with it."

"Fine." I stuck my bottom lip out. Derek grinned but declined to take the bait.

"Interesting story about Daisy and Clara," he said instead.

I rolled my bottom lip back in. "How they married men who fought on opposite sides in the Revolution? Very interesting. Wonder how that came to be."

In thinking about it, I realized I didn't know much about what had been going on in Maine during the American

Revolution. Everyone knows about the events in Massachusetts and Philadelphia—the Boston Tea Party and the battle of Concord; Benjamin Franklin and the Liberty Bell—but had anything been happening in Maine?

"Oh, sure," Derek said. "Lots of stuff happened in Maine. The various acts—the Sugar Act, the Molasses Act, the Stamp Act; you know, taxing imports and exports and everything else—affected Maine every bit as much as they affected Massachusetts and New York. The residents of Falmouth rioted, too."

"Where's Falmouth?"

He grinned. "These days we call it Portland."

"Oh." Silly me.

"York harbor had its own Tea Party in 1774. In 1775, British ships shelled Falmouth and caused a lot of damage. A lot of Mainers went north on the Canadian campaign."

"What's that?" I shifted the canned cat food to my other hand.

"The British were assembling an army at Quebec, and Benedict Arnold took a bunch of men up the Kennebec River in the fall of 1775 to stop them."

"*The* Benedict Arnold?"

Derek nodded. "In the early days of the war, he was a patriot. It wasn't until he was passed over for several promotions while other people took credit for his accomplishments that he became bitter and defected. That wasn't until 1780. In 1775, he hoped that the Canadians would join the Americans and kick British butt. Unfortunately, winter came early, and they had to eat their dogs to survive. Some stories say they ate their moccasins, as well."

"Yikes."

He nodded. "One division returned home in October. Benedict Arnold and the rest made it to Quebec and hooked up with Generals Montgomery and Schuyler, who had led their armies north from Montreal. They attacked the British in the middle of the night on December thirty-first—because the enlistment term for many of the American soldiers ended on January first—and failed miserably. About a hundred men died and at least three hundred were captured. General Montgomery died. Benedict Arnold got shot. And because it was the middle of winter, and winter is cold up here—"

I nodded. Having just lived through my first Maine winter, I could attest to that.

"—what was left of the American army decided to wait it out instead of trying to get back home. So they camped near Quebec and probably ate the rest of their shoes to survive. In the spring, they marched south to Montreal and from there to Crown Point, with the British army on their heels. Barefoot, probably. Turns out the American leadership had totally misjudged anti-British sentiment in Canada. Instead of rising up against the British and kicking them out, Canada remained loyal to George. And that's the story of the Canadian campaign."

"Interesting."

"Only if you like history," Derek said with a grin.

"I like history." Sort of. When it's got something to do with fabrics. Or when it's personal. Like when it applies to one of the houses we're renovating. Or when my boyfriend is holding forth and I get lost in listening. While he'd been talking, we'd passed from sunshine and the meadow into the shade of the trees. In just the few days since I'd walked through these woods on my way from our house to Gert Heyerdahl's—from Sunrise to Sunset and back—more patches of snow had melted, and here and there, small, sturdy flowers with bright yellow heads had pushed their way out of the ground and into the sun.

"Coltsfoot," Derek said. "*Tussilago farfara.*"

"I've never seen them before." I bent to pick one and hold it to my nose. It had a very distinctive smell. Strong. Spicy. Almost medical.

"They're native to Europe. Probably brought here at some point by settlers as a medicinal item. They were used to treat coughs and lung ailments until someone discovered there are pyrrolizidine alkaloids in the plants, that cause liver failure."

"Oops." I let the flower drop from my hand down on the forest floor.

"Picking and sniffing it isn't dangerous. Just don't eat it."

I promised I wouldn't. Derek looked around.

"Do you think you could find your way back to that little saltbox you told me about last week? The one you found on your way back from Gert Heyerdahl's house?"

"The one Mrs. Harris said used to belong to Mr. van Duren? I can try. It's right around here somewhere. It's locked up tight, though."

"I just want to take a look at it," Derek said easily. "But it's no big deal. If we miss the path, I'll just find it another time."

Because we were looking for it, the path wasn't hard to find, though, and about ten minutes later, we found ourselves standing outside the little saltbox again.

It looked exactly like it had last week: shuttered and still, like it was asleep. And between you and me, I didn't find it to be all that impressive. It was small and unkempt, with peeling paint, and it seemed to tilt forward, like it was bracing itself against the stiff wind coming off the ocean. Derek, of course, was mesmerized. His eyes as dreamy blue as the sky overhead, he walked around the house, touching the wood, cooing about the craftsmanship and age.

"Nice location, too," he said eventually, shading his eyes to look out to sea. "Just at the end of a quiet little cove with a narrow opening. None of the big ships could follow him in here. And it's an easy walk from the beach up to the house with whatever he was bringing in."

"Smuggled goods, you mean?"

He nodded. "The house is definitely old enough to be Mr. van Duren's. Mid-seventeen hundreds, I'd say. Wonder if he built it himself?"

"No idea. Mrs. Harris might know." I shifted from foot to foot. It was my turn to feel impatient. I'm as excited as the next girl about a decrepit house with potential, but it wasn't like we could buy this one. We already had a project, and this house wasn't even for sale. And after renovating Sunrise, I didn't think I'd want to tackle another house on Rowanberry Island anytime soon. Next time, I wanted to find a nice, easy flip right in Waterfield. One that we could walk to, where I didn't have to brave the cold and the ocean every morning, and one it wouldn't take the best part of six months to finish renovating. Plus, I was concerned about my kitten. What if it was hungry? What if it missed me? What if something had happened to it in the time that we'd been gone?

"Don't worry, Avery," Derek said when I expressed this. "Cats always land on their feet. He took care of himself before you started feeding him."

He started walking away from the saltbox, though. We hadn't taken more than a couple of steps before we heard a loud bang behind us. I jumped. Derek turned around, scanning our surroundings.

"Must be a loose shutter on the back of the house," he said eventually, moving off.

"If you say so." I hurried to catch up. "Why did you call my kitten a he? Have you looked at him?"

"When would I have gotten a chance to look at him? He runs every time one of us steps on the porch. I have no idea whether it's a he or not. We can try to catch him and take a look when we get there."

"OK," I said happily. "You know, Gert Heyerdahl's house has a very nice little stoop made from big slabs of stone. Do you suppose there's a stoop like that under our front porch, too? If the houses were identical . . ."

"Could be," Derek said. "They may not be identical to quite that degree, though. I've never had a good look at Gert's house, but I think it sits lower than ours. It's probably built on rock. The west side of the island is a little higher than the east."

"Can we look?"

"Sure," Derek said. "The porch does look like it was added after the house was built, so maybe there is something different underneath. I'll tear up a couple of planks. Once we get the cat out."

"Or you can tear up a couple of planks while I stand ready to catch the cat." Once Derek started ripping up the porch floor, the cat would run for sure.

He glanced at me. "Just make sure you wear gloves, OK? I doubt the little guy's been declawed."

I nodded. "Maybe I'll just put some food in a bowl and try to lure it out. Then one of us can crawl under the porch and see what's there. That way we won't have to worry about ripping anything out. Just in case there is no stone stoop underneath."

"It's gonna need repair anyway," Derek said with a shrug.

—15—

Fifteen minutes later, we were ready to put the plan into action. We were at our own house and had made it across the porch without rousing the cat. I had opened a can of salmon cat food and mixed it with some crunchy bits in a bowl, and I was ready to try to lure the cat out from under the porch. I was wearing gloves, and I had a cardboard box lined with an old curtain that I planned to put the kitten into once I caught it.

"What about bathroom breaks?" Derek had asked, watching me make my preparations.

"For the cat, you mean? I didn't think about that." Jemmy and Inky do their business out of doors, so there's no litter box at Aunt Inga's house; the idea of kitty litter just hadn't crossed my mind. This kitten must be used to doing its business in nature, as well, since nature was where it had lived so far. But it would need a way to get in and out of the box in order to do it. "Can you cut a door in the box?"

"Big enough for a cat?" He reached for an X-Acto knife. "Give it here."

I did and watched him carve out a rectangle, exactly big enough for a young kitten to make its way through.

"Once we close the flaps on top," Derek said, tucking the knife away, "it'll be nice and warm in there. He's been all right under the porch all this time; he'll be fine inside the box with the curtains to sleep on. And when he needs to go, he can go. Ready?"

"Ready. Let's do it." I hoisted the box and followed him outside to put Operation Cat into motion.

Once again, we managed to make it across the porch without spooking the little creature, and Derek walked to the side of the porch, where the kitten came and went between the rotted boards. He squatted. "I'll just get rid of some of these"—he ripped off a couple of pieces of wood and tossed them to the ground—"and then we'll see what we've got. Flashlight?"

He held out a hand. I fumbled the bowl of food over into my other hand, fished the flashlight out of the box, and handed it to him. He stuck his head and shoulders under the porch floor and shone the light around. "Let's see . . ."

"Is there a stone slab under there?" I wanted to know, leaning down. I remembered Gert Heyerdahl's front steps, and our discussion about whether we had something similar hidden under our wooden porch.

"Sure is. And . . ." In the blackness deep under the porch, a pair of glowing red eyes stared back at us. "Whoa," Derek said, the flashlight beam wavering for a second. "Devil cat."

"Is it coming?"

He shook his head. "It's disappeared. Probably hiding in the corner on the theory that if we can't see it, we'll forget that it's there."

"Maybe if you go to the other side of the porch and rattle the boards?"

"I'll try," Derek said, getting up. "Are you ready to catch it when it comes?"

I nodded. "Ready."

Except I wasn't, of course. The kitten shot out between the boards and ran right into me. I squealed and sat down with a thump. The kitten changed direction. Then it saw Derek and changed direction again. And instead of heading for open ground, down the meadow toward the water, it zipped up the porch steps and through the front door, which we had left open.

Derek muttered a curse and charged after it, flashlight in hand, the beam still waving. I picked myself up, leaving both the box and the cat food where I'd dropped them—the salmon and crunchy bits were mostly in the dirt—and followed.

Derek was standing in the hallway, his back stiff and his eyes narrowed, as he scanned the entry and what he could see of the dining room and living room through the open doors to the right and left. I closed the front door behind me and joined him.

"I don't see it."

He spared me a glance before going back to hunting pose. "It's here somewhere."

Well, duh. We'd both seen it run inside, so that kind of went without saying.

"I think it must have gone that way." I pointed into the dining room. "Those are paw prints, aren't they? In the dust?"

Derek squinted. "More like skid marks. Let's go."

He stalked toward the dining room, flashlight gripped in one hand, looking like he was preparing to face down a crew of burglars instead of one rather small kitten.

There were three rooms downstairs: a formal parlor or living room to the right of the entrance hall, a dining room to the left, and a cavernous eat-in kitchen stretching the width of the back of the house. Rather an unusual setup from what I knew about Colonial houses. Usually they're very symmetrical, with matching rooms on either side of a central hallway. We did have the central hallway, but it ended in a blank wall enclosing the enormous chimney instead of going all the way through the house to the back door. I mentioned it.

"You're right," Derek said, head weaving from side to side as he scouted for the cat, "usually these places are pretty symmetrical. I'm surprised this isn't. They must have converted a couple of other rooms into a kitchen at some point. In Colonial times, the kitchen was a separate building at a distance from the house. That way, if it caught fire, the whole thing wouldn't go up in flames."

"That fireplace is original, though, isn't it?" I pointed to it.

It was massive, perfectly centered in the long room, and longer than I was tall. Longer than Derek was tall, too. A cavernous opening with a couple of smaller openings in the brick next to it. One was for baking bread, I thought—I'd seen similar holes before, with big wooden spatulas in them—while the other had a hinged iron cover. Two or three old brass and cast-iron pots hung from a rail in the main fireplace.

"The big fireplace was for heating water and soup and stew and things like that," Derek said. "The two smaller holes were for baking bread and cooking other things. This does look original. Maybe Mr. van Duren knew that Daisy really liked to cook, and so he gave her an inside kitchen."

"Or maybe the weather is so bad up here in Maine in the winter that an outdoor kitchen wouldn't work. Opening and closing the door constantly would let all the heat out of the house, and they may even get snowed in and not have a way to feed themselves if they couldn't get to the detached kitchen."

"That's a good point," Derek said, still looking around for the cat. "I didn't think of that."

"You're not a woman." I shivered at the idea of having to go across the lawn for my morning coffee every day. Of course, they'd probably had to go across the lawn to use the privy, too, since indoor plumbing was but a dream at the time when this place was built.

"Thank God," Derek said, grinning. "So much for the good old days, huh? Any sign of the cat?"

I looked around. "None I can see. I'll check the bread oven."

I bent to peer into it, but no pair of eyes looked back at me.

"Probably went in here," Derek said, walking over to the wall beside the fireplace, where a piece of paneling hung open a few inches. "Original built-in cabinets. Very well made. If the door wasn't open and you didn't know they were there, you'd miss them."

I nodded, watching as he grabbed the edge of the door and pulled. It looked just like a panel, and he was right; if it hadn't been open a crack, I wasn't sure if I would have noticed that it was a cabinet. At least not without a more thorough examination.

I expected there to be shelves inside, but there weren't. A stack of boards on the floor indicated that there may have been shelves at one point, though. Removable ones. Brows lowered, Derek hunched and stuck his head and shoulders through the opening, flashlight already moving. "That's weird," his disembodied voice said, hollowly.

"What's weird?" And where was the kitten? I would

have expected it to come shooting out the moment he started flashing the light around.

"Looks like there's another opening of some kind in there. Or maybe I'm just crazy." He backed out, his hair gray with cobwebs and dust. "Have a look."

I took a step back. "I don't think so. Where there are cobwebs, there are probably spiders."

"There are cobwebs?" Derek said, brushing at his hair. "Oh yeah. Didn't notice. But I'm a lot taller than you are, Tink. If I've already brushed all the cobwebs away with my head, there won't be any way down on your level."

This was true. Squaring my shoulders, I took a step toward the dark opening. "Go on," Derek said, a hand on my back nudging me forward. "Here. Take the flashlight. You'll need it."

I took it and—ducking my head—passed into the dark.

"Wow," I said after I had waved the flashlight around, "that *is* weird."

Derek was crowding in behind me, pushing me toward a slim opening in the far back wall of the closet, just at the edge of the fireplace. I shone the flashlight beam in that direction. "Looks like that piece of wood right there—one of the shelves, I guess—must have gotten caught and kept the panel from closing. Otherwise, we'd never have noticed that there was anything back here."

"Definitely built to stay hidden," Derek's voice said behind me. I could feel the heat off his body behind me, and his breath stirring the hair on the top of my head.

I glanced back at him. "A secret room?"

"Most likely. Mr. van Duren probably built it. Betcha he stored some of his goods here."

"Or maybe he wanted his daughter's family to have a panic room in case the British came back to fight again?"

"That's possible, too. Here—" He squeezed by me to

go and grab the edge of the panel with both hands in an attempt to open it farther. It didn't budge.

"There's probably a lever somewhere, don't you think?" I started shining the light around the closet, looking for one.

"Try that hook over there," Derek wheezed, still trying to force the panel to move. "It doesn't look like it has another function."

I reached out and jiggled it. Up, down, up again. Derek staggered when the panel moved, sliding back into the wall with the grating sound of wood on brick. I shone the light into a square room, no more than six feet by six, half of it taken up by a mattress with a couple of dingy blankets thrown across it. The kitten was blinking at me from the tangle of blankets. As soon as it saw me coming, it ran, straight past us and out. We didn't try to catch it. Too busy looking around. The walls were brick in here, the ceiling was brick, and the floor was the same wide planks as in the rest of the house.

"Mr. van Duren's storage room," Derek breathed. He was leaning over my shoulder, peering into the dark space.

I nodded, directing the flashlight. "Must be. What's with the mattress, though?" I focused the light beam on it. "That's not Colonial."

It looked old, but not that old. Faded nylon, blue with ugly kidney-colored flowers. No mattress pad or sheet. And the blankets were mass-produced in the last ten or twenty years, probably in China. They were thin, gray—either from dirt or poor washing—and frayed along the edges. The single pillow looked lumpy.

"This is creepy," I said.

Derek's hands settled on my waist. I guess he was trying to give comfort, but it made me jump.

"Sorry."

"No problem." I got my breath back. "What do you think this is?"

"Originally? Mr. van Duren probably thought it'd be a good idea to put a secret room into the house when he built it. Either because he thought he might want a place to store contraband, or because he was afraid that the British were coming back and Daisy's family might want somewhere to hide. This is built between the chimneys, obviously. There's a space behind each chimney and behind the run-around stairs. Just big enough for this room."

I nodded. Made sense. "What about now, though? This stuff hasn't been here since Daisy's time."

"Nope." Derek hesitated for a second. "The old guy who lived here might have gotten a little paranoid in his old age. He was almost a hundred when he died. By then, he was tucked away in a nursing home in Boothbay Harbor. Refused to sell the place, though. Kept saying he was going to move back home." He shrugged.

"I know. Irina told me. Maybe he was afraid they'd come and take him away while he was sleeping, and he didn't want to go. So he'd hide in here. That way they couldn't sneak up on him." Poor old guy.

"I think I see a lamp," Derek said. "Shine the flashlight over in the corner behind the mattress, would you?"

I did as he asked, and he left me to walk, crablike, around the mattress. A second after he bent, the room lit up. I closed my eyes against the brightness, and it took a few seconds for my eyes to adjust to so much light again.

"Nothing else here," Derek said, hands on his hips, master of all he surveyed.

I shook my head. "I guess we need to get this stuff out of here. Don't want any mice to get in and build nests in the mattress. How do you suppose he got it in?"

"Very carefully," Derek said. "It's just a twin, though,

so with some brute force, it would bend enough to go through the closet."

I looked around in the now fully illuminated room. "There may be nothing else here now, but something was here recently. Look at the marks in the dust."

Along the whole of one wall, the dust on the floor had been scuffed, as if something had been put there and then picked up again. Several somethings, by the looks of it.

"This looks like a footprint," Derek said, putting his own size eleven construction boot next to it. "Smaller than mine."

I went to join him. "Bigger than mine, but not by a whole lot. Either a woman or a young boy, probably." I suppressed a shudder at the thought. "You don't think this is one of those horrible situations where someone kidnapped a boy and kept him hidden for years, do you? Like that creepy guy in Missouri a couple of years ago?"

Derek shook his head. "I think we would have heard something. This is down east Maine; boys don't disappear without a trace around here. At least not for very long."

Maybe not. It was still creepy, though. But maybe the former owner had just had exceptionally small feet.

"I'll just get this stuff out of here right now," Derek said, watching the emotions chase one another across my face. "You'll feel better once it's all gone." He bent and grabbed the mattress, setting it on its side and dragging it toward the low door.

"I don't know . . ." I said.

He glanced at me. "Why?"

"What if this is a crime scene? Shouldn't we leave it alone and let Wayne see it?"

Derek stopped. "Do you have any reason to think it's a crime scene?"

I had to admit I didn't. "It's just creepy. I want to get out of here."

Derek leaned the mattress up against the wall. "We can leave it for another day," he said. "You're right. We should concentrate on finding the cat, and then get back to the ferry. I forgot all about it."

"Me, too." I turned to look at the small brick room one more time before we exited, and stopped. "What's that?"

Derek turned, too. "What's what?"

"On the floor right there, where the mattress was. Looks like a little sliver of paper?"

Derek walked over to it and bent. After a moment he straightened, though, pulled a knife out of his pocket, and squatted.

"What?" I said.

"It's a piece of paper. Bigger than it looks. Someone tried to shove it out of sight into a crack between the planks and didn't quite get it all in."

"Or maybe they just used it to stop a draft," I suggested.

Derek grunted. "Looks like a piece of newsprint. I've got it. Almost . . . there."

He put the knife away first and then brought the paper to me, carefully unrolling it as he went. It was brittle and a little discolored but otherwise not in bad shape.

"Comics?" Derek said, eyebrows arching.

"Looks that way."

"Damn. I guess they *were* just trying to block a draft."

"Maybe. Look at the date, though." I pointed. "Two weeks ago, just before we started working on the house. After we bought the place, and long after Mr. What's-his-name left."

"Huh. That's interesting." He turned it over in his hands. We noticed the writing at the same time; a faint scribble along one edge, written in pencil so light that we both squinted.

"I can't make it out," I said.

Derek shook his head. "Looks like chicken scratches. Let's get out of here and take a look in natural light. You go first." He put a hand at the small of my back and pushed me toward the door. I ducked through, into the closet and from there out into the kitchen. There was no sign of the kitten, but the sunlight flooding through the windows was nice.

Derek shut the paneled door behind us and turned to me. "Let's have a look." He held the paper into the sunlight. We both bent over it.

"I still can't make it out," he said after a moment.

My pulse quickened. "I think it's written in Russian. Cyrillic. Same as the writing on that scrap of paper the girl in the water had in her pocket."

He shot me a look. "You're kidding."

"Nope. It's the same kind of letters. That word right there"—I pointed to it; it started with a *p*—"is Irina's last name, I think."

"Really?" He twisted the paper, looking at it from different angles.

"I'm not sure. But it looks like it. At least what I remember from last time I saw it."

"I didn't see it last time," Derek said. "Or the time before that. But if you're right, I think we should give it to Wayne." He handed the scrap of paper to me. I stuffed it in the pocket of my jacket.

"If it's the same handwriting, that would mean there's a connection between the girl in the water, Irina, and this house."

"There's already a connection between the girl in the

water, Irina, and this house," Derek said. "The girl in the water had Irina's name and address in her pocket, and Irina helped us buy this house."

"You know what I mean."

He looked at me over his shoulder as he walked through the dining room toward the hallway and the front door. "You mean a direct connection between the girl and this house."

I thought about it. "Yeah, that's what I mean."

"That's what I thought you meant," Derek said, holding the front door open for me. I was just about to step through when a streak of gray fur shot between my legs and out through the opening. I staggered.

"Damn cat," Derek said, but without heat.

I found my balance. "It went back under the porch. Let's leave the box outside, and maybe it'll investigate once we're gone."

"Doubtful," Derek said, locking the door behind us.

I shrugged. "We can try to catch it again tomorrow. Right now, let's hurry so we don't miss the ferry. I want to give this piece of paper to Wayne as soon as possible."

"You and me both," Derek said, and took my hand to pull me along behind him as soon as we hit the grass. The last thing I saw before we turned the corner of the house was the gray kitten inching out from under the porch toward the spilled salmon and crunchy bits on the ground.

—16—

By the time we got back to Boothbay Harbor and the truck, it was dinnertime.

"Where are you going?" I asked Derek when he turned the truck away from the harbor and the road to Waterfield, in the direction of Burns Salvage and the neighborhoods north of town.

He glanced at me. "Angie is Ukrainian, right? I want to ask her to translate the words on the paper."

"Are you sure we shouldn't just get it to Wayne as soon as possible? And let him deal with it?"

"Twenty minutes isn't gonna make a difference," Derek said.

"Ian closed the business, though. Remember? When we left?"

"I know where he lives," Derek said, and stepped on the gas. The words had a vaguely threatening sound to them, I thought.

Ian turned out to live in a saltbox—a big one—a mile

or two outside Boothbay Harbor. He had a couple of acres of mostly woods around him, and we had to spend several minutes bumping over a rutted track full of tree roots and big rocks to get there. Only to be met by a sign that read "Trespassers Will Be Shot on Sight."

"Surely not?" I said.

Derek glanced at it. "Probably. Maybe I should call and warn him we're here. Wouldn't want him to shoot first and ask questions later." He pulled out his phone.

I could tell from Derek's half of the conversation that Ian was doing everything in his power to say no, he didn't want to see us, but when Derek reiterated—for the fifth or sixth time—that we were right outside and it would only take a minute or two, Ian relented and came to the door. I stood listening as one, then two, then three locks were unlocked, a chain was unhooked, and a deadbolt was slid aside. Either Ian was seriously paranoid or someone was out to get him.

"I swear this is only gonna take a minute," Derek said again when Ian stood in the doorway, outlined by light from behind. It made him look even bigger and more menacing, his beard bristling.

I snuck a peek past him into the house—I'm a renovator; I like looking at other people's houses—and saw old wood floors, painted, paneled walls, a set of antlers hanging above what must be the basement door, and what looked like a rifle leaning up against the wall beside the door. I gulped.

Derek was still trying to talk his way inside. "One minute, I promise. We just want to ask Angie about a few words on a piece of paper. That's all."

Ian didn't answer.

"How *is* Angie?" I asked. "Is she feeling better?"

He looked down on me. Way down. "She's all right. I don't want her upset any more today."

"I don't think this'll upset her," I said. "We just need someone to translate six or seven words on a piece of paper we found. Here." I pulled it out of my pocket and showed it to him. "See? Right there, along the edge? It won't even take a minute. Can you at least ask her?"

Ian hesitated, considering before saying, "Wait here. I'll ask." He took the piece of paper with him and disappeared, closing the door in our faces.

I turned to Derek. "What now? Will he bring it back?"

"I'm sure he will. He didn't lock the door." But the look he shot at it was troubled. "I told you, he's a little socially backward. I'm surprised he's letting Angie inside."

"Did you see the gun?"

He shook his head. "But I'm not surprised. Ian likes to hunt."

"This looked like a rifle. With a little thingamajiggy that you look through. A scope. And it was sitting right inside the door. Does he like to hunt from the privacy of his own front porch?"

"I can't imagine he does," Derek admitted, "but maybe he has a problem with skunks or coons or something. Getting in the garbage. That happens sometimes around here. Could be just bird shot."

I nodded. Could be.

Ian opened the door again after a few more seconds. Now there were two pieces of paper in his giant hands: the newspaper we'd found in the house on the island and a piece of paper towel with a few words scribbled on it in blue pen. "Here."

He thrust them both into my hands.

"This is the translation?"

He nodded. "Now please go. And leave Angie alone. She's delicate."

"Of course."

"I'll be in touch," Derek added, trying to inject some normalcy into the situation, I guess. "Next time I need something for a project."

Ian nodded. Before we were even off the bottom step, the symphony of locks, chains, and bolts had started up again behind us as Ian made his home secure from intruders.

• • •

"What does it say?" Derek asked when we were back in the truck. It had gotten dark enough now that I had to turn the ceiling light on in the cab to read the scribbled words on the paper towel. My eyes popped.

"What?" Derek repeated.

I swallowed. "Assuming Angie is right, they're names. Three of them. Katya Pushkar, Olga Kovalenko, and . . . um . . . Svetlana Rozhdestvensky."

Derek glanced at me. "So you were right."

"About what?"

"About what you thought was Irina's last name."

"Except it doesn't refer to Irina."

He shook his head.

We rode in silence down the road toward Waterfield, both probably pondering the same question. What do you get when you put three Ukrainian girl names together with a dead woman with no identification wearing Russian jeans, and a dead ICE agent?

"Smuggling," Derek said.

I blinked at him. I hadn't realized I'd said it out loud.

He continued, "These girls are paying someone to bring them into the U.S. illegally. Somehow they must have made it to Canada, and from there, someone brought them by boat to Rowanberry Island. That someone stored them in our house, in our secret room, and then when we started working on it, he or she moved them somewhere else."

"Where?"

"Who knows," Derek said. "You didn't go through Irina's house when you and Wayne were there last week, did you? What do you want to bet they were there? In the other rooms? The two of them that are still alive, that is. I wonder whether Katya or Olga is the dead one?"

I was too shocked by what he'd said to even begin to speculate. "Irina? You think Irina is behind this?"

"Who else?" Derek said with a glance at me. "She was familiar with our house and knew it was empty. The girl—let's call her Katya; it's simpler, and she looked like a Katya to me—Katya had Irina's contact info in her pocket. Just in case they got separated, I guess, so she'd know where to go. And when she fell overboard on the trip from Rowanberry Island to the mainland, and they looked and couldn't find her, and she never showed up at the house, it wasn't like they could report her missing. She was illegal and they were breaking the law. If they said anything, they'd all get caught. And probably deported."

I didn't answer. I wanted to tell him he was wrong, that Irina couldn't have—wouldn't have—done this, but I couldn't find the words. His scenario made a horrible sort of sense, and I had no proof, nothing to show why it couldn't have happened this way; just my feelings of liking Irina too much to want to believe this of her. Her worry when she hadn't been able to get in touch with her sister in Kiev had seemed genuine, and her reaction to the girl's—Katya's—body in the morgue had seemed sincere.

"And don't forget that it was Irina that Agent Trent was looking for the day she was killed," Derek added, speeding down the road. "We spun a nice scenario about Ian and Angie, but it's pretty obvious, Avery. Irina killed Lori Trent to keep her from finding the other two girls. Or from finding out about the smuggling. Somehow she got

Svetlana and Olga out of her house, and now she's gone to join them. And they're all loose somewhere in Maine. Or New England. Or anywhere in the country by now." He looked disgusted.

"I have a hard time believing this," I told him.

He looked at me as the scenery beside the road went by in a blur. "Why? It makes perfect sense."

"On paper. But I like Irina."

Derek rolled his eyes and turned his attention back to the road. "I like her, too. But that has nothing to do with it."

"You're accusing her of murder!"

"Manslaughter," Derek said. "Unpremeditated and in a panic to cover up what was going on. But if it makes you feel better, maybe Irina didn't do it. Maybe Svetlana or Olga did. Or Katya, if Olga is the dead one. And then Irina helped them get rid of the body. By dumping it in the harbor."

I didn't answer. Just bit my lip and tried to think of a reason—a good reason, a reason I could use to convince him he was wrong—that it couldn't have happened that way. Surely there was another explanation. . . .

After a few minutes' silence, he turned back to me.

"You OK, Avery?"

"Not really," I admitted.

"I'm sorry. It makes sense, though. Even Angie's reaction. She seemed almost nervous when we mentioned Irina's name earlier today, didn't she?"

"Maybe."

"She must have come over last year. Maybe they smuggle in a batch of women every winter. Irina herself came over three years ago—isn't that what she said?—maybe on a tourist visa that ran out or something. . . ."

"I doubt that." I knew that such is the most common way for illegal aliens to make it into the United States. They enter on a tourist visa and just never go home. But

Ukraine wasn't one of the countries from which such entry was possible. From what I'd understood from my research the other night, only people from well-to-do countries in Western Europe—countries with a standard of living similar to that of the United States—are awarded tourist visas. People from developing countries, or war-torn countries, or communist countries, can whistle after any kind of visa, unless they can get entry as refugees. Ukraine was one of those places that people probably couldn't wait to leave, and so tourist visas from there were few and far between. It's a way for the ICE to keep down on illegal immigration.

"Whatever," Derek said. "She got here somehow. You can't argue with that. And once she was here, then she started working on getting other women over. Angie last year; there may have been a few other women at the same time. And then Svetlana, Olga, and Katya this year."

I didn't answer. I didn't want to believe it, but in spite of myself, I was starting to. It made sense. At least enough sense that I couldn't ignore it.

"We're gonna have to tell Wayne this, aren't we?"

Derek looked at me. He didn't say, "Well, duh!"—but his expression did. "I'm afraid so, Avery. I know you like Irina—I like her, too—but we can't let her get away with something like this."

"Right." My hand tightened around the piece of paper towel, and I had to concentrate on straightening it out.

• • •

"Interesting," Wayne said thirty minutes later, after we'd managed to track him down at home.

Home for Wayne these days is the newly renovated carriage house behind the Waterfield Inn. It's a place where Wayne can get away from the rigors of crime fighting, and Kate can get away from the relentless pace of smiling and being available to her guests, and where they can both kick back and relax and remember their honeymoon in Paris, courtesy of my Parisian-inspired decor.

Wayne was definitely kicked back when he opened the door: He was dressed in jeans and a T-shirt, with his feet bare and his hair messy.

"Oops," Derek said with a grin, "we're not interrupting anything, are we?"

"Dinner. I'm cooking." He turned back into the house, leaving the door open. I stepped through and Derek followed. Wayne wandered back toward the compact kitchen, where something was sizzling on the stove.

"Kate's across the way." He nodded toward the main house, stirring whatever was in the wok on the stovetop. It gave off an aroma of garlic and other vegetably things that made my mouth water. It was a long time since lunch, with a lot of exercise in between. "What's going on?"

"We found a secret room in our house on the island," Derek said. "It was probably old John's storage room for the stuff he smuggled in two hundred years ago."

"Where is it located?" Wayne glanced up at us both, still stirring.

"The entrance is through one of the built-in kitchen cabinets. Right next to the fireplace. The room itself is behind the fireplaces and the staircase in the hallway. Turns out the staircase doesn't butt up to the back of the chimney; there's six feet of space between them. Just enough for a twin mattress and a few feet to walk around in."

"Interesting," Wayne said.

I rolled my eyes. "That's not why we're telling you. I mean . . . yeah, it's interesting. I'm excited about it. But it's what we found there . . ." I dug in my pocket.

"What did you find there?" Wayne squinted at it. "Comics?"

"Not just any comics," Derek said. "The comics page from the *Boothbay Register* three Sundays ago."

Wayne thought for a moment. "Didn't you own the place three Sundays ago?"

"We sure did."

"So someone was in your house. If you're reporting a B and E, Brandon can file the report for you. I'm off duty tonight."

"We're not reporting a B and E," Derek said with heavy patience. "I don't care that someone was in our house three weeks ago." He paused. "Well, actually . . . yes, I do. But that's not what this is about. Show him, Avery."

"Look at this." I held the paper up to his nose, indicating the scribbles along the side.

"Looks like the writing on that other piece of paper," Wayne said. "The one the dead girl had in her pocket. That's Irina's name right there, isn't it?" He used the spoon to point.

"Yes and no. It's actually Svetlana's name."

Wayne lowered his eyebrows. "How do you know?"

"That's something else we have to tell you. We drove up to Boothbay Harbor for lunch and stopped by Burns Salvage to see if Derek's friend Ian had any Colonial hardware we could use at the house."

"And?"

"He has a new wife," Derek said. "She's Ukrainian."

"No kidding?"

"No. He also had Agent Trent's business card in the office."

"And a baseball bat behind the counter. And a rifle just inside his front door at home."

Wayne glanced at me but addressed Derek. "Did you ask him about it?"

Derek nodded. "He said he and Angie—that's the wife—spoke to Agent Trent a month ago. During a home visit. Trying to make sure she's legal. He said they haven't seen her since."

"I'll make a trip up there tomorrow. See what I can find out. Tell me more about the words on the . . . What is that, a paper towel? I take it you asked Angie to translate for you?"

I nodded. "Ian took the piece of paper inside the house to her and brought the paper towel back. According to Angie, they're names. Three names. First and last. All Russian. All female."

Wayne was just as quick on the uptake as Derek. Quicker. "Trafficking," he said.

Derek nodded. "That's what we're figuring, too."

He went through the scenario he had come up with during the car ride home, casting Irina as the main bad guy. I waited for Wayne to start picking holes in the theory, to point out why Irina couldn't be guilty, but he didn't, just nodded as he played with his stir-fry.

"What happened to innocent until proven guilty?" I muttered.

Both men turned to me. "I'm not about to put out an arrest warrant on her, Avery," Wayne chided me. "I just want to talk to her. This explanation doesn't have to be the true one; there are others that might fit, as well. But as a theory, it covers all the bases."

It did, unfortunately.

"And as such, I have to take it seriously. Just like I have to look at all the other options. Including getting Brandon to take this piece of newsprint down to Barnham College and double-check that your friend Angie gave us the right translation."

"Why wouldn't she?"

"I don't know," Wayne said, "that's what I want to find out. I'm also going to have Brandon take another look at Irina's house to see if he can find evidence of anyone else having stayed there recently. We'll put out an APB on three foreign women traveling together anywhere in the New England states, in case someone happens to take notice of them. I'll call the police in Kiev myself and see if they have any information about these other two women. And I'll have Brandon contact the bus station and the train station and every hotel, motel, bed-and-breakfast, and inn in a three-state area to see if anyone fitting the description of these three women is staying there. Anything else you two have learned today that you want to share?"

The food in the wok was starting to smell like it was ready, and outside, we heard a door close at the same time as the clock on the wall sounded the hour. Kate must be on her way across the grass for dinner, and Wayne was very obviously trying to get rid of us. The marble-topped table in the dining alcove was set with china and wine goblets and tall candles in silver holders . . . there was even a bunch of flowers in the middle. Carnations.

Derek took my arm. I thought about the other thing I had wanted to mention—Gert Heyerdahl's Russian blue cat—and decided Derek was right; I was making something out of nothing. There couldn't possibly be a connection between a Russian blue cat and missing Russian, or Ukrainian, women. That was just too far-fetched. It certainly wasn't important enough to bother Wayne with when he so obviously wanted to be alone with his wife.

We withdrew, giving Kate a hug on our way across the grass to the truck.

"Dinner?" Derek said when we were back in the cab.

I did my best to shake off my feelings of gloom. Maybe Irina hadn't had anything to do with Agent Trent's death. Maybe she'd just gone camping. And in any case, it wasn't Derek's fault either way, and I shouldn't take it out on him. "Chinese sounds good."

He grinned. "As it turns out, I, too, make a mean stir-fry."

"You're gonna cook?"

"If Wayne can do it, I can do it. Let's stop at Shaw's for some stuff and go back to the house."

"My house?"

He glanced at me. "Of course your house. I don't have a wok."

"And you think I do?"

"Don't you?"

"I'm sure there's one somewhere." I sat back against the seat. "If not, I have a big frying pan."

"That'll work," Derek said, and put the truck into gear.

Shaw's Supermarket was fairly quiet on a Saturday evening at dinnertime, and it didn't take long to walk through the produce section and fill a basket with sugar snap peas and carrots, broccoli and garlic. In the refrigerated section, Derek snagged a package of already sliced steak, and from the dry goods, we grabbed a bag of rice. I glanced at the floor, remembering how last time we'd been here, I'd been with Irina. Where on earth could she be? And was it actually possible that she had smuggled her sister into the United States and had bashed Agent Trent over the head and dumped her in the harbor?

"What do you want for dessert?" Derek said.

I pulled my eyes away from the place on the floor where Irina had been squatting, picking up the pieces of glass from the broken tomato sauce jar, her face averted. As if she didn't want anyone to get a good look at her face.

"I don't care, as long as it's chocolate. Whoopie pie?"

"Why did I even bother to ask?" Derek said, heading for the bakery.

I followed, after a last look at the floor.

As it turned out, I *did* have a wok in a box in one of the kitchen cabinets, and Derek *did* make a mean stir-fry, dripping with garlicky goodness and crisply perfect veggies. I ate until I couldn't eat another bite, and then I sat back and groaned. Derek grinned.

"Good?"

"Do you even have to ask?" I'd all but licked my plate. "Why didn't you tell me you could cook?"

"Because I can't," Derek said. "This is it. And stir-fry isn't exactly cooking. It's just tossing a bunch of stuff into a pan and making sure it doesn't stick."

It seemed like cooking to me. More, it *tasted* like cooking. He'd definitely be doing this again.

"How about I build a fire in the fireplace in the living room," Derek said, getting up, "while you clean up, and then we can watch a movie?"

"Sure." I started to clear the enamel-topped table while he sauntered out of the kitchen, down the hall, and out the front door to the porch, where I—or rather, Derek—keep a small stack of firewood. I could hear him come back inside while I ferried the used plates to the bright blue resin counter. Jemmy and Inky looked up at me from the floor, their eyes fixed and demanding. Jemmy, the more vocal of the two, opened his mouth in a yowling demand. I rolled my eyes and dropped a couple of pieces of meat into their bowls. Silly of me to try to buy their affection with treats, but it was a shame to let the food go to waste, and they obviously wanted it. The cats went to work, tails twitching. I moved the other leftover meat into a ziplock baggie, intending to take it to the island in the morning. Maybe the Russian blue kitten would appreciate some of it, too.

By the time I was done, the fire was crackling, and Derek had found an old James Bond movie on cable. I curled up in a chair and he stretched out on the sofa as we both lost ourselves in Sean Connery and *From Russia with Love*.

That's irony.

—17—

Derek's phone rang at an ungodly hour the next morning, but like most practicing and former doctors, he goes from dead sleep to full wakefulness in less than a heartbeat. "Yeah?"

I rolled over into the warm spot left by his body and snuggled in.

"You're kidding," Derek said.

The voice on the other end quacked. I opened my eyes and squinted. It was still dark outside.

Derek sighed. "Yeah, yeah. I'll be there in thirty minutes."

He put the phone back on the nightstand and got to his feet.

"What's the matter?" I asked, watching sleek muscles ripple as he moved.

He shook his head in the process of pulling on his jeans, his voice disgusted. "That was Brandon Thomas. Someone reported seeing three women, two of them fitting the descriptions of the Rozhdestvensky sisters, going onto the Appalachian Trail yesterday afternoon."

"Isn't that in the South?" North Carolina? West Virginia? When you heard people talk about it, it was always down there somewhere.

"The Appalachian Trail runs from Maine to Georgia," Derek said. "The mountain range reaches all the way into Canada. Two hundred and eighty-one miles of trail is in Maine. We have some of the most difficult hiking of any state."

"And Irina and her sister went there?"

"Looks that way. Wayne has called in help from the state police in Augusta. Daphne and Hans are going, along with Brandon. He wants me to come with them as well. Both because I've hiked the trail a bunch of times before—in the summer, though, not in April; my God, it can still snow in April!—and because if someone gets hurt, I can help set a broken bone or diagnose a concussion."

I nodded. "Give me a minute to take a shower, and I'll come, too."

He shook his head, scouting for the rest of his clothes. "No offense, Tink, but we'll have our hands full without having to worry about you."

"Oh, that's nice."

He stuck his arms through the sleeves of his T-shirt and pulled it over his head. I watched, just a little sadly, as all those lovely muscles disappeared behind blue cotton. When his head popped out on the other side, he said, "How much hiking have you done in your life? Do you have hiking boots? Real ones? Sneakers won't be enough for something like this, and those cute, little boots you wore this winter . . ."

"Fine. I get it." I grimaced. "This is for the big boys, and I'm just a weak little woman."

He sat back down on the edge of the bed. "Don't be that way, Avery. You wanna go hiking on the Appalachian Trail, I'll take you. Just not today. Sometime this summer, when I know there isn't gonna be snow at the higher altitudes, and sometime when we're not trying to track down three fugitives or criminals or whatever they are. I can't worry about you, too."

"Fine."

But I didn't feel fine, and Derek knew it. He pulled me into his arms. "I love you, Tink. I don't want anything to happen to you. It snowed on the mountains overnight. If we find them at all, they could be dead. If they're not, if they survived the night and they're determined to get away, they could be desperate. They could have guns. People could die. And I don't want you to be one of them."

"OK," I murmured. It's hard to say no to Derek when he's holding me close, and his voice is rough, and I can hear the beat of his heart under my ear and feel the warmth of his body and smell his soap and shampoo and detergent and concern.

"Thank you." He let me go with a kiss on top of my head. "I have to run. You'll be OK without me today, right?"

"Of course. I'll probably just hang out here. Do some cleaning or something." The kind of things that women do. "Maybe I'll go visit Kate. Or go out to Rowanberry and see if I can catch the cat."

"Just be careful," Derek said, pulling his boots on. "I'll call you when I get back, OK?"

I nodded.

"See ya, Tink."

And with that, and another quick kiss, he was gone. I heard the front door slam behind him and—a few seconds later—the sound of the truck's engine cranking over. I buried my face in the pillow and groaned. Dammit.

I was awake, though, wide awake, and after lying there futilely trying to get back to sleep for fifteen minutes, I gave up and crawled out of bed. After a shower and change, with my hair still damp and kinking wildly around my face, and with a cup of coffee in my hand from the coffee maker in the kitchen, I padded down the hall to the front parlor and booted up the computer.

If everyone was hunting down Irina and her two companions on the Appalachian Trail, then no one was doing much of anything else, it seemed to me, and I thought I might use the time to dig up some background on Olga and Katya. Yes, I know Wayne had said he'd contact his colleague in Kiev for information, but A) Wayne was with the other searchers and wouldn't be back in Waterfield for hours, and B) the information Kiev came up with—if any—might not be the kind of information I was looking for.

I started by searching both names, without much to show for my trouble. Yes, there were people sharing those names. Plenty of people. One of the Katyas was listed, as far as I could tell, as a student with the university in Kiev. So that might be a connection to Svetlana. The problem was that I couldn't read the websites, which were in Cyrillic, and when I tried to use an online translation program, I got gibberish.

So I turned to the Russian-bride websites again, starting with the one where I had seen Svetlana's listing. There were a few Olgas there. One of the Olgas might have been the dead girl from the water. It was hard to tell, but she was blond and blue-eyed, with lots of makeup, dressed in virginal white. Her picture was one of the handful I had handed over to Brandon after my earlier search.

There were also quite a few Katyas, Katya being one of those fairly common names in the Ukraine; I guess like Kathy or Katherine or Kate is here. You don't stumble over one every time you turn around, but there are enough that you don't have to wait too long between each, either. I printed out profiles for all the Katyas to give to Brandon. One or two of them might have been the girl from the water; blue-eyed blondes with sweet faces and too much makeup.

This particular website offered a way to search for available women by name—in case you saw one you liked one day, I guess, and you wanted to go back to her later—and I typed in the name Angela—as in Angie Burns.

Angela, it turns out, is not a common Russian name. Angelina is more common, or Aneta or Anichka. An Angela did come up; however, the website noted that she was no longer "available," and so I couldn't view her listing. *But we have others!* the website proudly proclaimed.

I glanced at the clock in the corner of the screen. It was getting close to nine o'clock. Not too early to call, even on a Sunday. I dialed.

"What's up?" Josh said. "Isn't Derek's phone working?"

I wrinkled my brows. "As far as I know, Derek's phone's working just fine. Why?"

"Why are you calling me? Why aren't you calling him?"

"Because I want to talk to you?" I suggested.

"Oh." I pictured him blushing. "Sorry. I thought . . . Derek's just up ahead. I thought maybe you couldn't get hold of him, and so you tried me instead."

"No," I said, "I'm actually trying to get you." Although if I'd realized he'd be with the search party up on the Appalachian Trail, I wouldn't have bothered. "I need some computer help, but I guess if you're up in the mountains, you're not gonna be able to do that, are you?"

"Not until I get back. Unless it's something simple that I can just walk you through. What do you need?"

I explained the situation. "The listing is blocked. Archived or something. I'd like to look at it."

"Might take a little bit of hacking. Probably too complicated to do over the phone." I could hear him breathe as he walked; the terrain must be steep. "Tell you what," he continued after a moment's thought. "Send Ricky an e-mail. This is his e-mail address." He rattled it off; I scribbled it down. "Send him the link to the website and tell him what you want. He's even better at this kind of thing than I am, and he's home. He'll access it for you. I'll give him a call and tell him to look out for it."

"Thanks," I said. "Are you sure he won't mind?"

"Of course not. Ricky lives for this kind of thing. It won't take him long to do."

"What's going on where you are?"

"Oh, you know. The usual. Walking straight up the sides of mountains. Derek's fine, but I spend too much time sitting on my butt to be comfortable being this active."

I smiled. "Any sign of them?"

"Nothing yet. We haven't gone very far. Terrain is too steep to hurry."

"I'll let you go," I said, "so you can concentrate on climbing. Be careful. Tell Derek to be careful, too."

Josh promised he would. We both hung up; Josh to call Ricky, and me to e-mail him.

While I waited for Ricky to get back to me with what I assumed would be Angie's Russian-bride profile, I did as I had told Derek I would and turned my hands to straightening and cleaning the house.

An old house—and Aunt Inga's house is old; a Second Empire Victorian built in the 1870s, with ten-foot ceilings and old plaster walls—produces a lot of dust. I'm sorry to have to report that there was a layer on all my flat surfaces: tables, chairs, mantels, baseboards. I spent thirty minutes just walking around with a dust cloth, and that was before I started vacuuming.

In my opinion, a perfectly clean house is a sign of a wasted life. I even have a refrigerator magnet that says as much. I've found, however, that a time of doing mindless housework is a good time to think. And I had plenty to think about.

The connection between the Russian women, Gert Heyerdahl, and the Russian blue cat still bugged me, and so did Irina's reaction to Gert's caretaker that day we went to Shaw's Supermarket.

A splotch of red on the floor by the love seat caught my attention for a second before I realized it wasn't blood, just ketchup. Or maybe tomato sauce from the last time we'd eaten spaghetti in here. And there I was, right back on the case again.

True, that jar of tomato sauce might simply have slipped out of Irina's hand and shattered on the floor the other day—sometimes they do that; the jar might have been slick or her hands cold—but what if she'd seen or heard something that had startled her?

I stuck the wand of the vacuum under the love seat and sent a mouse sailing across the floor. For a second, my heart jumped, until I realized it was just a cat toy, something that Jemmy or Inky must have left there. I picked it up—by the tail—and put it into the box beside the door.

Back to that night in Shaw's Supermarket. Someone's voice had rung out right then, hadn't it? Just as Irina reached for the jar? And after it dropped, Irina had looked up, beyond my shoulder. What if she had seen Gert Heyerdahl's caretaker behind me and recognized him? Maybe they'd been working together on smuggling these young Ukrainian women into the country. Irina would have needed help; she didn't have access to a boat. And Gert's caretaker had one; a nice, unremarkable, unnoticeable, oldish wooden boat, with a little cabin below deck. A cabin cruiser. A boat that people were probably used to seeing in the waters around Rowanberry Island.

So maybe Irina had connected with him and had arranged for him to bring the girls ashore there. And she had used our house to hold the girls until she could make arrangements to get them into Waterfield. If this was the case, it'd be no surprise that she'd be startled when she saw him, since he could probably identify her. And if there was ever a time when Irina wouldn't want to be identified, it would be then, with a suddenly dead Russian girl in the hands of the police that day.

I stopped, vacuum still grinding away, my eyes fixed on nothing. Gosh, what if Derek and Wayne were right and she was a murderer? What if she'd decided she needed to kill the caretaker . . . ? Wipe out anyone who could connect her to the human trafficking before disappearing into the Appalachian Mountains with her sister and friend?

I hadn't seen Gert's caretaker since that night; for all I knew, he was lying somewhere with his head bashed in. Maybe Irina had tried to get to Angie, too, and that was why Ian kept a baseball bat behind the counter and a shotgun beside the door. Maybe that was why Angie was so terrified she wouldn't leave the house or let anyone in. She was afraid that Irina was gunning for her.

The vacuum was making desperate choking sounds while sucking so hard on the old Persian that the rug wrinkled. I started moving again, slowly, while my mind scrambled along.

Maybe I was on the completely wrong track. I mean, it wasn't like I *wanted* Irina to be guilty. Yesterday, I hadn't even wanted to believe Derek when he suggested it. Maybe there was another explanation that made at least as much sense.

Assuming Irina wasn't guilty, who was? If Irina's

reaction at the morgue was sincere, then she truly hadn't known Katya, or Olga, or whoever our dead Russian girl was. If she'd truly been surprised and worried when she hadn't been able to get in touch with Svetlana in Kiev, then Irina hadn't had anything to do with bringing Svetlana here. And I thought Svetlana must be here. The three names on the piece of newspaper in our house, coupled with Irina's contact information in the pocket of the dead girl, coupled with the fact that Svetlana hadn't shown her face in the Ukraine for three months, at least . . .

So maybe someone else was bringing Russian girls into the country illegally. Maybe Irina had been smuggled in the same way, and that was why she had reacted the way she did in the supermarket. Maybe she had recognized the man I knew as Gert Heyerdahl's caretaker as her own transporter. Maybe he was using the time while Gert was away each winter to smuggle Russian women onto Rowanberry Island and he was hiding them in our house and then, when we bought the place and went to work, in Gert's house. Where the shutters were closed and he wouldn't let me look around inside. The girl in the water—Katya or Olga—had shown up the day after I stopped by Gert's house. Maybe the girls were held there against their will, waiting for someone to come and buy their freedom. Relatives, future husbands, or worse. Several articles I'd come across when I originally did my Internet search for Russian women had detailed how lovely young girls and women from East European and Southeast Asian countries were brought to Western Europe and Britain as prostitutes and sex slaves.

Maybe they had heard me outside that day and had realized that there were people nearby they could go to for help. Maybe they had waited until it was dark and had somehow managed to get one of them out of Gert's house and over to ours, but of course we hadn't been there, and instead of going back to Gert's house, Katya (or Olga) had tried to swim to shore and find Irina. But she had underestimated the temperature of the water and the distance to shore, and she'd died instead, and we'd found her.

Maybe Irina had realized—from recognizing her sister's handwriting on the scrap of paper—that Svetlana was somewhere in Maine being pimped. Maybe she had recognized the caretaker from Gert's house in Shaw's Supermarket. She had asked me who he was. Maybe she had gone to look for him. And then maybe she had killed him and had found Svetlana and whichever other woman wasn't in the morgue right now, and then she had killed Agent Trent when the agent had stumbled onto the girls in Irina's house, and then all three of them had lit out for the Appalachian Trail.

I turned off the vacuum and tried to call Derek to run my theory past him and, through him, past Wayne, but by now they must have moved out of range of cell towers, because none of my calls went through. I tried Derek's phone, I tried Wayne's, I tried Josh's again. . . . They all refused to cooperate with me. In desperation, I called Kate, only to get her voice mail, as well.

"Thank you for calling the Waterfield Inn. I'm afraid I'm away from the phone and can't take your call right now, but if you're interested in making a reservation, please leave your name and number and I'll get back to you as soon as I can."

As I stood there, wondering who else I could call, finally my e-mail program dinged to let me know I had a message. It was from Ricky.

Here you go, he wrote, followed by a link. I clicked it and found myself—not unexpectedly—looking at Angie

Burns's beautiful face. She looked ethereal, with her enormous, melting brown eyes, dainty face, and a cloud of long, dark curls falling over her shoulders. She wasn't pregnant when this picture was taken but was dressed in a skimpy bikini. I made a mental checkmark on the air. Point to me: Seems like all these women were connected through this one website.

Can you tell me anything about the owner of the website? I shot back to Ricky, quickly.

Gimme 5, was the response I got.

While I waited for five minutes to pass, I went back to the listing for Angie, who turned out to be just twenty-two and from the small village of Nemyriv, whose chief claim to fame is being the birthplace of Nemiroff vodka. She liked moonlight, walking in the woods, and listening to music.

Ricky, bless him, hadn't sent me only Angie's unlocked page, but he had done something that allowed me to enter the rest of the website from there, as well, and to cruise to my heart's content though all the pages, archived as well as active. And that was how I found Irina's Russian-bride listing.

It was old, from four or five years ago, but Irina looked much the same as she did now. A few years younger, perhaps, but other than that, she hadn't changed much in the past half-dozen years. Her hair was still long and dark, although in the picture, she had it unbound. These days, she keeps it pulled straight back from her face into a tight bun or braid, and she makes as little as possible out of herself. In this picture, she was wearing what I can only describe as slut-wear. The hot pink top was low cut and skin tight, and the leather miniskirt ended just below her butt, nowhere close to meeting up with the black, thigh-high boots. Her hair was down, falling over her shoulders, and her lips were dark red. There was so much makeup on her eyes that she couldn't seem to keep her eyelids all the way up but looked ready for bed. Maybe that was the point.

Irina is thirty-one, the caption said, *and from Kiev. She likes to dance, visit museums, and go to the theater and ballet.*

The computer signaled another e-mail.

Funny thing, Ricky wrote, *you'd think a website hawking Russian women would originate somewhere in Eastern Europe. This one doesn't. It's here in Maine. That's as close as I can get right now, but if you give me a little time I can probably get you a name and address for the owner.*

I wrote back and told him to go ahead if he wanted a challenge. Surely it couldn't hurt to have that information.

By the time I finished dusting and vacuuming and had emptied the dish drainer of last night's dishes, it was going on eleven o'clock in the morning. Ricky hadn't gotten back to me with any details about the website owner. Either it must be harder than he thought to get the information, or he'd gotten sidetracked with something—probably Paige—and had gone out. I pulled on my pink Wellies and a coat and headed outside, too.

The weather had turned colder again. Derek had mentioned that snow had fallen on the mountains overnight, and even here in Waterfield, it was chillier than it had been just the day before. The sky was gray with low-hanging clouds. I didn't think we'd get any snow down here on the coast today, but I was glad I hadn't relegated my puffy blue winter jacket to the attic quite yet. It was nice and warm, and I snuggled into it as I wandered down the hill from Aunt Inga's house on Bayberry Lane.

It wasn't that I was worried, I told myself as I headed for the harbor and the ferry. After all, if Irina was the murderer, and she was safely on the Appalachian Trail, halfway across the state from where I was going, there'd be nothing to worry about, would there? I just wanted to check up on my kitten and maybe stop by Gert Heyerdahl's house on the way back to the ferry dock to see if the caretaker was still breathing. If he was, then no harm done. And if he wasn't . . . well, that'd be another nail in Irina's coffin, I figured. If he wasn't there at all . . . maybe I'd just try to take a closer look around.

It must have been Ned the ferry conductor's day off, because another man—old and gnarled—was doing Ned's job. I paid him the fare and went to sit on one of the benches near the steering house, where I'd be as protected as I could be on the ride. The weather had turned exceedingly nasty: much colder, with froth-capped waves and a stinging wind that blew my hair back from my face and then curved around and came back to whip it forward. The horizon was gone; all I could see in front of the boat was shades of gray, as waves, clouds, and fog blended into a messy whole. Great. Just what Derek and the rest of the rescue team needed: a proper pea-souper to make navigating the Appalachian Trail even more treacherous. I grimaced.

Rowanberry Island was just as desolate and depressing as the previous day. More so, with the overcast sky, the fog in the distance, and the stinging mist. I buried my hands in my pockets and ducked my head, wishing I'd brought my winter hat, gloves, and a scarf along with my winter coat.

There was no one abroad today, not even Pepper the Russian blue, and the small general store was dark and closed. It *was* Sunday morning, so maybe the owner had gone to church. On the mainland, since Rowanberry didn't boast a church. As I slogged past the village toward the woods, I wondered idly if any of the other islands did, or if everyone had to get into Boothbay Harbor or Waterfield to go to church. The place looked like a ghost town, so maybe everyone had headed for the mainland, en masse, this morning. And then I put the thoughts aside and set out for Sunrise and Sunset.

—18—

All the salmon and crunchy bits from yesterday were gone.

I peered into the darkness under the stairs but saw no evil red eyes staring back at me. No eyes of any other kind, either. And jumping up and down on the porch didn't bring forth the little monster. I unlocked the front door and went inside to get Derek's flashlight. I was on my way back out when it occurred to me to look inside the cardboard box we'd placed on the porch, and lo and behold, the kitten was curled up inside in a corner of the box in a nest of old curtains. Of course, as soon as I opened the flaps on top of the box, he or she shot out of the opening Derek had cut, between my legs, and made a beeline for the safety of the underside of the porch again.

Fine. If that's the way it wanted it.

I filled another bowl with more crunchy bits and cat food, added one filled with clean water, and put them both on the porch in the corner by the box. When I left, the kitten would probably come back out and would eat and go back to sleep inside the box again. Meanwhile, I had more important things to do.

The fog was starting to creep in for real now, trailing white fingers through the trees as I set out for Gert Heyerdahl's house. The atmosphere was eerie, with a sort of hollow and echoing quiet. Except for the mournful sound of a foghorn somewhere in the distance, and the wind rustling above my head, causing pine needles to whisper and still-bare branches to crack together, everything was still.

There was no sign of life at Gert's house, and the dock was empty. *Calliope* was gone. Gert's caretaker must not be working on Sundays. Lucky break, if one I had sort of counted on. Or at least hoped for.

I climbed the stone steps and peered through the sidelights. The entrance hall looked exactly as it had the last time I was here. Dark and quiet. The door was locked, of course, and no one answered when I knocked. Not that I'd expected anything different.

I stood for a second, biting my lip, thinking about what to do next. The shutters were still covering the windows downstairs, although they'd been turned back from the windows on the second floor. Maybe Gert's caretaker was doing one level at a time. Or maybe the Russian women had been kept up there, hidden away until Irina came and got them, and now there was no sense in keeping the shutters closed anymore. That didn't explain why the shutters on the main floor were still closed, of course. It did mean that I would be able to look into the second floor if I could get up to it.

Would I be able to pull Derek's ladder from our house over here? If I went back and got it? And if I did, would I be able to raise it? Or maybe Gert had a ladder sitting around somewhere? I could have a look around for it, maybe.

Decisions, decisions. I mulled for a second, weighing

the time it would take to run back to our house and drag, literally, a ladder all the way back over here against the time it would take to check the property for one. One that might not exist. Just because the place was deserted now didn't mean Gert's caretaker wouldn't be back soon. And it would behoove me to be finished and gone by the time he got here. Unless he was dead, of course. And he might be. Maybe even somewhere inside the house.

Something moved behind the upstairs window. I took a couple of steps back, the better to see. I blinked. Stared. Shaded my eyes. Blinked again.

Maybe it had been just a patch of fog floating by.

No, there it was again. The outline of a person. Between the six-over-six panes and the ancient, wavy glass, it was difficult to make out details, but it looked like a woman. Pale face, long dark hair . . . The ghost of Clara van Duren, or whatever her married name had been? Or maybe Gert had a live-in housekeeper as well as a caretaker, making the place ready for him?

Or could it be Svetlana Rozhdestvensky?

What if I'd been looking at the situation wrong? What if Irina hadn't gone hiking on the Appalachian Trail with her sister and Katya/Olga? What if she hadn't run away at all? What if she had come here to rescue Svetlana and the others. Here, where Gert's caretaker found her and killed her. The way he'd killed Agent Trent? Maybe I'd find Irina's body floating in the harbor one of these mornings. And now Svetlana was upstairs, with no hope of rescue. While Derek, Josh, Brandon, and Wayne were wasting their time trekking the Appalachian Trail looking for three other women who fit the general description of Irina, Svetlana, and friend.

Given the circumstances, I decided to sacrifice the wavy glass in one of the sidelight panes in order to find out who was upstairs. It would take too long to go back for the ladder, and what if she—whoever she was—needed help? If I used a rock to knock out one of the sidelights, I might be able to reach my hand in and turn the locks and bolts on the inside of the door.

I was on my way up the stoop again, rock palmed and ready, when the door opened.

For a second, my hand wavered as I considered the idea of lifting the rock to use as a weapon in case I needed one. Then my fingers twitched, and the rock dropped. It hit the stoop with a crack and rolled off into the grass. I didn't watch it. I was staring at the woman in the doorway, my eyes threatening to roll, too, straight out of my head.

"Oh, my God!" I managed. "What are you doing here?"

It was Irina—not Svetlana, Irina herself—dressed, as Arthur Mattson had described, in jeans and a green sweatshirt with the white Maine Association of Realtors® logo on it.

For a moment I wasn't sure what to do, and more, what to think. I'd always liked Irina, ever since the first time I'd met her. I didn't want to believe her guilty of what Derek and Wayne suspected her of. At the same time, the fact that my boyfriend and the chief of police thought she was a murderer was sobering. And more than sobering, it was scary. What if they were right and I was wrong? What if I was standing face-to-face with a cold-blooded killer? What if she was thinking of killing me, too?

I took a step back—just a precaution—and stumbled, off the stoop and onto the ground, ending up on my butt on the wet grass.

"Are you all right?" Irina said. She was still standing inside the door in the shaded front hall, where she couldn't be seen from outside. I don't know who she was afraid would see her, since we were clearly the only two people here and since visibility was becoming less and less as the fog settled in. By now, even the dock was starting to disappear.

"Fine, thanks." I got myself to my feet and brushed my rear clean. As well as I could, since there's nothing anyone can do to brush away water that's already seeped into fabric. I'd be walking around with a wet bottom for the next few hours until I could make it off the island and into a dry pair of jeans.

"What are you doing here?" I asked again. "I thought you were on the Appalachian Trail."

Irina blinked. "Why would you think that?"

I moved a little closer, up to the stoop but not onto it. "When you disappeared, Brandon Thomas put out an APB on you. He got a tip that someone who matched your description, and your sister's, went on the trail yesterday afternoon."

Irina paled. "My sister?"

"She's here, isn't she? Svetlana? In Maine?"

Irina glanced past me, into the fog. She did a sort of sweep with her eyes of the area in front of the house. "Where's Derek?"

I rolled my eyes. "Where do you think? Hiking the Appalachian Trail looking for you."

"He let you go out here alone?"

"He didn't let me. I went." And what was up with the question, anyway? Was she worried that something might happen to me? Or did she want to make sure I was alone, in case she was planning to do something to me herself? "And you never told me what you're doing here."

"You never told me what you're doing here," Irina shot back.

I sighed. "Not looking for you. I had no idea you'd be here. I was just having a look around."

Irina scanned the fog again. There was nothing to see. Just me, standing here with my wet butt and my arms folded across my chest. Her eyes returned to me. "It's a long story. You'd better come in."

I hesitated. Did I trust her enough to walk into Gert's house when I'd maybe never walk out? Or did I trust her more, enough to believe that she didn't—couldn't have—killed anyone?

I stalled. "Do you know about what happened to Agent Trent?"

Irina nodded. I'd been hoping she'd say no; that way at least I'd know she hadn't had a hand in killing the ICE agent.

"How did you hear?" Had it been on television? Or in the newspaper? Had Tony the Tiger gotten hold of the story and run with it?

"My"—Irina hesitated—"friend was in Waterfield yesterday and heard the news."

Her . . . friend? "Would that be the guy we saw at Shaw's Supermarket the other day? When you dropped that jar of tomato sauce?"

Irina nodded. She was still peering worriedly into the fog. "Please come inside, Avery."

Her fear was infectious, and I found myself looking around, too, the small hairs on the back of my neck prickling.

From out of the fog, the sound of a boat motor reached us. It was impossible to tell where it was coming from or which direction it was heading, but it was getting louder, so at least it was coming closer. Irina twitched. I made up my mind.

"OK." I may as well go in; she wasn't coming outside, and she didn't seem willing to tell me anything while we were standing here half in, half out of the house. Plus, I wanted the opportunity to look around the place. And maybe to see if I could open Gert Heyerdahl's secret room. If the houses were exact replicas, and ours had one, it stood to reason that his would have one, too.

So I squared my shoulders and took a deep breath and walked through the door, while the *chugga-chugga* of the boat motor echoed through the fog.

The inside of Gert's house was fabulous, even in the semidarkness with the shutters closed. Gleaming wood floors, intricate paneling, high-end furniture. Once upon a time, I worked for—and dated—a reproduction furniture maker, very good at what he did, and this stuff looked like it could have come from Philippe's studio.

"This place is gorgeous."

Irina nodded, looking around. "Mr. Heyerdahl has a lot of money."

No kidding.

Aside from the fact that it was finished, and beautifully, the layout of the house was exactly the same as in our house on the other side of the island. Parlor to the right, dining room to the left, tight run-around staircase in the middle with—just maybe—a secret room behind it, accessible from the kitchen.

"Where are you going?" Irina asked when I strolled, oh so casually, into the dining room.

"Just having a look around." I did just that, admiring Gert's dining room set in dark wood with demure blue, yellow, and white stripes on the cushions. It was tasteful and elegant, although personally, I would have rather seen a pattern of white daisies with bright yellow centers on a spring green background.

The kitchen was updated. Totally, top to bottom. Tile floor, granite counters, stainless steel appliances, brass pots hanging above the island where the stove was. The fireplace was still there, though, and the built-in cabinets next to it. I opened the nearest cabinet door and stuck my head in.

"What," Irina repeated, her voice more strident now, "are you doing?"

I pulled my head back out again and explained over my shoulder. "In our house, there's a secret room behind the chimney. I just wanted to see if there was one here, too."

"I have no idea," Irina said, folding her arms across her chest. There was a knife block on the counter a few feet away from her, bristling with wooden handles. I glanced at it and then glanced away. Better not to give her any ideas.

The hidden room could wait. I straightened up. "Why don't we go sit down somewhere. This is going to take a while."

We ended up upstairs, in one of the bedrooms; the same one where I'd seen Irina's reflection through the window earlier. She must be staying there, because the double bed looked like it had been slept in, and there was a backpack, empty, tossed in the corner. A sleeping bag, still rolled up, lay next to it. One of the drawers in the bureau was open a crack, where a piece of clothing—what looked like another pair of jeans—had gotten caught and kept the drawer from closing all the way. A hairbrush was lying on top of the bureau, the couple of long, dark hairs caught in the bristles identifying it as belonging to Irina.

She sat on the rumpled bed while I curled up in a small, white chair over in the corner, with a plastic bag tucked under my butt so the mud on my behind wouldn't stain the pristine whiteness of the fabric. It made a crinkling noise every time I moved. Irina kept her hands tightly folded in her lap and kept shooting glances out the window, where the fog was now pressing against the wavy glass.

I watched her, trying to decide where to start, how to broach the various subjects and questions I had. What to say so I didn't freak her out or—scary thought—make her feel like she had to do something to shut me up. And there were so many questions to ask, so many things I needed to know. Where was Svetlana? Who was the dead girl in the water? Had Irina killed Agent Trent? Did she know Angie, Ian's girlfriend?

Probably better to start with something less confrontational, though.

"How long have you been here?"

She glanced around the room. "Here? Since Friday night."

"I spoke to Arthur Mattson," I said. "He told me he'd seen you leave and that it looked like you were going camping. That's why we thought, when we got the tip about the Appalachian Trail, that it might be you. Is Svetlana there? On the trail?"

Irina shook her head, lips tight.

"Where is she?"

"I don't know," Irina said, and from the expression on her face, I don't think she was happy about admitting it.

"Have you seen her?"

Another head shake.

"But she's here? In Maine?"

Irina pried her lips apart. "I think she must be. She's not in Kiev."

"But you don't know where?"

She shook her head.

"The writing on that piece of paper the dead girl had in her pocket? Was it Svetlana's handwriting?"

Irina shook her head, but not in negation. More like resignation or disgust or despair, closing her eyes for a moment. "I think so. But it was hard to tell. The paper was wet. Everyone else in my family is where they are supposed to be, though. All except Svetlana."

I nodded. "Did you talk to Agent Trent the other day? Or did you run away—come here—to avoid talking to her?"

Irina's lips thinned again. "I spoke to her."

I tried to soften my voice, to sound friendly and nonconfrontational. "What happened?"

"Nothing happened," Irina said. "She called me at work. Mr. Mattson had told her where I work, and she called the front desk and got transferred. She asked me to meet her."

"At the Waterfield harbor?" Where Irina had conked her over the head and tipped her into the water?

"In Portland," Irina said.

"Oh." I bit my lip, my cheeks pink. Well, duh. That made a lot more sense, didn't it? Agent Trent had come to Waterfield to talk to Irina, but Irina wasn't there so Lori Trent tracked her down in Portland instead.

Irina shook her head at me. "You don't really think that I killed her, do you, Avery?"

"I think the police think so. That that's why you ran away. So you wouldn't be arrested."

"I didn't," Irina said.

"I believe you. So what did you talk about? You and Agent Trent?"

Irina sighed, rubbing her hands over her face as if she were tired. She looked tired, with dark rings under her eyes and tight lips. "I told her everything. That it was Svetlana's handwriting on the piece of paper, that I suspected she and a friend had come into the country illegally and were being held somewhere, and that the friend must have been trying to get away. . . ."

"So you didn't have anything to do with smuggling them into the U.S.?"

She shook her head.

"Oh. I thought maybe . . . you know, that you . . ."

"I came here illegally," Irina said. "Someone contacted me online, through a website I'd signed up for."

"The Russian-bride one?"

She nodded. "He offered to get me into the United States for a price. I didn't have the money, so he suggested an alternative."

"What was the alternative?"

Irina just looked at me, and after a moment, the pieces aligned themselves in my head. Russian brides, attractive women from Eastern Europe and Southeast Asia smuggled into the West . . . to work as prostitutes?

I managed to bite down on the exclamation before it slipped out, though I couldn't quite keep the shock from showing on my face. Irina looked uncomfortable, ashamed, and then defiant.

"I'm sorry," I said, and meant it. "So you told Agent Trent about it?"

Irina nodded. "Everything. How I came here, what happened, all I knew or had learned about the people in charge. It wasn't much. I spent a few weeks with them, and then I was . . . sold to a man in Skowhegan who was looking for someone to cook and clean and . . . do other things."

Right. I suppressed a grimace. "Do you know a woman named Angie? Angela? From the Ukraine? Early twenties, very pretty, with brown hair and brown eyes? Pregnant?"

Irina shook her head. "Who is she?"

"Just a friend of a friend. I wonder if she isn't one of you, too. She's very skittish."

Irina nodded. "Traveling halfway around the world for a chance at a new life only to end up in a brothel can do that to a person."

No kidding. "How did you get away? Did you have to escape, or did the guy let you go?"

"I escaped. The same night he brought me there. He had a heart attack, and I called nine-one-one and then I ran away. I didn't want to be sent back to Ukraine."

"Oh, my God." I sat up straight, the plastic crinkling under my butt. "What did you do?"

I couldn't imagine finding myself in that situation: practically broke, in a strange place, knowing no one and unable to go to the police for fear of being arrested and deported.

Irina avoided my eyes. "Walked to Augusta. Slept outside for a few nights until I found a shelter. They sent me to Portland. Eventually I found a job and a place to stay."

There must be a lot more to the story than those few terse sentences, but it was beyond obvious that she didn't want to go into detail. "What happened to the guy?"

"Mr. Eagan?" Her lips thinned. "He died. The ambulance got there too late."

"Did you tell Agent Trent all this?"

Irina nodded. "And then I told her about that night at Shaw's Supermarket, and that I recognized the voice of a man from"—she hesitated—"the organization. The people who brought me here. One of the men in charge."

I nodded.

"You told me the man behind you was Gert Heyerdahl's caretaker, so I told Agent Trent that. She said she was going to take the ferry from Portland to Rowanberry Island and have a look around. Pretend to be a visitor, you know? I told her about you and Derek, and that she could say she had come to see you if anyone asked."

"Makes sense."

"I thought so," Irina said, her eyes shiny now. "I asked to go along, in case she found Svetlana, but she said no. If I had recognized the man, he might have recognized me, too, and she didn't want us to be seen together. So I let her leave and found my backpack and sleeping bag and took the next ferry from Waterfield. I thought I could follow her, you know? I thought she might get into trouble, and maybe I could help. I've known about the smuggling for three years, and I haven't done anything to stop it. I've been too afraid. But this time I wasn't. I wanted to help. So I followed on the next ferry. But I didn't see her on the way, and when I got here, she wasn't here, either. She never came."

I wrinkled my brows. "How do you know that?"

"He told me," Irina said.

"He? Who?"

"Me," a gravelly voice said from the doorway. It added, precisely, "Or rather, I."

—19—

I froze. I hadn't even heard him come inside, let alone up the stairs and over to the door. And he looked threatening standing there, still in those padded coveralls and with that ski mask on his head, ready to pull down over his face. It was grim. The face, I mean. The really scary part, though, was the gun. It wasn't pointed at me—not precisely—but it wasn't exactly pointed anywhere else, either. It was in his hand, sort of hanging there, ready to come into play at any moment.

"This is Avery," Irina said into the silence.

He nodded, those muddy brown eyes flickering over at her for a tenth of a second before coming back to me. "We've met."

"Of course."

Silence reigned for another moment, only punctuated by the beating of my heart, surely loud enough for them both to hear. I tried not to look at the gun, but it was difficult.

"You won't need that," Irina added.

"You sure?"

She nodded. "Just put it away, please. It's making Avery nervous."

No kidding. As soon as the gun was out of sight in a pocket of the coveralls, I felt myself starting to breathe easier.

Even so, it took me a few seconds to get my voice to cooperate.

"What's going on?" I looked from one to the other of them.

They looked at one another.

"I think I'm missing something," I explained. "See, I thought *you*"—I looked at the man in the doorway—"were helping Irina smuggle Svetlana and her friends onto Rowanberry Island and hiding them in the secret room in Derek's and my house, and then, when we started fixing the place up, you moved them here, since Gert Heyerdahl was away until summer and the place was just sitting here, empty, and that's why you were so standoffish when I came and asked to see the house. And then, when one of the girls got away and drowned, and ICE was called in, and Lori Trent caught on to what was happening, I thought the two of you killed her. But now I'm not so sure anymore."

They looked at one another again. After a second, Irina smiled. Her friend blushed.

"Avery"—Irina turned to me, her lips twitching—"this is Gerhardt Heyerdahl. He's been staying here all winter."

"You're kidding." I stared at him, up and down a few times. "You don't look anything like the picture in your books."

"You've read my books?"

"My boyfriend's read your books. I like cozy mysteries."

"Ah." He nodded. "That picture is fifteen years old. I don't look like that anymore."

No kidding. He must have lost fifty pounds, easily, and he'd shaved off the beard, which had obscured most of his face, and cut his hair. It was amazing the difference it made.

"Here." He stuck his hand in his pocket—I stiffened—and came out with a wallet (not the gun). "My driver's license."

It was from Florida, and the face was the one he sported now, sans beard and with a healthy tan. The name identified him as Gerhardt Heyerdahl, with an address in Miami.

"Thank you." I handed it back. So he really was Gert Heyerdahl. But did that mean that he wasn't involved in the smuggling?

Not necessarily, I thought.

"Gert realized something was going on last year," Irina explained while Gert put the driver's license back in his wallet and the wallet back in his pocket. "But he didn't know what. So this fall, he decided to make it look like he'd gone back to Florida, but instead he'd stay on the island and try to figure things out."

I looked around. "You've been living here all winter? With the shutters closed?"

Gert Heyerdahl nodded.

"I guess that explains Pepper. I thought it was strange that you'd leave her here when everyone said you always take her with you when you leave."

"You've seen Pepper?"

"Yesterday. In the village. I think I have one of her kittens living at my house."

"You can bring it here," Gert said.

"That's OK. I think I'll keep it, if that's OK. I have two cats at home that I inherited from my aunt, but they're not very friendly. I'm hoping maybe the kitten will be nicer."

Gert nodded.

"So if you didn't kill Agent Trent"—I looked from one to the other of them—"who did? And what's with the gun?"

They looked at each other.

"Protection," Gert said. "Bad stuff going on."

For a bestselling author, he wasn't very eloquent.

Irina nodded. "When we find Svetlana, they may not want to let her just walk out. The gun will help."

"You have a permit for it, I hope? If not, you're not supposed to have it."

Gert informed me that he did. The gun was owned fair and square, leftover from a period a few years ago when he'd acquired a rabid fan who wouldn't leave him alone.

"I realized that something strange was going on last year," he explained. "I was doing some research into smuggling, because my next book has to do with human trafficking, and I was looking into the history of Rowanberry Island. Did you know that John van Duren, who built both our houses, was a smuggler?"

I nodded. "I saw your signature on the list of people who had taken out the file from the Historical Society before me. Have you explored your secret room yet?"

"I didn't know I had a secret room," Gert said.

"Well, I don't know that you do. But the houses are supposed to be identical. And we have a secret room. Just a little one. Behind the chimneys. The entrance to ours is from a built-in cabinet in the kitchen."

"Show me." He turned and walked down the hall, without waiting for me to answer. I glanced at Irina, who was still sitting on the bed. She shrugged.

"Sure." I uncoiled myself from the chair and crinkly plastic and trotted after Gert. Irina got up from the bed and followed.

The houses *were* identical, at least originally. But when

Gert's house went through remodeling before he moved in, he'd had someone redo the built-in cabinets along with the rest of the kitchen to where the shelves were now securely fastened to the walls and didn't come out. I guess they hadn't realized the shelves were loose for a reason. There was no way into the cabinet anymore. At least not for Gert, who—even pared down—was much too big to squeeze between the shelves. Even Irina had a problem fitting herself in. I was small enough to slither through, though, on my belly on the floor, like a snake. Clutching a high-powered flashlight.

The lever—in the same spot as ours—was stuck from years of no use, and the secret door opened with a grating squeal of dry hinges. But it opened, enough that I could squeeze through and into the secret room.

It wasn't until I was inside that I realized that they could lock me in here and no one would ever know where I was. If the Russian girls had been kept in the secret room in our house and hadn't been able to get out, then chances were there was no egress. No matching lever on the inside. If John van Duren and his sons-in-law had used the rooms for storage of illicit goods, it wasn't like they'd need a way to open the door from inside, was there? Although, just in case something went wrong and they accidentally locked themselves in—if the secret door slammed closed from a gust of wind or something—or if John thought he might have to hide his family in the room to keep them safe while something was going on outside, and he was worried that something might happen to him before he could get back and let them out . . . surely he would have incorporated a second lever inside? Wouldn't he?

I never had occasion to find out, because Irina and Gert made no move to lock the secret door behind me. They just stood at the entrance to the cabinet, peering into the darkness after me. "Anything?" Gert said.

I got to my feet and flashed the light around.

The inside of Gert's secret room looked just like ours. Small and square, with red-brick walls, a brick ceiling, and wide plank floors. There was no mattress here, though. No one had been living here, at least not recently. There was a layer of dust, like velvet, thick on the floor and on a couple of boxes over in the corner. Wooden boxes, not cardboard. Crates. I walked over to them, noting the marks my footsteps made in the dust. No one else had been here in the time—years—it had taken for almost an inch of dust to settle on everything.

I raised my voice. "A couple of crates in the corner. Too heavy to carry. I'll push them out to you."

I started maneuvering the closest box across the floor toward the door. From the faint tinkling noises it made as I shoved it, it sounded like there was glassware inside. Maybe some long-ago householder had used the secret room as a butler's pantry or storage room, for the "good" china.

Gert stood ready to grab the crate and pull it the rest of the way into the kitchen, and I went back for the other while he and Irina opened the first. I could hear the nails scream as they pried off the wooden lid.

"Bottles," Irina announced.

"Rum," Gert added.

"No kidding?" I was pushing the second crate across the plank floor now. It was making the same tinkling noises as the first. "Must be Mr. van Duren's stuff."

"It's not old enough," Gert said. "This is from the prohibition. 1920s. Rum-running."

"How do you know?"

"Haven't you read the file from the Historical Society?" He took the second crate from me and hauled it into the kitchen. I went back to make sure there were no more.

"Not very well," I admitted as I flashed the beam around.

No, nothing else in here. "I looked at it a little over lunch yesterday, but after that we got busy, and I left it in Derek's truck overnight. The truck that he took to the Appalachian Trail this morning."

I got down on my stomach and elbows and slithered back through the cabinet, under the lowest shelf, into the kitchen, leaving the secret room open behind me.

"More liquor," Irina explained when I came out, brushing dust and maybe even some cobwebs off my hair. Brrr.

"Jeb Perkins was a rumrunner," Gert said, peering at a bottle he'd lifted from the crate and held up to the light. "He owned this house in the early part of the century. In fact, all of Rowanberry Island was involved. Everyone benefited from the smuggling Jeb did, so everyone kept their mouths shut and helped out. Were there bottles in your secret room, too?" He glanced over at me.

I shook my head. "Just an old mattress and some blankets. And a piece of paper with Cyrillic writing on it."

"What did it say?" Irina wanted to know.

I glanced at her. "Your sister's name. And two others. Katya and Olga. I can't remember their last names."

"They were there."

I nodded. "Must have been. A couple of weeks ago, anyway. The names were written on a page from the Boothbay Harbor newspaper, and it had a date on it. Late March. But we started work on the house on April first, and the girls must have been moved somewhere else. I thought they were here"—I looked around—"but obviously they're not."

Gert and Irina both shook their heads. I looked closely at Gert—I still didn't quite trust him the way Irina seemed to; unless Irina just seemed to and they were both playing me—but if he was lying, I couldn't tell.

"Why would you suspect me?" he asked, plaintively.

"Other than the fact that you were extremely standoffish when I first met you? And that the house was tightly shuttered? And you had a boat with a cabin below deck, perfect for transporting illegal cargo? And that it was the night after I was here that that poor girl drowned?"

"Ah," Gert said, following my reasoning with no problem, "you thought she'd heard you outside and realized someone was nearby, and she tried to find you?"

I nodded. Trust the thriller writer to figure out that sequence of events without being told. Unless the dead girl really had been here, and that's how he knew exactly what had happened. . . .

My head was starting to spin from the various permutations of possibilities. Could I trust this guy? Was he telling the truth? Was Irina? Had he duped her, too, or was she in on it with him? Or was he truly just trying to figure things out, too?

I've always been a pretty trusting type of person. Naive, if you prefer. I tend to see everyone the way they present themselves to me, and I'm not particularly good at looking past the obvious and suspecting nice people of doing bad things. That's the biggest reason why, until I met Derek, my love life was one long line of disappointments as the nice guys I thought I knew turned out not to be nice at all. The cheating bastards.

Anyway, I'm not good at being suspicious. I take things at face value and proceed accordingly. Much as I wanted to, I had a hard time putting aside the fact that I'd always liked Irina—and the fact that Irina seemed to like Gert—and go on the assumption that they were both trying to fool me.

"Did you go anywhere else that day?" Gert asked, obviously following his train of thought to its logical conclusion. If the girl had seen or heard me that day—and that was by no means a sure thing; it might have been a coincidence, pure and simple—but if she had, and it hadn't been here at Gert's house, then she must have seen me somewhere else.

I shook my head. "Just here and back. Derek and I came out in the boat that morning, I didn't take the ferry, so all I did was walk from our house to yours and then back again." I paused, remembering. "Except . . ."

"Yes?"

"I took a wrong turn on the way back and ended up in front of a little saltbox house. I think it used to belong to John van Duren. You know, the original van Duren house. Where Daisy and Clara grew up."

"I know what you're talking about." Gert nodded. "A little overgrown saltbox about halfway between our two houses. Lon Wilson owns it, but he's usually away in the winter."

"So . . . if someone used our house while it was empty, you think it's possible that they might have used Mr. Wilson's house while he's been away, too?"

"You suspected them of using my house while I was away," Gert pointed out, "so yes."

"I suspected *you* of using your house while you were away. It's not exactly the same thing."

Irina was looking from one to the other of us, impatiently. "Who cares who thought what about whom? Where is this place? I want to see it."

"They're probably not there anymore," Gert warned even as he walked toward the door to the dining room. Irina followed and I brought up the rear, brushing ineffectually at my pants. Between the mud earlier and the dust now, I looked like I was growing mold.

"I'm sure as soon as that poor girl died," Gert added, "they would have moved the other women out. Maybe even off island."

"I still want to see it," Irina said stubbornly.

"Of course." Gert held the front door open for her. I scuttled through, too, and we headed around the house, aiming for the path I knew was there, even if I couldn't see it in the fog.

By now, the pea soup was thick enough that unless we stayed together, we'd lose one another in a matter of seconds. Irina and I held hands as we stumbled through the woods, and the flashlight I still carried from earlier did nothing except illuminate Gert's back five feet ahead of us as he led the way down the path. Trees and branches came and went nearby; once in a while one of them would materialize out of the fog fast enough to make me jump, my heart accelerating nervously.

Irina was jumpy, too. Her palm was sweaty, and whenever something unexpected would loom out of the fog—like a big branch close to the path—she'd catch her breath fast and tighten her grip on my hand.

"Where do you think Svetlana is right now?" I asked after a few minutes of stumbling along in Gert's wake.

Irina glanced at me over her shoulder. "If I knew that, don't you think I'd be there?"

"I didn't mean specifically. Although . . . was there something about the place where you were, for those couple of weeks before you were taken to Skowhegan, that you can remember? Anything at all?"

"It was a basement," Irina said. "Stone walls. No windows. Lightbulb in the ceiling. A bed, a toilet, and stairs going up to a door in the floor upstairs. It was locked, except when someone came with food or to . . . um . . ."

"I get it. So you couldn't see much."

She shook her head.

"What about sounds? Could you hear anything?"

"Footsteps," Irina said. "Upstairs. Sometimes voices."

"Could you hear what they were saying?"

She shook her head.

"And what happened when you were . . . um . . . moved? To Skowhegan?" Surely down east Maine didn't have some sort of underground slave market? A human trafficking ring was bad—and surprising—enough.

"Something in my food," Irina said. "When I woke up I was in Mr. Eagan's house."

The same sort of tranquilizer the girl in the water had been given, maybe.

"That's too bad." That Irina hadn't seen anything to pinpoint where she was held, I meant. But it was certainly understandable. If these people had sold her to some abusive lecher wanting a house slave, they'd want to make damn sure she wouldn't know where to find them later. Just in case she got to a point in her life—like now—when she was no longer afraid to tell people what had happened to her.

"You said you recognized someone's voice," I added after a moment. "At Shaw's Supermarket."

Irina nodded. "I have no idea who the man was, though. When I turned around, Mr. Heyerdahl was there, and I thought it was him. Now I don't know who spoke."

Figures.

"What happened when you got here on Friday? To Gert's house? You didn't say." And although I wanted to yell at her for being so stupid—to follow a man she thought was a human trafficker to the place where he lived—I held back.

"I told you," Irina said, a little defensively, "I wanted to help Agent Trent. And if Svetlana was here, I wanted to find her."

"But you never saw either of them. Right? And instead you ran into Gert."

Irina nodded. “I took the ferry out and came to the house straightaway. I didn’t see anyone. Not until I was looking through the windows—the tall ones next to the door . . .”

“The sidelights. Right.”

“And Gert . . . Mr. Heyerdahl came out and saw me.” She blushed. “As soon as I heard him speak, I knew he wasn’t the man I had heard three years ago.”

That made sense, up to a point. At least it explained why Irina hadn’t been afraid of him. “What did Gert think when you showed up on his doorstep?”

“I realized she might be part of what I was investigating,” Gert said over his shoulder. “I recognized the Ukrainian accent. We got to talking, and she told me the whole story. I stumbled over what I thought might be smuggling last year, when I was doing research for the next Mischa Nemov thriller.”

“Your book?”

Gert nodded. “I spoke to a few of the locals last summer about Rowanberry’s history and smuggling up and down the coast and got the idea that something might still be going on. I had no idea it was human trafficking, though. I figured it was drugs.”

“Any locals in particular?” It might be helpful to pinpoint who Gert had spoken to, who had given him the idea.

But Gert shook his head. “The ferry crew, the guy at the general store, a few of the people in the village when I’d run into them . . . It wasn’t anything specific, or even definite, just a general sense of secrecy, of people sticking together against the outsider.”

I nodded. Made sense.

We reached the little saltbox house a minute or two later, stopping to catch our breath just at the end of the path. The house itself looked eerie, like something out of

Sleeping Beauty, all shuttered as if sleeping, overgrown and wreathed around with fog. That mournful sound of a foghorn came again, and I shivered.

"I didn't even know this was here," Irina said.

"I'm not surprised. Apparently it's been in the same family—Lon Wilson's—since time immemorial, so it's never been on the market, and it isn't like it's marked or anything. Or even visible from the water, all overgrown like this. Mr. Wilson must like his privacy."

"I don't think Mr. Wilson has been here for a couple years," Gert said over his shoulder. "At least I haven't seen him. He retired to Sarasota. Came up in the summers for a while, and then stopped."

"Do you know him?"

He looked at me. "Well enough to know that he wouldn't be a part of something like this. If someone's been using his house, it was without his knowledge."

"So you were here the same day you were at Mr. Heyerdahl's house?" Irina asked.

I nodded, wondering why she called him Mr. Heyerdahl and not plain Gert. True, he hadn't told me to call him Gert, so maybe she was just too polite to use his first name without being told.

"Can we get inside?"

"Lonnie keeps a key around," Gert said. "Once in a while he'll call and ask me to go check that everything's all right. It's right here." He reached up and fumbled along the top of the pediment above the door. After a second, he came away with a key. A big one, skeleton type. That was all that was on the door, a big, old-fashioned lock. No Yale locks, nothing newer than 1950.

"Not very concerned with security, is he?"

Gert glanced at me as he fitted the key into the lock.

"There's nothing here worth stealing. Lonnie would come out here to get away from civilization, to rough it, and only when the weather was good. There's no electricity here, there's only cold water—anything warm would have to be heated in the fireplace—and there's no TV, no cable, no telephone, nothing at all to remind him of the real world."

"Lord," I said. Last summer I'd been feeling like living in Aunt Inga's house without a shower for a month was roughing it.

Gert nodded. "Maybe not so strange that he's not making the trip up here anymore, after all." He pushed the door open. It creaked, of course.

Irina and I looked at each other. One of us would have to go first; Gert was holding the door open and obviously waiting. Irina looked apprehensive, so I took the first step across the threshold.

"Lord!" I said again as I looked around. I'd thought our house was basic; this was barely more than a shack.

All right, so it had floors. Not all houses of that vintage did, or so Derek had taken great pains to tell me. Some were built straight on the ground with rushes or sand covering the dirt. This place at least had rough planks. But beyond that, it was dismal. The walls were leaning, the ceilings were low—Gert, though not overly tall, had to duck his head to avoid braining himself on the cross beams—and the windows were minuscule. Everything was dark, with all the shutters closed, and of course there were no lights, as Gert had already warned us. I turned on the flashlight and shone it around.

No, I didn't blame Lonnie Wilson at all for preferring to stay in warm and civilized Sarasota. Not if this was what he had to look forward to on Rowanberry Island. And it was equally obvious why he didn't bother installing better locks or a security system. Nobody in their right mind would try to steal any of this stuff.

The furniture was mismatched, thrift-store pieces mixed with what were probably Lon's own furniture from childhood. Most of it looked to be at least fifty years old and not in good shape. The kitchen, in the lean-to part of the house, looked worse than Aunt Inga's had when I first inherited my house. I'd told Derek at the time that my aunt's kitchen cabinets looked like they were made from driftwood she'd picked up on the beach. I'd been exaggerating, of course: They were fifty-year-old cabinets, crooked and worn, but they weren't that bad. These were. They really did look like they were made from driftwood, weathered and unpainted, open shelves with no doors and a half-circular sink on the wall where all the water came out rusty. And cold. The kitchen counter was Formica, the original, with a stainless-steel edge, and there was no stove, no fridge, no microwave or dishwasher, or any of the other things we've pretty much come to take for granted in our day and age. It was like being back in the Stone Age.

There were two rooms on the first floor, plus the lean-to with the kitchen, and two more upstairs. Tiny rooms under the eaves, each with barely enough room for a twin bed and a chest of drawers. The drawers were empty, and the beds inexpertly made, with blankets tossed over the mattress and no apple pie corners in sight. The sheets smelled musty. Someone had been here recently, though: The dust on the floor was scuffed, even though it was impossible to make out individual footprints.

"Help me to look around," Irina said. "In case there's something here."

"Something . . . ?"

"I don't know. Just something." She started looking.

I shrugged and did the same, although I had no idea

what I was looking for. Or if I'd be able to recognize it if I saw it.

We spent the next two hours meticulously going through the house, checking the pockets of every pair of pants in the drawers and every coat and jacket in the closets. We stripped all the beds and turned all the mattresses over. We opened every door to every cabinet in the kitchen and bathroom. We checked the inside of coffee canisters and medicine bottles, as well as inside the toilet tank. Gert, who had given some thought to weird places to hide things, given his profession, helped out by knocking on walls and stepping on loose floorboards.

In the end, we found . . . nothing. Nothing at all to indicate that Svetlana, along with Katya and Olga, had ever been here.

"Maybe it was just a coincidence," I offered. "The fact that the girl chose that particular night to try to get away. Maybe it wasn't because she saw me or heard my voice."

Because if she hadn't been here, and she hadn't been at Gert's house, then I had no idea where she's been.

"Or maybe they were here, but whoever removed them just did a fine job of making sure there were no clues," Gert added.

I nodded. That was possible, too. There *had* been that sharp bang the day Derek and I had been here, as if someone was trying to get our attention. "So what do we do now?"

Irina looked exhausted. "I don't know," she admitted. "I hoped we would find something here. Maybe even Svetlana."

"Maybe we should check the village," Gert said.

I nodded. Irina had said she'd been held in a basement. If she'd been on Rowanberry Island, the village was the only place where such a thing might exist. Not down here on the south end. "Why don't we take a walk in that direction? I'm gonna have to go there anyway to catch the ferry. The two of you can walk me there, and maybe you"—I looked at Irina—"will notice something familiar."

Irina looked game, if not exactly hopeful.

—20—

Walking across the island in thick fog was a trip, and I mean that in every way. We couldn't see more than a few feet in front of us, and if the person on point—Gert—didn't keep his eyes on the ground, we'd wander off the path in no time. Once or twice we ended up staring at a tree that had suddenly materialized directly in front of us. And then we had to backtrack, to figure out where we'd gone wrong and try to pick up the path again and hope we were going in the right direction. A walk that would normally have taken twenty minutes took close to an hour. We didn't meet a soul along the way; although then again, someone could have passed us just a few feet away on either side, and we wouldn't have known it. Not only couldn't we see, but it was even difficult to hear with the fog, since everything sounded sort of hollow and it was hard to determine where any sound originated.

Eventually, we made it through the woods, across the meadow, and into the village, where things were even more freaky. The fog lay so close to the ground I felt I almost had to kick it out of my way when I walked. And poor Irina, who desperately wanted to look around to see if there was anything here she recognized, couldn't see a blessed thing. Houses rose up on both sides of the cobblestoned street, but we could barely see them as we stumbled along.

"The ferry's probably stopped running," Gert muttered.

I turned to him. "Excuse me?" Surely he hadn't said what I thought he'd said?

He glanced at me. "The fog's too thick. Most likely they've canceled departures until the fog lifts."

I looked around. "How long will that be?" This soupy mess certainly looked like it had settled in to stay.

He shrugged. "Could be later tonight or could be tomorrow. You're welcome to spend the night with us. Me." He glanced at Irina and then away, quickly.

I glanced at Irina, too. Was something going on between them? I hadn't picked up on anything like that, not in her behavior, but it sure sounded like . . . I mean, "us"? And look, she was blushing.

"Thanks," I said, "but . . ."

No thanks. And not only because I didn't want to interrupt anything, but because I still wasn't a hundred percent sure I trusted them. Either of them. Together or separately. I wasn't worried right now, awake and upright, in the middle of the day and with people around—even if I couldn't see any of them, they'd hear me if I screamed, or if, God forbid, Gert shot me—but if I went to sleep in Gert's house, I might never wake up, and that'd be sort of bad. Derek didn't even know where I was, and I had no way of calling him, with the cell phone signal missing out here in the middle of the ocean.

"There's a lady here somewhere who has rooms for

rent," I added, looking around at the fog. "I've seen the sign before. It was here somewhere. . . ."

"Who'd run a guest house on an island like this one?" Gert asked. "Monhegan is one thing—they get a lot of tourists—but whoever comes to Rowanberry? There's nothing here."

"*You're* here. Don't people follow you around? You're famous, aren't you?"

Gert looked at me like I'd lost my mind.

"You did say you had a stalker," I pointed out.

"In Florida. Not here. That's what I like about Maine. Nobody knows me, and nobody cares. And other than the occasional nutjob, readers don't tend to go on pilgrimages to their favorite authors' homes, anyway. We're not rock stars, you know."

I nodded. So Gert wasn't a big enough draw to bring tourists to Rowanberry Island. And there was nothing else here that would interest anyone. No museum or important historic building, no ancient battlefields, no bird sanctuary, no artist colony . . . What *did* bring people out here? In enough numbers to support a guest house?

"Maybe the owner keeps the sign out in case someone happens to come by needing a room," Irina suggested. "Like, if the ferry stops running and they can't get back to the mainland until the next day."

Maybe. "I saw it in the window last week. It was gone yesterday, though."

"So maybe someone rented the room. Or maybe family came in to visit or something. For the holiday."

I blinked. "Holiday?"

Irina nodded. "Sure. It's Palm Sunday. The beginning of Easter."

"Oh." I bit my lip. I should have known that. "Speaking of Easter, that Ukrainian Easter egg of yours . . . where is it?"

It was Irina's turn to blink. "The paperweight? Isn't it on the coffee table? I didn't take it anywhere."

"Maybe it is." Probably just my imagination gone haywire. It does that sometimes. "Back when I thought you'd killed Agent Trent, it was the murder weapon."

Irina looked at me.

"Sorry," I added. "It made sense at the time."

She nodded. "I liked her. She said she'd find Svetlana and make sure that the people who have her go to jail for a long time. I didn't want her dead."

"I'm sure you didn't. You know, that's something that maybe we should talk about."

"What?"

"Agent Trent. You said you told her everything, right? About coming here three years ago and everything that happened to you? And you told her to go to Rowanberry Island. Because you thought you recognized Gert's voice that day in Shaw's Supermarket?"

Irina nodded. "Except it wasn't Mr. . . . Gert's voice. It was someone else's."

"Right. But you thought it was Gert's, so you sent Agent Trent out here to talk to him. Except she never arrived."

I looked at Gert for confirmation. He shook his head.

"So somewhere between Irina's office in Portland and Gert's house on Rowanberry Island, Agent Trent was killed."

"It happened in the harbor, don't you think? Wasn't that where you found her?" Gert looked at me.

I nodded. "We did find her there. But not until yesterday morning. And it was Friday afternoon when she left Irina's office. It was still daylight. I don't think she could have been floating in the Waterfield harbor that whole time without someone noticing her. Do you?"

Gert admitted that I had a point. "So what do you think happened?"

It was Irina who answered. "Maybe she got on the ferry to go to Rowanberry Island. And when she got here, she asked someone for directions to Mr. . . . Gert's house, and that person killed her."

I nodded. "Or maybe she never even made it this far. Maybe someone on the ferry realized who she was and killed her."

Like cute little Ned Schachenger. Maybe he was working as a ticket taker on the ferry because he helped smuggle Russian women into the country every winter and it let him keep up with anything that went on around the islands, including anyone coming and going. Like ICE agent Lori Trent. Ned could have met her on the ferry; he looked so sweet and innocent that she wouldn't have thought twice about asking him questions about the Russian women. *I* had asked him questions about the Russian women. Of course, he hadn't killed *me*. Then again, I wasn't an agent with Immigration and Customs Enforcement.

So maybe Lori Trent had buttonholed Ned on the ferry, and maybe Ned had gotten spooked. Maybe he had admitted something he shouldn't have, and maybe he had realized it and had whacked Agent Trent over the head with something—surely there were plenty of smooth, round objects on board the ferry that he could have used—and then he had stashed the body somewhere and waited until the ferry got back to Waterfield late Friday night, before he heaved the body over the railing and into the water. He wouldn't necessarily realize that Waterfield wasn't where she belonged. Or maybe it even happened on Saturday morning; Agent Trent's body could have been kept on the ferry, docked in Boothbay Harbor, all night, until the first run the next day. Where Waterfield was the first stop.

I turned to Irina. "Who was the conductor on the ferry when you came over on Friday night?"

She blinked. "No idea. I wasn't paying attention."

"Young kid? Blond hair? Sweet smile?"

"I really couldn't say. Sorry, Avery."

"No problem." It didn't really prove anything either way. But if I was right—and it did all hang together, including the fact that Ned had been at Shaw's Supermarket the night Irina and I had seen Gert there—then maybe the thick fog was a good thing, because it kept the ferry away and Ned off Rowanberry Island tonight. He probably had an accomplice, but with Ned gone, at least we wouldn't have to worry about both of them.

"Maybe she asked for directions at the store," Gert suggested. "If I came here for the first time, that's where I'd start."

I nodded. "Me, too. Derek and I were in there yesterday, though, to buy cat food for the kitten, and the owner said he hadn't seen a visitor since August. I guess you"—I turned to Irina—"haven't stopped in?"

She shook her head. "Should I have?"

"Not necessarily. It isn't very nice. Dust all over everything except the floor, and canned goods that looked like they'd been sitting in the same spot on the shelves for a year, at least. I made sure Derek checked the expiration dates on everything we bought. Although . . ." I trailed off.

"What?" Gert said.

"Nothing. Just . . . he said he hadn't seen anyone new since last summer, but someone must have bought a snow globe recently. You know, one of those touristy things with a scene inside that says 'Memories of Maine' or 'Greetings from Rowanberry Island' on the base? When you shake it, fake glittery snow falls on everything."

They both nodded.

"There was a thick layer of dust all over everything,

and I could see where there had been a snow globe until recently. There was a hole in the dust, you know, next to the others? So if there haven't been any tourists around for six months at least, who'd have bought a souvenir snow globe? Surely none of the locals."

Gert and Irina looked at one another. "Maybe it fell?" Irina suggested. "And broke? When he was . . ." She broke off.

"What?"

"I was going to say when he dusted, but he didn't dust, if you could still see where the snow globe had been sitting."

I shook my head. "Other than the floor, no one's cleaned that place for months. Someone could have picked it up and dropped it, though. And then he had to mop. It would explain the clean floor, when everything else was so dusty. And"—I thought back—"that actually makes a lot of sense, because the floor wasn't just clean, it sparkled. Like there were tiny specks of something on it, between the floorboards maybe. Like the sparkly silver snow inside the globe."

"It couldn't be very well made," Gert opined, "if accidentally dropping it would make it break open."

"They're souvenirs. You know, made in China. So no, probably not. Although I picked one up, and it was actually a lot heavier than I thought it would be. Not as heavy as Irina's Easter egg, but not a lot lighter, either. The glass must be really thick. And they're big, too."

"As big as the Easter egg?" Irina wanted to know.

I thought back. "A little bigger, actually. With a heavy base. Maybe it's something the guy makes himself—or someone on the island does—because I haven't seen anything like it anywhere else. We can go take a look if you want. If the store's open. There were several others still left on the shelf."

"No," Irina said, "I don't think I want to do that."

"Why not?" Gert and I both turned to look at her.

"Because"—she hesitated—"well, what if Agent Trent did make it all the way to Rowanberry Island, and she did stop at the store to ask directions . . ."

"And she picked up a snow globe and accidentally dropped it?"

Irina shook her head. "And the snow globe didn't fall, but someone used it to hit her on the back of the head?"

Gert blinked. So did I. It was one of those *ding-ding-ding* lightbulb moments when you realize that—duh!—maybe you've been looking at things wrong.

I found my voice. "That's . . . interesting."

"It would explain a number of things," Gert said. He looked at Irina. "You know, Hal was in Shaw's Supermarket that night when you thought you recognized my voice. I saw him and ducked out of the way so he wouldn't see me, since I go into the general store all the time in the summer, and I didn't want him to recognize me and realize I was still around."

And that was also interesting.

"He was one of the people you said you spoke to last summer about the smuggling, right?"

Gert nodded, and I could see the same dawning realization in his eyes that I figured was in my own.

"Maybe we need to see if Irina recognizes *his* voice," I suggested. "I know that you two both have good reasons for why you don't want him to see you, but maybe I could just open the door and stick my head in, you know, and just ask sort of offhandedly if he knows whether the ferry is still running. If I keep the door open, maybe you'd be able to hear his answer."

Gert and Irina exchanged a look. "Fine with me," Gert said. Irina nodded.

"Just be sure to stay back far enough that he won't see you. Or lurk over to the side, or something."

They both nodded.

"I think it should be a little farther down this way." I started making my way carefully down the cobblestoned street.

The lights were on inside the store now, making it easier to find in the fog. Irina and Gert faded to one side, while I tried the knob. It didn't budge. But the light was on, so although the sign in the window was still turned to Closed, I knocked. If I'd truly wanted to ask whether the ferry was still running, that's what I'd do.

The first couple of knocks didn't produce any result, so I knocked again, harder. After a moment, the store owner's face appeared behind the counter, popping up like a jack-in-the-box. What the heck had he been doing back there; taking a nap on the floor?

I put an ingratiating smile on my face and waved. He glanced over his shoulder before he came out from behind the counter and started walking toward me. Slowly, like he hoped that if he took too long, I might give up and disappear.

Fat chance. I waited, that same big-eyed, apologetic grin on my face, until he'd woven his way between the shelves and over to the door and had unlocked it. He pulled it open just far enough to speak to me through the crack.

"Yes?"

"I'm sorry to bother you," I said. "Remember me? My boyfriend and I stopped by yesterday to pick up some cat food? We're renovating the old Colonial on the other side of the island?"

He nodded. So much for trying to get a few words out of him for Irina to hear.

"I came out this morning, you know, to make sure the kitten was OK. And then the fog came in, and now I've been waiting for the ferry for a while, but it's not coming, and I was wondering, you know, how long it's gonna be before I can get off the island and back to the mainland."

He looked at me in silence as the seconds ticked by. I started to worry that he wouldn't answer when he finally opened his mouth. "Ferry gets canceled when the fog's this bad. Won't run till morning."

"Seriously?" I made a face, trying to make it look like I hadn't already heard this information.

He nodded.

"What am I supposed to do?"

He shrugged. "Can't do nothing but wait."

"Do you have a phone that can reach the mainland? Or a computer?"

He shook his head.

"Does anyone else? How about that lady who has the rooms for rent? Mrs. Harris? I met her yesterday. D'you think she might rent me a room for the night? I'm not sure I want to spend the night sleeping on the floor back at the house."

"Glenda's off the island for the day," Hal said. "Went to church on the mainland this morning and can't get back with the ferry not running. Only Calvin's home."

The implication was that I wouldn't want to ask Calvin to rent me a room and risk being stuck in an empty house with him overnight. Which was absolutely correct. I had a sort of *a-ha* moment when I realized that that's why the name Harris had sounded familiar; it was Calvin's name, as well. Glenda must be Calvin's mother.

"Can I at least buy something to eat from you? If I'm going to be stuck here overnight?"

He hesitated. "Whatcha want?"

"How about a jar of peanut butter and a loaf of bread and maybe a bottle of Diet Coke? Oh, and a candy bar."

I expected him to open the door for me, but instead he told me to wait. And locked the door while he gathered the things I'd asked for. While I waited, I made sure not to look to my left, where Irina and Gert were skulking.

"Ten bucks." He handed me the brown bag. I dug in my wallet and produced a ten. The price was outrageous, but this wasn't the time to haggle. "Thank you. Guess I'll just head on back to the house now. If you're sure about the ferry?"

He nodded. I turned on my heel and walked away. And kept walking, even after I heard the door close and the lock catch. And then I kept walking some more, just in case he had followed me to make sure I was actually going back to the house.

"Pssst!"

The summons came from the opposite side of the street. I walked closer and saw Gert gesturing to me from a narrow space between two houses. I could just barely make out Irina behind him.

"Well?"

She nodded. "It's definitely him."

"The same guy whose voice you heard in Shaw's Supermarket last week? The guy who brought you into the U.S. three years ago?" Just making sure . . .

Irina nodded again. "It's him."

"So do you think your sister is there somewhere?" Gert looked at her. "In the store? Above, perhaps?"

"More like below," I said, realizing for the first time what I'd seen earlier. "Listen to this. When I first knocked on the door, I couldn't see the guy anywhere. So I knocked a few more times, and suddenly he pops up behind the counter. Like he was crouched down or something, you know? And I guess he could have been, except what if there's a door or something back there, in the floor, that goes down to that room you mentioned?"

"That's . . ." Irina stopped. Somewhere in the fog we could hear a sound. All three of us held our breaths as we faded farther into the narrow space we were occupying.

The sounds were footsteps. And it sounded like they were coming closer. In fact, it sounded like they were coming straight at us. Dammit, he must have followed me from the store. Far enough behind that I hadn't heard him.

Except we didn't see anyone. And then the steps stopped, and we heard a knock. A sort of special knock. First three short taps, then a pause, then two more.

After a moment, a door or window opened. A voice said something; I couldn't hear what, or who it belonged to. I did recognize the other voice, though. We'd just been discussing it.

"It's time."

The other voice said something more, maybe an objection or a query, because Hal the shop owner answered, "Even if someone was around, they couldn't see nothing. It's like the inside of a cloud out here."

The voice inside the house said something else, and then Hal spoke again. "Ten minutes. They're ready to go. I'll bring 'em up."

The door closed again, and the footsteps faded into the fog. We looked at each other.

"Them?" I whispered.

"Up?" Irina added.

Obviously we were all thinking the same thing. That "them" was the Russian women and "up" meant out of the storage room we'd just postulated existed under the floor of the store. Mr. Shopkeeper and his accomplice were planning to move the women under cover of the fog. Either to another location on Rowanberry Island or maybe somewhere else entirely. Maybe to someone like Irina's Mr. Eagan. And once that happened, we'd never be able to find them.

"We should probably follow him, don't you think?" I whispered.

Irina nodded.

"What about this guy?" Gert gestured with his thumb toward the house we were skulking beside, the one where the window had opened and the shopkeeper's accomplice had answered.

"Hal said ten minutes. If we hurry, maybe we can get back to the store and overpower him before his friend shows up."

Irina was already moving toward the corner of the house and the cobblestoned street.

Gert glanced over his shoulder. "Maybe I should stay here. . . ."

I shook my head. "You're the one with the gun. We need you. How else are we going to make him give us the girls?"

"What if this guy decides to show up early, though?" He indicated the accomplice in the house beside us.

"That's why we have to hurry," I said.

Gert demurred. "I'm not really sure about this. I mean, I've been having fun skulking around this winter, playing superspy, but I'm not really very brave, you know. I'm a writer. All my daring is on the page."

"At least you're daring somewhere. I'm quaking in my boots right now. But Irina needs us. If we don't go after her, she's going to take on the guy on her own. And then he'll have three of them. Now stop arguing and go." I gave him a push.

He went. We scurried off down the street, back in the

direction of the general store. The lights had been turned off by now, so it was harder to find in the thick fog, but we did make it to where Irina was hugging the wall.

"What now?" Gert whispered. "Doesn't look like he's coming out. What do you want to bet he's waiting for his buddy to show up first?"

Damn. That was a scenario I hadn't considered, and probably should have.

"I know!" Irina said. "We'll knock on the door. The same way he did. Three knocks, then two more. The signal. Maybe that's what he's waiting for."

Gert and I looked at each other. Made sense.

"I'll go," Gert volunteered.

"I'd be happy to . . ."

He shook his head. "It has to be me. I know he won't be able to see much with the fog and no lights, but he'll see my outline, and no offense, but you look nothing like a man."

No arguing with that. Plus, the guy had just looked at me less than fifteen minutes ago. There was no way he wouldn't recognize my outline and realize I was back.

"I think it should be me," Irina said. "She's my sister."

We both ignored her, since she was the absolutely last choice of who should go.

"So what if this guy recognizes me?" I argued. "As long as he opens the door?"

"I'm not giving you my gun. And I'm not letting you go over there without one!"

"I don't want your gun. And you let me go over there without one earlier."

"That was before we knew for sure that he's a trafficker and a criminal," Gert said.

I opened my mouth, but then closed it and looked around instead. "Where's Irina?"

"What?" Gert looked around, too. Not that we really had to ask; even as we were standing there craning our necks, we could hear the knocks on the general store door. Three, then two.

"Damn!" Gert breathed. He started forward. I followed, just as the door opened.

"What . . . ?" Hal began, before Irina launched herself forward into the store, plowing right over him, voice raised. "Svetlana!"

"Hell." Gert fumbled for the gun as he picked up speed. I ran after him.

Hal was only taken aback for a few seconds; as soon as we made it to the door, he had gotten his hands on a gun of his own and was aiming it at Irina, who was tearing into the store, between two aisles of dried goods. I guess maybe the owner was loath to risk shooting any of his merchandise, or maybe he was worried that she'd bleed on his stuff, because he didn't pull the trigger. Or maybe he simply figured that since she'd stupidly walked into his lair, he'd just close and lock the door behind her and then deal with subduing her. I'm sure that's what he intended to do when he turned toward the front door. Where he came face-to-face with us.

Or rather with Gert, who had managed to get his own gun out of his pocket and was pointing it straight at the bad guy.

"Put the gun down, please."

"Mr. Heyerdahl." Of course Hal didn't. "She pushed her way in here, did you see that? Just knocked on the door and pushed me aside. I should call the police."

"Yes, why don't you do that?" I said, and appeared next to Gert. "In fact, I'll do it. Just show me phone."

Hal's eyes flickered to me for a second, and then back to Gert's gun. Couldn't blame him for that. Meanwhile, somewhere inside the store, Irina seemed to have found her sister. We heard squeals and what was either sobbing or laughter. Maybe both.

Hal glanced over his shoulder. Glanced back at Gert's gun, and then took off. Back into the store toward where the commotion was. He tried to slam the door shut in our faces, but of course it didn't work. The door coming at us served to slow us down for a vital few seconds, though, as we both took an instinctive step back.

I don't know what Hal thought he was gonna do, but it was obvious what Gert thought: that Hal would shoot Svetlana and her friend, and Irina as well, before letting them get away. The author burst through the door with a roar, gun at the ready, and tore down the aisle in hot pursuit.

I scurried after, not quite believing that I was running toward a man with a gun. I'd been lucky four months ago—Melissa had gotten shot and I hadn't—but there were two guns at play here, in the hands of two men who were both probably pretty desperate—one to avoid going to jail for a long time, the other to prevent the slaughter of a woman I was beginning to think he'd rather come to like a lot—and so the chances for getting caught in the crossfire were doubled. And yet there I was, hurrying behind Gert.

Hal must have been in the process of moving the girls out of the storage room when Irina knocked, because we found them all just in front of the counter. The girls were dressed to travel, in jeans and jackets, their eyes dilated almost black. Some kind of date-rape drug, maybe; something to make them docile and cooperative. It wouldn't do to have them belligerent and wanting to get away while they were transported, maybe even by boat, somewhere else. And they were handcuffed together, probably so that one of them couldn't try to escape without the other. It would be impossible for them to swim, and they'd have to, to get off the island. Svetlana, at least, understood some of what was going on and had recognized her sister. Although her face was totally impassive, there were tears leaking from her eyes, running down her cheeks, and she was clinging to Irina, who clung right back. The two of them really did look very much alike, in spite of the ten-year age difference. Both tall and angular, with long dark hair, broad Slavic faces, and high cheekbones. The other young woman, attached to Svetlana's other side, was shorter, with light, mousy brown hair and the biggest breasts I'd ever seen. At least in real life. No mystery why the bad guys had chosen her from among the available Russian brides.

Gert rocked to a stop at the end of the nearest aisle. I skidded into place next to him.

"Drop the gun," Hal snarled. He had reached Irina's other side and was holding her by the upper arm and pointing his gun at the side of her head. "Drop it, or I'll blow her away right now!"

Gert hesitated. He had a clear shot, there was nothing to stop him from pumping a bullet straight into Hal's heart, assuming his aim was good enough. . . . The problem was that Hal's finger might tighten on the trigger if he got hit, and although Hal would be dead, Irina would be, too. And that would be bad.

I glanced to my right, at the line of snow globes on the shelf. If the criminals had used one to kill ICE agent Trent, maybe I could use one to bash Hal over the head. I'd have to get closer, though. I took a step back to see if maybe I could sneak out of sight and come back around the other way, but his eyes flickered to me. "Don't move!"

I stopped. "So what happens now? We stand here and wait for your buddy to arrive?"

He blinked.

"I mean, unless you're planning to shoot all of us, it's not like you're gonna get away with this."

"Don't give him any ideas, Avery," Gert said, eyes and hands steady.

"I wasn't. I was just saying how, if all three of us turn up dead, someone's gonna notice. It's not like Wayne and Derek won't put it together. They know about the trafficking."

Gert nodded. And then we stood in silence while a few more seconds ticked by. Any moment now, Hal's accomplice would arrive. Through the door we'd considerately left unlocked when we burst through earlier. And we'd be sunk.

The others must be thinking the same thing, because I saw something move in Irina's eyes. There was no time to interfere, and to be honest, I'm not sure I would have even if I'd realized what she planned to do. Something had to happen, someone had to do something, and Irina had obviously decided it was up to her. I guess maybe she thought if she had to sacrifice herself for her sister, then that would be all right.

At any rate, she looked at Gert for a second, whether to try to communicate something or maybe just to take one last look before going to her death, I'm not sure. And then she threw herself sideways, away from the man with the gun, starting a domino effect as she knocked over first Svetlana, and then Svetlana's friend. They landed in a heap on the floor. Hal's finger did tighten on the trigger of the gun, but the bullet flew over their heads and hit a dusty can of chicken broth on a shelf against the opposite wall. The can started pouring broth through a perfectly round hole in the side. Meanwhile, Gert hurled himself forward and slammed into the bad guy, knocking him to the floor.

"Run!" he yelled.

I didn't need to be told twice. I started forward, giving the two men a wide berth, and grabbed Irina. She's a half foot taller than me, but somehow I managed to haul her to her feet. It must be true about fear giving people supernatural strength. Between us, we managed to sort out Svetlana and her friend and get them both upright, and then we all tumbled toward the front of the store.

"Gert . . ." Irina protested as I pushed her.

"He's fine. Go."

Of course, he wasn't fine. He was rolling around on the floor while Hal did his best to beat the crap out of him. Both of their guns had gone flying, and I thought for a second about running back and scooping one of them off the floor to take with us. It might come in handy as we tried to make our getaway. Then again, unless I was willing to use it—and I wasn't sure I could shoot someone in cold blood, even in self-defense—it would be time better spent running like hell. I ran like hell.

—21—

We were just a few yards up the cobblestoned street, not far from the general store at all, when a shot rang out.

Irina stopped dead, and the rest of us faltered, too. When she made to turn back, though, I grabbed her. "No."

"But Gert . . ."

"He said to run." I gave her a push.

"But . . ."

"He's probably right behind us. That was probably him shooting. Just keep moving. Get the girls away from here before the other guy shows up." I pushed her again, harder. She stumbled on.

"I'll catch up," I called after her and dashed back toward the store.

It's difficult to move stealthily and carefully when your heart's threatening to knock a hole in your chest and you expect bullets to come flying at you with every step you take. I managed, though. I slipped back into the store and crept toward the back, keeping close to the shelves of groceries the whole way.

Everything was quiet. Maybe a little too quiet, as they say in the movies. Some painful groaning might have been nice; at least that way I would have known that someone was alive. As it was, I got the shock of my life when I came upon Gert, lying facedown on the floor next to the counter in a widening pool of blood.

OK, so the fact that the pool was widening was probably a good thing. It meant he wasn't dead yet. And if I wanted to keep him that way, I had no time to waste. I bent and dug my heels in and managed to turn him over. At least if he was lying on his back, the blood might sink to the bottom and not spill out the front.

The damage looked pretty extensive—the whole front of his jacket was red—but I could see his chest move. And as far as I could make out, the bullet had hit him in the stomach, not the chest. That was probably good.

If I could have called Derek for advice, I would have, but we had dealt with a gunshot just a few months ago, and I'd seen him put pressure on the wound to keep the blood loss to a minimum. I looked around and spied a stack of souvenir towels on a shelf. They were as dusty as everything else in the store, but a little dust was probably the least of Gert's worries right now. Ripping open his jacket, I slapped the towels against the wound in his stomach and pushed down.

Gert groaned. His eyelids fluttered and then he opened his eyes. For a second, they looked glazed, like he couldn't remember who or where he was, or what had happened. Then he recognized me. "A'ry?"

"Yes, it's me."

"'Rina?"

"Running. With the other girls."

He lifted a limp hand. "Go."

"I will. I just want to help you first."

He shook his head. "No time. Go."

"Fine." I added the rest of the souvenir towels to the stack on Gert's stomach—the blood was already soaking through the first few—and zipped up his jacket again. "Keep pressure on this if you can. I'll get you some help as soon as I can."

There was hardly any power at all behind his voice anymore. "Go."

I went. Back out the door and up the cobblestoned street, dashing after Irina and the other Russian women. Before I left the little village behind, I thought I heard footsteps through the fog, heading toward the store. Not much time left, then.

I caught up to Irina and the others after a few minutes. They hadn't been able to move as fast as I was, and they didn't know the terrain as well, either. Svetlana and her friend were weak from malnutrition and from sitting around without getting any exercise for several weeks. Plus, they were handcuffed together and woozy from the drugs. Irina was wearing heavy hiking boots. Great for navigating tricky terrain, but not so good for running a race. Not to mention that she was reluctant to leave Gert and was sluggish as a result.

"Gert?" she asked when I caught up, her voice frantic.

"Shot. Stomach." I couldn't manage more than a syllable at a time. "He'll live." I hoped.

We made tracks the best we could away from the village, but between our various handicaps and the thick fog, we didn't move very fast. It didn't take long at all for the remaining bad guy to pick up our trail.

Although the fog turned out to be a blessing as well as

a curse. Yes, it slowed us down, we couldn't see where we were headed, and every so often one of us would stumble and even fall, and we'd all have to slow down enough for her—or them, in the case of Svetlana and her handcuffed friend—to get up. And we were about as stealthy as a herd of buffalo thundering through the countryside.

Thankfully we heard the footsteps before we saw anyone, and before he got close enough to see us. The Ukrainian girl whose name I didn't know had fallen and dragged Svetlana down with her, and Irina and I had come to a fidgety stop while we waited for the two of them to pull themselves back up so we could keep running. And that's when we heard someone behind us. Rapid footsteps, coming closer.

"Gert!" Irina said.

"Doubt it." He hadn't been in any condition to run when I left the store, and he'd be in worse condition now. That is, if he was still alive. The second bad guy might have decided to assure his getaway by putting another bullet in Gert before he left. Hopefully he'd been too preoccupied with tracking us to think of it, though. Either way, it wasn't something I felt I ought to mention. "Better not let him see us. Whoever he is."

Svetlana and her girlfriend stumbled in one direction while Irina and I scurried in the other. We flattened ourselves in the grass off to the side of the path, holding our breath and hoping against hope that our hearts weren't beating loud enough for him to hear. And this was where the fog became more of a blessing than a curse: Bad guy number two loped past, close enough that we could see him, like a dark shadow against the swirling yellow white mist, but not close enough for him to notice us.

We waited until he was gone, swallowed up by the fog and out of sight and hearing, and then we scrambled into a group again. All of us were soaked from lying in the grass, and my previous annoyance with my wet bottom seemed like it had happened a million years ago.

"What now?" Irina asked. She looked over her shoulder. "Go back?"

"To the village? No way."

"But what about Gert? We can't just leave him."

"He wanted us to get away," I said. I didn't want to leave him, either, especially after seeing the damage that bullet had done, but he'd told me to run. He had sacrificed himself to give us a chance to get away, and I intended to make full use of it.

"But there are boats in the village we could use to go to the mainland."

"There are people in the village, too. Bad people."

"What about the man in front of us?"

"We'll go slowly," I said. "That way we'll hear him if he comes back."

"Where are we going?" Svetlana asked, her accent similar but heavier than her sister's. She seemed to be waking up a little, while her well-endowed friend was still stumbling along in a daze. The busty one was shorter, so maybe the drugs had affected her more severely.

Irina and I looked at each other. "Off the island?" Irina said.

"Ideally." We couldn't go to Derek's and my house, because the bad guys knew who I was and would probably expect us to head there. We couldn't go to back Gert's, either, since they'd recognized him, too. Or at least the shopkeeper had recognized him. We couldn't call anyone for help, since there was no cell service. That left taking to the water and trying to make our way to the mainland. "Gotta find a boat."

"The village . . ." Irina tried again.

I shook my head. "We don't know how many people know about this whole trafficking thing. The whole village could be in on it and turning a blind eye. Just like they were doing during the prohibition. Gert has a boat. He brought it back earlier, right?"

Irina nodded. "Do you know how to drive it?"

"Not exactly. But I know how to drive a car."

"That is not the same thing," Svetlana said.

No kidding. However . . . "I'm sure we can figure it out. If it's between that and dying."

Nobody answered, so I figured we were on the same page. We started moving again, more slowly, breathing shallowly and listening for signs that our pursuer—who was in front of us at this point, so we were actually, technically, pursuing him—was on his way back toward us.

I figured he'd either caught a glimpse of us earlier, on our way out of the village, or his accomplice the store owner had been alive and lucid enough to tell him who we were. Either way, I thought he must know where we were headed. He was probably on his way to Derek's and my house to see whether we'd taken refuge there, or to Gert's house, to look for us there. When he didn't find us in either place, he'd either hang out and wait somewhere between the two, where he could intercept us when we got close enough, or he'd come back this way. I hoped he didn't hurt my kitten, and I hoped even more he wouldn't come up with the brilliant idea to torch both houses, just to prevent us from hiding inside them. On a clear day, I probably wouldn't have minded too much—I'd have been tempted to set up a signal flare myself, if it came to that, in hopes of attracting the coast guard—but on a day like today, nobody would see the smoke anyway, and if the house burned down, Derek would have a fit.

In the end, it took us longer to get back across the island

than it had taken Gert, Irina, and me to stumble to the village through the fog in the first place. And I thought *that* had taken a long time. What was especially ironic—and frustrating—was that while we were so desperate to get to the other side of the island and onto Gert's boat, we had to move at a snail's pace, with frequent detours into tall grass and between the trees to avoid being seen by our pursuer.

From time to time we'd think we heard him, and we'd split up and scurry to safety, flattening ourselves in the wet grass and holding our breath for long minutes while we waited for discovery, but there was never anyone there. He was still up ahead, and the closer we got to the south end of the island, the slower we moved.

Once we got near the path that connected our house with Gert's, I thought for sure we'd find him. Skulking somewhere, waiting for us. I mean, he couldn't know whether we'd try to hide out at our house or at Gert's, and it made sense that he'd station himself somewhere between the two to intercept us. I made sure we gave that stretch a wide berth, flitting from tree to tree in the foggy forest like a small band of Micmacs, two of whom were stuck together.

All in all, it was a harrowing experience. Not like facing down a man with a gun, knowing that he can pull the trigger at any moment and it's bye-bye Avery. That's a sharp, panicky sort of fear, quickly over with one way or the other. This was more like a nightmare, stumbling through a no-man's-land of fog and shadows for what seemed like years, never knowing when the axe would fall but always having to be looking for it. By the time we made it out of the woods into the clearing where Gert's house stood, I was almost wishing the guy would just show himself so I could stop anticipating.

But there was no sign of him. Not that we could see much, of course, but we left Svetlana and her friend standing by the back wall of the house, while Irina and I circled the house, going in opposite directions. If he was circling, too, he'd run into one of us sooner or later.

But he wasn't there. Neither of us came across anyone else until we met again at the front of the house. We tried the doorknob, of course, just to be safe, and the house was still locked up nice and tight.

"Are you sure we shouldn't just hunker down and wait until morning?" Irina murmured into my ear. "Or until the fog lifts?"

"Do you have a key?"

She shook her head. "We could break a window."

"I think we should try to get off the island. He's here somewhere—maybe down at Derek's and my house, waiting for us—and if we don't show up, sooner or later he'll get over this way. I'd hate to be squatting inside while he's pouring gasoline around the foundation."

Irina turned pale. Paler. "You don't think he'd do that, do you?"

"I hope not. But just in case he does, I'd rather not be inside."

Irina nodded. "I'll go around this way." She pointed in the direction she'd been headed, the way I'd come from. "I'll see you on the other side of the house."

I nodded and continued in the direction I'd been going.

Part of me had worried that by the time we got back to the two Russian women, the bad guy would have come out of the woodwork to join them, but he was nowhere to be seen, and Svetlana assured us they hadn't seen a sign of anyone. Her friend was starting to look a little more with it now, too. Enough for me to ask, "What's your name?"

"This is Olga," Svetlana said.

"So Katya was the one who died?"

Both women's eyes filled with tears. Obviously their

captors hadn't bothered to tell them about the drowning. I gave myself a hard mental kick. *Way to go, Avery.* Just what we needed, for the two of them to be distracted and weeping in addition to shackled together and drugged.

Irina was explaining the situation—at least I assumed she was—in rapid-fire Russian. Or maybe Ukrainian. That's assuming there's a difference. I waited for her to finish and then told her to tell them that if it hadn't been for Katya getting away and us finding her body, we wouldn't have known that the two of them were there on the island, and we wouldn't have come to rescue them. So although it was sad that Katya had died, she had been instrumental in helping them get away from the bad guys.

"And we're not away ourselves quite yet, so let's wait to talk about this until we're safe, OK?"

They nodded.

"Does either of you know how to drive a boat?"

They shook their heads.

"What about you?" I turned to Irina.

"Sorry."

"I don't, either, but I've watched Derek drive the motorboat a lot. It's small and has an outboard motor in the back, with a string that you pull to start it. And a steering wheel. Have you been on Gert's boat at all?"

She shook her head. "I've seen it, though. Sitting at the dock. There's no motor."

"I'm sure there's a motor somewhere. Just not hanging off the back. Down below, maybe. It's much bigger than ours. If there's a key and a steering wheel, I'm pretty sure I can figure it out."

I was less sure than I made out to be, but really, what was the alternative? Sitting on the island and waiting for rescue? When no one knew where we were and when they were all probably stuck on the Appalachian Trail?

I wondered if there was fog there, too. If so, they might have had to stop walking and hunker down to wait it out. They could be there until tomorrow. And really, how hard could navigating a boat be? If I could drive a car, surely I could drive a boat. The water was deep around here, I didn't have to worry about hitting any sandbars, and as long as I stayed clear of the islands, I ought to be able to get us back to Waterfield. The fog would make things more difficult, since I wouldn't actually be able to see where I was going, but it's amazing what one can accomplish when the alternative is certain death. As long as there was a key on the boat, things looked good. I wouldn't know how to hotwire it if there wasn't—is it even possible to hotwire a boat?—but we'd cross that bridge when we got to it. If it came down to that, we could at least push off from the dock and float away. Go out a few yards and drop anchor, far enough off the island that no one would risk swimming out to the boat in the frigid water to get to us. And then we could hang out there and wait for the fog to lift and someone to spot us. Sooner or later Derek would realize that I was gone and come looking for me. It might take a couple of days, especially if he was stranded on the Appalachian Trail overnight, but he'd get here. All we had to do was survive until then.

We started moving again, around the corner of the house, all in a cluster now. And all of us even more hyper-aware of our surroundings than before. We were so close, and it was so tempting just to make a break for it and get to the boat as quickly as we could, but we couldn't afford any mistakes. Not when we were almost safe.

We made it around the house unchallenged and started crossing the small meadow in front of the house, going down to the water and the dock. Under other circumstances I'd be freaking out about having to cross open ground. That wasn't an issue now, with the fog. Even if the guy was hunkered down among the trees, gun at the ready, he had to see us to aim. An automatic weapon would take us all out, of course, with one quick *rat-a-tat* of a trigger finger, but I didn't think we were talking about that kind of criminal. These guys weren't professionals, just a couple of amateurs who had managed to run a human trafficking ring for a few years without getting caught. Probably because it was such a small operation—two or three women once a year—out here on the edge of the world . . . just amateurs. Yes, my heart was beating double time, but I wasn't worried about walking into a hail of bullets. I was worried about maybe *one* bullet, but I comforted myself with the knowledge that if we couldn't see him, he couldn't see us, either. At least not well enough to hit any of us.

We reached the dock unchallenged and crept onto the slick planks.

"Careful," I muttered as Olga slipped and threatened to slide into the water and pull Svetlana with her. Irina grabbed them both and kept them upright, and did it with a minimum of noise.

The cabin cruiser was up ahead; we could see the dark outline getting clearer through the fog with every step we took. Just another minute now, and we'd know whether we'd have a chance to get off the island or not. Gert might have the key in his pocket, and if he did, we were SOL.

Irina helped me to hold the boat steady and I slithered over the low railing and onto the wet deck, where I stood weaving for a few seconds, arms out for balance, teeth gritted against the need to squeal, while my legs got used to being on the water and my shoes struggled for traction on the slippery wood. Once I felt fairly confident in my ability to stay on my feet, I slip-slid toward the below-deck steering house. Maybe I could peek in and see whether . . .

Yes! There was a steering wheel, and—even better—there was a key. Already in the ignition. I turned to the others and beckoned, smiling for the first time in the past two hours, at least.

The others scrambled on board, too, less carefully now, while I swung myself down into the steering house. There were four low windows in the front, letting me look out onto the deck and the fog, and behind me, a set of doors leading into what had to be the little cabin that made this thing a cabin cruiser. The doors were closed. While I turned the key in the ignition—holding my breath and praying—Svetlana pulled the doors open and pushed Olga inside. Irina, meanwhile, stayed on deck, keeping an eye on the fog and getting ready to cast off.

The engine caught, and Irina started to lift the rope that held the cruiser tethered to the dock. I hunted for the maritime equivalent of a gearshift to put the boat into reverse, and I had just found it when Svetlana and Olga came back out of the cabin. Moving backward, and with their hands in the air.

A few steps behind them—or rather in front, seeing as they were coming out butts first—was a man with a gun. I gulped.

I guess I'd realized, sometime after standing in the village with Irina and Gert what felt like a lifetime ago, that Ned Schachenger wasn't the second bad guy in this scenario. Ned lived in Boothbay Harbor. Our Bad Guy Numero Uno, Hal the shop owner, had knocked on the door of someone right here on the island. I just hadn't given much thought to . . .

"Calvin!"

He glanced over. "Hi, Miss Baker."

Great. He remembered me, too.

I waited for him to order me to turn the key in the ignition and shut the boat back down, but it didn't come. Instead he just stood there, with that nasty little gun pointed at my stomach, and waited for Irina to cast off. I opened my mouth to let her know what was going on—maybe she'd, at least, get away and back onto shore if, as it seemed, he was planning to take the rest of us into open water—but he shook his head and wiggled the gun. I closed my mouth again.

Irina finished her part of the job and came toward the steering house. As soon as she had swung herself down, the gun moved away from me and in her direction.

It didn't really matter which one of us he was aiming at, and he must have realized it. I mean, yeah, if it came down to the bottom line, and only one of us could survive, I didn't want to die. But as long as there was a gun pointing at any of us, we were all likely to do what he wanted.

What he wanted, in the first instance, was for Irina, Svetlana, and Olga to go back into the cabin and sit down, side by side, on one of the built-in bunks along the curved wall. Then he turned to me.

"Go."

"I've never driven a boat before," I protested. The added incentive of having a loaded gun pointed at me didn't make it any easier. Yeah, it made me want to succeed, so I wouldn't get shot, but on the other hand, it didn't make it any easier to concentrate.

"You drive a car?"

I nodded.

"Same thing. Except you don't have to worry about staying between the lines." He chuckled at his own wit.

Until I could figure out a way to take advantage of the situation, cooperating seemed like the best course of action. So I grabbed the gearshift handle and moved it toward reverse and managed to get away from the dock without flooding the engine or doing whatever the maritime equivalent is.

"Go away from the island," Calvin said.

I moved the shift back to neutral and then forward. Slowly. The boat started picking up speed. Very little speed, since I had no idea where I was going and what might be in front of me. We couldn't be more than a few yards out from land, but there was fog everywhere, and I'd already gotten turned around. I didn't know whether he was taking us toward the mainland or out to sea.

I decided to ask. "Where are we going?"

He glanced at me. "Boothbay Harbor."

Good to know. "Why?"

He arched his brows. "I have buyers for these two girls. And money to make."

Yowch. "Won't they . . . I mean, with the fog and all, are you sure they'll still be there?"

"Oh, they'll be there. Just concentrate on driving."

I concentrated.

On boats they build these days, there's probably lots of newfangled electronic stuff: computers and radar and satellite systems that tell you where you are in relation to everything around you and let you know when you're about to run aground. Gert's boat was an antique; it lacked all those helpful things. There had to be some sort of navigational thingy somewhere, because Calvin kept ordering small adjustments, a little to the left, a little to the right, but I couldn't figure out how. We didn't run into anything, though, so he must have known what he was doing. I was getting more of a feel for the controls, too, which gave me more confidence that we might make it out of this situation with our lives.

A few minutes ticked by as we crept through the fog. I had no idea what was going on in the cabin behind me; whether Irina was planning some way to overpower Calvin and take over command of the boat, or if she and the others were waiting for me to figure something out. I could hear the murmur of their voices—in Russian—but, of course, I couldn't understand what they were saying. And I was too worried about Calvin and the gun—and the fog—to look over my shoulder for more than a second at a time. Most likely they were just catching up with one another and with what had happened over the past couple months.

"How long have you and . . . um . . . your friend been running this racket?" I asked Calvin. Talking was better than listening to the silence, plus I was curious.

"My uncle." Calvin's voice was cold. "Three years."

"So Irina was one of the first women you brought over."

Calvin glanced at her. "Uncle Hal picked her. I wouldn't have. Too old."

"I guess you picked Olga and Katya, then." The cute little—dead—blonde and the buxom brunette.

Calvin confirmed that he had.

"What . . . um . . . Did you happen to go into the store earlier? Did anyone survive? Your uncle? Or Mr. Heyerdahl?"

"I think Uncle Hal might have made it," Calvin said. "I didn't see him." He shrugged.

"And Mr. Heyerdahl?"

"Lying in a pool of blood. I figured he was a goner."

"But you didn't check to see?"

"Excuse me, but I had some runaway merchandise to track down. I didn't have time to mess around."

Well, excuse *me*. I went back to steering the boat. Silently thanking God that Gert might still be among the living.

With that worry off my mind, I could turn my attention to other things. There had to be something I could do to stop this guy. I mean, there were four of us and only one of him. Yeah, he had the gun, which did even the odds a little, but I had control of the boat, and surely that had to count for something. Could I run it aground? Make him stumble and lose the gun?

Probably not. He knew more than I did about where the obstacles lay around here, and he was directing me clear. He'd shoot me before I got anywhere close to grounding the boat.

Could I haul back on the gearshift handle and stop the boat dead in the middle of the water? That might make him overbalance. Would it work, though? I didn't know enough about boats to be sure. So was there a way to push him overboard? Dropping him into the chilly waters of the Atlantic would take care of him. It had killed Katya. We'd make sure Calvin didn't come to that—I wanted him to survive to stand trial—but if he got a good dunking, maybe he'd be easier to deal with.

But for that we'd have to get him up on deck first, and how would we accomplish that?

It might be better to ambush him. For all four of us to jump on him and knock him down. And sit on him. Then again, if we did, if we somehow managed to communicate that plan to one another, and by some miracle nobody got shot in the process, and we got the gun away from him, and we tied him up and made sure he wasn't a threat anymore . . . then we'd have to navigate to shore on our own, and I had no idea how to do that. So long as this fog lasted, I depended on Calvin to tell me where to go.

So maybe the best thing would be to make use of him. He'd said we were going to Boothbay Harbor. He could be lying, sure—but I doubted it. If he had let us go instead of running after us earlier, he could have gotten away. There were plenty of boats in the harbor on Rowanberry Island he could have used to make a break for it. But he'd come after us. He must have wanted the Ukrainian girls back badly enough to take the chance.

So it seemed safe to assume that he'd told the truth and we were actually going to Boothbay Harbor.

Waiting until we got there before trying to tackle Calvin might be the best course of action. Once the harbor was within sight, I could open the throttle, aim straight for the nearest pier, and slam into it. That would take care of him. He might shoot me first, but if we were that close to shore, someone would hear the shot and come to investigate, and his chance of disembarking on the QT would be zero. I might even survive, if the nearest hospital wasn't too far away. Melissa survived getting shot back in December.

My mind made up, we spent the next fifteen minutes cruising in silence while I rehearsed the plan in my head, trying frantically and uselessly to consider unforeseen angles and plug any holes I could think of. By then Calvin's behavior clued me in that we were getting close to land. That and the fact that his cell phone was working. He used it to call someone and arrange to meet them right at the harbor to hand over the "merchandise."

It was time to make my move.

I had no idea how close to shore we were, but with Calvin's attention divided between me and the phone, and between the phone in one hand and the gun in the other, we wouldn't get a better chance. I pushed the shift forward, just a little, and yanked hard on the wheel. The boat banked. I yanked the wheel the other way. The boat bucked. Calvin stumbled. And here came Irina. She must have realized that I'd been planning something and been waiting just inside the doors, ready for the action to start.

She threw herself at Calvin from the door of the cabin, coming in low, so she hit him at the back of the knees. Calvin buckled and went down. The gun went off.

The sound of the shot was deafening, especially in such a tiny space. My ears were ringing, and I admit it,

I thought I might have been hit. From reading books and watching TV, I know that there's sometimes a moment or two between getting shot and realizing it, before the pain kicks in.

I didn't have time to stand still and take stock, though. I turned and flung myself on top of Calvin before he could get up. Irina got it together, too, and scrambled onto him as well. The gun had gone flying, and I saw it over in the corner. Calvin's hand was questing for it, fumbling like a giant spider across the floor. Until Svetlana, Olga in tow, stomped on it. Hard. Calvin howled.

"Check his pockets," I told Svetlana breathlessly as I clung to his other arm.

She stared at me until Irina prompted her. I guess maybe she didn't want to touch him, and who could blame her? But she bent to slide her hand into the pockets of Calvin's jeans, one after the other. The key chain was in the front right-hand pocket, and one of the keys fit the handcuffs. Svetlana unchained herself from Olga, and then used the cuffs to fasten Calvin's wrists together. Behind him, just in case he was some kind of champion swimmer who could get himself to shore with his hands cuffed together. To be safe, we trussed his feet, too, with a length of rope Irina found in the cabinet below the steering wheel.

I gave Svetlana the gun before starting the boat again, and we crept forward. While I concentrated on navigating, Irina opened my cell phone to call Derek, now that we were close enough to land to have cell coverage back. Only to find a voice mail message there from—of all people—Ricky Swanson. It had come in several hours ago, just after I'd arrived on Rowanberry Island. When I listened to it, I couldn't help but laugh. Talk about too little, too late.

"Avery, hey. It's Ricky. Look, I've tracked down the owner of that Russian-bride website for you. You know, the one that's based here in Maine. And you're not gonna believe this, but it's registered to Calvin Harris. You know, that guy you met at Guido's that night you were there? From Barnham? The one who said he'd heard people on the ferry dock talking about Russian women? He's been running it right from his dorm room at the college. Best I can figure out, he really was talking about it when I overheard him, and that story about the people on the ferry dock was just a story he came up with to explain it away. Man, do I feel stupid. I'm gonna try to call Josh now, see if I can get in touch with his dad. I'll call you later. And don't go near this guy, Avery, OK?"

He disconnected. I sighed, shaking my head.

—Epilogue—

"I'm never doing this again," Derek said.

It was the end of June, and we were sitting on the porch outside our house on Rowanberry Island, watching the sun rise while sipping high-octane coffee and petting Mischa the cat. We had just come off another all-nighter; the last in a long line of them lately. There had been times, many—and most of them wholly unrelated to that nightmare afternoon with Calvin and his uncle Hal and the Ukrainian women—when I'd been sure Rowanberry Island would be the death of me.

We'd made it into Boothbay Harbor without any problems that day, Irina, Svetlana, Olga, and I. Oh, and Calvin. By the time we got there, Irina had used my phone to call Derek, who had told Wayne, who had gotten hold of Reece Tolliver with the state police in Augusta, who had called the chief of police of Boothbay Harbor, who had been on the dock to meet us. He had already snagged the two buyers of Calvin's "merchandise": a pudgy fifty-something with moist hands and chapped lips, who was eagerly awaiting his nubile twenty-something mail-order bride, and a sleek and dangerous East European, who was there to pick up his latest CSW—commercial sex worker. I never found out which girl was supposed to be going with which man, and I was quite happy not to know.

Olga had long since gone back to the Ukraine. She'd accompanied Katya's coffin, in fact, just about a week after the ordeal, when Wayne and company released the body and sent it back to Kiev for burial. Any dreams Olga had had of starting a new life in the golden land of opportunity had been beaten out of her by the time Irina and I found her, and she just wanted to go home where she'd be safe. Wayne had asked his new contact in the Kiev police to keep an eye on her for a while, since she was clearly pretty traumatized by what had happened, and Wayne was worried that she might develop some issues as a result.

Svetlana was made of sterner stuff and was determined to stay in the United States. To help her sister, Irina made the ultimate sacrifice and found herself a rich American husband who was willing to sponsor both of them. She and her beard—a famous writer—tied the knot at the Boothbay Harbor courthouse just a week or so after that horrible Sunday on the island.

Yes, Gert Heyerdahl survived getting shot. He'd lost a bit of blood by the time the Boothbay Harbor police got to the general store to rescue him, but the bullet hadn't nicked any arteries or hit any vital organs, so the doctors cleaned him up, poured a few pints of blood back into him to make up for what he'd lost, and declared him good to go. He proposed from his hospital bed: ostensibly to keep Irina from being deported back to the Ukraine, but we all knew the truth. Later in the week, when the courthouse clerk said,

"You may kiss the bride," it wasn't a perfunctory peck on the lips that followed.

Calvin's uncle Hal was not as lucky, unfortunately. And I mean that sincerely, since I'd really have liked for him to have survived so we could make him pay for his crimes. But when Gert attacked him in the general store and the rest of us ran for our lives, Uncle Hal had somehow managed to get hold of Gert's gun. Gert had tackled him, and Uncle Hal had tumbled backward into the still-open basement storage room. He'd cracked his head on the edge of the floor going down, but not before he'd managed to squeeze off the shot that hit Gert in the gut. Gert hadn't been sure whether Uncle Hal was dead or merely biding his time before rising out of the hole like a phoenix from the ashes, so before I even got back to the store that afternoon, Gert had slammed the trap door shut and lain on it to make sure Uncle Hal couldn't get out.

And that was why Calvin hadn't seen his uncle when he arrived at the general store, and why he thought that Uncle Hal might still be alive.

As it turned out, the crack on the back of the head had knocked Hal out, and he died the same way Agent Trent had, from a busted cranium. By the time the police got there, he was well and truly gone. Nobody threw him in the water afterward, so he got off pretty easy, in my opinion. A whole lot easier than if he had survived to stand trial. The Portland police found Agent Trent's car in the parking lot in Portland, by the way, and determined that she'd gotten on the ferry there. When she got to Rowanberry Island and the general store, Uncle Hal had killed her, and then he and Calvin had dumped her in the Waterfield harbor that night.

Calvin claimed that the idea to smuggle East European women into the country had been his uncle's from the beginning. He might even have been telling the truth. Hal Spencer, like his sister Glenda—who was in on the trafficking up to her neck—was descended from a long line of smugglers, starting with John van Duren back in the days before the American Revolution. It was in his blood, if you believe in that kind of thing. Of course, if you do, then it was in Calvin's blood as well, and it wasn't like Uncle Hal was around to tell anyone that the whole thing was Calvin's idea, was it? The Russian-bride website was all Calvin's doing, anyway, and with Ricky and Josh's help, Wayne was able to prove it. The two guys the Boothbay Harbor police arrested on the dock were happy to implicate him, as well. Calvin and his mother pleaded guilty to a lot of things to avoid going to trial, and at the time Derek and I were sitting there enjoying the coffee and sunrise, both of them had been sentenced to quite a few years in a place where they hopefully wouldn't get to enjoy either. Or if either of them had coffee, at least they didn't get to drink it while watching the sun come up over the Atlantic.

Not that I was in a state to be appreciating the view. We'd been working through the night, and not for the first time. Hence Derek's declaration of "never again."

Renovating the house on Rowanberry Island had turned out to be a much bigger job than even Derek had anticipated. It was a huge undertaking, and it just seemed to go on and on. As soon as we fixed one thing, we realized that there was something else wrong that we hadn't known about. It didn't help, either, that we had to move all the tools and materials—everything we needed, including the granite counter for the kitchen, all two tons of it—from the mainland by boat.

Not that we weren't having fun, of course. It was tons of fun. It was just a really big job for two people. But the house was turning out gorgeous. The floors were spit and polished, the wide planks shimmering with the pearly sheen of satin polyurethane. The walls were painted in traditional Colonial colors: ochre and dark red, blue and green. Derek had matched and patched the worm-eaten paneling around the fireplace in the living room, while I had had some fun creating fake paneling upstairs with the use of different kinds of decorative moldings. Strips and rosettes and dentil molds, the ones that look like rows of teeth. It's a nice, easy way to get the look of hand-crafted paneling without the effort or expense. And it looked fantastic.

I'd painted a poor man's runner up the stairs to the second floor, but I'd cheated a little; we'd sanded the stairs, and instead of painting them in two different colors—one for the thread and one for the "runner"—I'd kept the outsides of the steps natural wood, and had painted a white stripe in the middle. And then I had added frilly edges that could have come straight off a doily. It was, in fact, a stencil, one I'd drawn myself on a piece of plastic and cut out with a razor blade. It looked pretty good, if I do say so myself.

And talking about painting, I'd also done a couple of sailcloth rugs: one for the living room and one for the dining room. The one in the living room had black and ochre checkerboard squares, with a little red flower in about every third or fourth yellow square. The one in the dining room was similar, but was green and white inside a black border, and instead of flowers, I'd had some fun and had painted actual checkers in a few of the squares. Red was winning at the moment, but black might pull through in a pinch. And—quite a surprise—a couple of people who had seen them had commissioned sailcloth rugs of their own, so I was starting a little sideline business.

I knew exactly what Derek was talking about, though. We were both suffering from burnout.

I nodded. "Next time, I want to renovate a small house.

One that won't take forever. And one we won't have to travel halfway across Maine to get to."

"Waterfield to Rowanberry Island isn't exactly halfway across Maine."

"You know what I mean. I want a house right in Waterfield. Preferably in the Village. A house I can walk to."

"That isn't gonna be easy," Derek said judiciously, stretching long legs out in front of him. Mischa the kitten latched onto a jean leg and started climbing. "Houses in Waterfield Village tend to be a little too rich for our blood."

I looked at him, and he clarified, "Priced too high to make any profit from renovating. We'd have to get whatever it is at a fire-sale price. And when we get it that cheap, it's usually something that needs gutting and starting over."

Mischa reached a spot where his tiny claws were hitting not just fabric but flesh, and Derek winced and peeled him off. Mischa hung on, complaining, and I had to reach over and gently unhook each of his tiny, needle-sharp claws from Derek's jeans.

"If you're gonna keep this monster, you need to get him declawed," Derek grumbled.

"He'll be all right." I put him down in my lap and started stroking him. He purred. "And I am keeping him. He's coming home with me when we're done here. When will that be?"

Derek glanced over his shoulder at the house. "Another few days. Just to make sure everything is ready."

"And then?"

"Then we start thinking about our next project."

"No rest for the weary." I stretched my legs out. "Have you come up with a house we can flip for Noel's TV show yet?"

Noel is my stepfather, and he's a TV producer in California. When he was in Waterfield over Christmas, he had run the idea by us of taking part in an episode of a home-renovation show his network produces, and Derek and I had said yes. Now Noel was ready, or at least he would be in the next few weeks. The show was called *Flipping Out!* and the premise of it was quick-flipping: slapping lipstick on the project, adding surface-gloss and curb appeal, in and out in a week flat. Fresh paint, updated kitchen cabinet hardware, new kitchen counter, new bathroom floor, new light fixtures . . . nothing invasive or time-consuming, just small changes that make a big difference.

As soon as I heard we'd have to renovate a whole house in just five days, I'd tried to bow out, but Derek had convinced me it would be fun; we just needed the right house.

Now he nodded. "Melissa has found us something."

Melissa. Just what I'd spent the past year trying to avoid: having Melissa James represent me in a real estate deal.

There was no way around it, though. Now that Irina was married and was accompanying her husband to Florida at the end of the summer, she had decided to quit the business. She didn't have to work anymore; Gert was making more than enough money to support them both in style. Or if she enjoyed it, maybe she'd get into condo sales in Miami, or something. Something more lucrative and easier than trying to beat out a living on the back roads up here in the frozen-half-the-year north. So Melissa was our only hope, as well as our salvation, it seemed.

"What is it?" I asked.

"Tony Micelli owns a little cottage on Cabot Street," Derek said. "Eleven hundred square feet, two-one—"

A two bedroom, one bath.

"—that he's been renting out for years. The tenants just moved out—the college semester ended—and now Tony wants to try to sell it. He's allowing us to go in and make it look good."

"Big of him."

Derek shrugged. "I've seen it, and it'll be great for what we want. He's footing the bill for the materials, even paying us a little for the work, and then Melissa will list and sell it once it's finished. Everyone wins."

"And it's a good candidate for a quick flip?"

"Oh, sure," Derek said. "Tony hasn't done anything to update it, so most of the original features are there. Fireplace, millwork, hardwood floors. The roof's good, and it's been sided, so we won't have to mess with the outside much, and the kitchen cabinets are original. . . ."

And we both knew how much Derek liked original kitchen cabinets.

I shrugged. "If it's good enough for you, it's good enough for me."

"That's my girl." He grinned. After a minute he added, "I hear that Judith and Mamie Norton over on Green Street are thinking of selling their house."

I rummaged in the files in my mind. "The two old ladies in that big craftsman bungalow on the corner? The one with the lace curtains in all the windows?"

"That's the one. Those same curtains have been there for as long as I've been alive. I don't think the house has been renovated or updated since it was built. It'll have all those original features, untouched for ninety years. And it's gonna cost a pretty penny, especially if they go ahead and have a Realtor list it. But maybe we could talk to them before they get that far, see what they say. . . ."

"It's a big house," I pointed out. "One of those rambling craftsman bungalows from—what?—the 1920s? It's a good two thousand square feet, wouldn't you say? And if it hasn't been updated since then . . . I thought you didn't want to take on another big project again so soon."

"They won't be ready to do anything for a couple of

months, at least. By then, maybe we'll have a contract on this, and we'll have had time to rest up."

"Whatever you say." I leaned back on my elbows, with Mischa still curled into a ball in my lap, vibrating cozily.

Derek lay back on the porch floor and closed his eyes as the sun rose higher in the sky. "I'm gonna take a nap."

"That sounds like a good idea." I moved the cat off my lap and curled up next to him. "Wake me when it's time to go home."

"No worries," Derek said, his voice already fading, "I will."

I smiled and snuggled in. After a moment, Mischa crawled on top of me and went back to purring.

—Home-Renovation— and Design Tips

Creating an Authentic Canvas Floorcloth

– A Little History –

Floorcloths date from fourteenth-century France, but they reached their height of popularity in the sixteen hundreds in England, where they usually replicated the look of expensive marble tile. The earliest floorcloths were the simplest, often displaying a tile design. Some of them look amazingly like 1950s linoleum. As time progressed, the designs expanded, as did the range of colors: from the original black, red, and white to a range of hues. Authentic floorcloths were—and are—constructed from canvas sailcloth made impervious by the application of oil-based paints. They're hypoallergenic and pet friendly, and they clean easily with soap and water.

TOOLS AND MATERIALS

- Sailcloth—big enough for the "rug" plus a one-inch border all around
- Oil-based primer
- Oil-based paint in colors of choice for pattern
- Miter
- Hide glue or other glue substitute (Dr. Jekyll's Hyde Glue is supposed to work well)
- Paintbrushes
- Pencil
- Polyurethane
- Stencil, if desired

DIRECTIONS

1. Cut canvas sailcloth to desired size plus one-inch allowance/border.
2. Cover both sides of canvas sailcloth with two coats of oil-based primer to prevent shrinking.
3. Fold a one-inch border all around, miter, and bind with glue.
4. Apply three coats of base color to top of floorcloth, using oil-based paint.
5. Draw pattern on top of base color, freehand or by use of stencils.
6. Color pattern using oil-based paint.
7. Apply many, many coats of polyurethane to seal the design. The professionals use eight.
8. If desired, you can "antique" the floorcloth after you're finished, to make it look old, by applying a crackle finish (available in hardware and home-renovation stores) or by distressing paint with a hard brush.

Using Stencils

Avery used stencils to enhance the painted poor man's runner on the stairs in her house as well as to make her Colonial floorcloths. Stencils are great when you need to keep things looking the same across a large surface, like a staircase, a floor, or a wall.

TOOLS AND MATERIALS

- Low-tack masking tape or stencil adhesive
- Stencil brushes or foam brushes
- Paint (and palette if desired)
- Level
- Ruler or tape measure
- Cloth or paper towels, for cleanup

DIRECTIONS

1. For best results, make sure any cracks or holes in the surface have been filled in and smoothed down.
2. If the surface needs painting, make sure you allow it to dry thoroughly. A flat base paint is best. If your stencil paints are not sticking to the surface, you may need to sand the area lightly.
3. Determine where you want your stenciled picture to be, using the level and ruler or tape measure. If you are stenciling a wall or very large area, begin in the least noticeable corner.
4. Tape your stencil to the surface using a piece of low-tack tape across each corner or by applying stencil adhesive to the back of the stencil. If you are working on a flat horizontal surface (like Avery's stair steps), you may find it easier to use weights instead of tape.

5. Apply paint to the stencil openings (islands) using an up-and-down dabbing motion. If you use a back-and-forth brushing motion, the brush will push paint under the stencil and cause smearing.
6. Begin with the part of the stencil that is farthest away from you to avoid accidental smudging, and start at the edges of each island/opening and work your way toward the center.
7. Allow paint to dry thoroughly before applying additional coats of paint for a deeper color or shading.
8. When you are satisfied with the color(s) and the paint is completely dry, remove the low-tack tape and carefully lift the stencil.
9. Do any touching up that needs to be done.

– Helpful Hints –

Resist the temptation to load up the brush with paint so that you don't have to do a second coat. More color is achieved by repeated coverage, not by using more paint.

A brush that is on the dry side will keep paint from seeping under the stencil and smearing or running. If paint is seeping under the stencil or you are not getting clean edges, you are using too much paint.

When your brush is properly loaded, an even powdering of paint is left when blotted on a paper towel.

Making Your Own Stencils

TOOL AND MATERIALS

- Tracing paper/drawing paper
- Clear plastic
- Pencil
- Scissors
- Sharp razor blade

DIRECTIONS

1. Choose an image you'd like to use for a stencil or draw your own. Keep in mind that simpler is better. The best images have high contrast with few variations. Wallpapers and fabric patterns are some good places to look for patterns.
2. Draw or copy your image onto tracing paper or clear, fairly thick plastic. If the image you're tracing doesn't have disconnected parts, you'll have to draw those in yourself.
3. Different areas of the stencil should have clear boundaries that allow bridges to appear around the islands (openings) where paint is to be applied. Make sure the bridges are wide enough to keep paint from seeping under and smudging your image.
4. Consider making your stencil out of clear, fairly thick plastic; some people say presentation covers work well. That way, you can use your stencil more than just once or twice.
5. If you prefer working with paper, there are ways you can protect your paper stencil for future use:

   – *If you can get your hands on some clear contact paper, you can cut a piece the size of your stencil, remove the backing, stick it to the paper stencil, and cut out the islands.*

- *Packing tape works, as well. Place your stencil on a flat surface with the front facing up. Run strips of packing tape over the stencil while making sure to overlap the edges so that the entire surface is covered. Run the tape past the edges and trim the excess with a pair of scissors. Cut out the islands.*
- *It helps to put the protective surface on the front of the stencil, because having a slick surface on the back increases the chance for paint smearing underneath.*

Installing Fake Paneling

Authentic Colonial homes often had beautifully paneled rooms, and if you want to replicate tongue-in-groove Colonial-style paneling, you can certainly do that. Be sure to use knot-free, select-grade pine, and start by measuring the wall you're paneling and drawing a detailed schematic replica of what you want it to look like.

Colonial paneling consisted of three sections of wood: stiles—medium-thin vertical pieces; rails—medium-thin horizontal pieces; and panels—bigger square or rectangular pieces to go between the rails and stiles. You make panels by gluing and clamping boards together.

Rails and stiles have grooves cut into their sides, while panels have tongues, making for a tight fit. You start by cutting all the stiles, then all the rails, then the panels, since they take different saw attachments.

Dry-fit them together first to make sure they go together perfectly before hanging them with eight penny-finish nails. Or, if this sounds like too much work, you can buy kits of precut Colonial paneling from lumber yards or online providers, if you don't feel like doing so much cutting yourself.

However, if you want the look of fancy paneling but you don't have the time, money, or patience to put together the real thing, there are easy ways you can make your walls look paneled for a lot less money and with a lot less effort. This works especially well for doing sections of walls—say, to install wainscoting below a chair rail in a dining room—but you can do whole walls this way as well, by continuing the same process all the way up to the ceiling. All you'll be doing is nailing a grid of trim pieces to the wall in a pattern, and then painting it to look like expensive paneling.

TOOLS AND MATERIALS

- Measuring tape
- Pencil
- Level
- Wooden wainscoting panels of desired width
- Table saw
- Nails and hammer
- Construction adhesive
- Top cap
- Baseboard
- Crown molding (if doing a whole wall)
- Caulk
- Primer and paint
- Paintbrushes or paint roller

DIRECTIONS

1. Roughly lay out where the panels will be on the wall and locate any fixtures, such as light switches, plugs, receptacles, vents, etc. You'll have to cut holes for these, or avoid them.

2. Determine how much material you'll need. As a general rule, the bottom rail is wider than the top rail, and the stiles are narrower than both. Quantity will depend on how close together you put the stiles, i.e., how big the panels are. As a general rule, narrow panels make the ceiling look higher while wide panels make the wall look longer and the room bigger.
3. Measure the desired height of the wainscot and draw a level line the whole way around the room to mark the reference point for installation. If you're doing a whole wall, or the whole room, repeat the process all the way up the wall to the ceiling.
4. Carefully lay out and mark on your walls where all the pieces that will form the wainscot (horizontal rails and vertical stiles) will go.
5. Use the table saw to rip all your stock ahead of time to the size you've determined you need. You're essentially building a grid, so make sure the stiles fit snugly between the rails.
6. Use nails and construction adhesive to secure the top (horizontal) rail along the level line.
7. Secure all of the vertical stiles in place. Use the level to make sure that the corners are square.
8. Secure the bottom rail below the stiles.
9. Secure the top cap—the decorative piece that finishes off the wainscot. If you're planning to panel the whole wall, skip this step and add more stiles on top of the top rail for the next section of your paneled wall.
10. Cut and secure the baseboard.
11. If you're going all the way up the wall, cut and secure the crown molding to finish the wall.
12. Sand any saw marks and sharp edges.
13. Caulk joints.
14. Prime and paint.

– Helpful Hints –

If you're limiting yourself to doing a wainscot, a fancy crown molding adds balance under the ceiling. You can spend money and effort on putting together a multi-tiered crown molding, or you can fake it: By adding a decorative trim piece or two to the bottom of the existing crown molding, if needed, and by adding a piece or two of decorative trim a couple of inches farther down the wall, and then painting the trim pieces and the wall between them the same color, you give the impression that the whole area is crown molding. Works like a charm!